FOR MANY A LONG DAY

*The continuation of the spellbinding
Hamilton saga*

Sam Hamilton and Robert Scott are now in
their fifties, with families of their own, and are
grateful to have work at a time when there is
much unemployment. But they have little joy
in their lives. Set in the Ulster of the 1930s, the
saga of the two families continues through that
troubled decade. This is a tale of courage and
friendship, of disappointment and achievement, and ultimately of the triumph of love...

FOR MANY A LONG DAY

Anne Doughty

Severn House Large Print
London & New York

This first large print edition published 2013
in Great Britain and the USA by
SEVERN HOUSE PUBLISHERS LTD of
9-15 High Street, Sutton, Surrey, SM1 1DF.
First world regular print edition published 2009 by
Severn House Publishers Ltd., London and New York.

British Library Cataloguing in Publication Data

Doughty, Anne, 1939-
  For many a long day.
  1. Families--Northern Ireland--Down (County)--History--
  20th century--Fiction. 2. Nineteen thirties--Fiction.
  3. Down (Northern Ireland : County)--Social conditions--
  20th century--Fiction. 4. Large type books.
  I. Title
  823.9'14-dc23

ISBN-13: 978-0-7278-9993-4

Severn House Publishers support The Forest Stewardship Council
[FSC], the leading international forest certification organisation. All
our titles that are printed on Greenpeace-approved FSC-certified paper
carry the FSC logo.

MIX
Paper from
responsible sources
FSC
www.fsc.org   FSC® C018575

Printed and bound in Great Britain by the
MPG Books Group, Bodmin, Cornwall.

For Canadian friends and cousins known since childhood or recently discovered.

Acknowledgements

I must begin by apologizing to the inhabitants of both Armagh and Peterborough, Ontario, for taking liberties with their commercial activities. Freeburn's in Armagh and Robinson Lumbering in Peterborough are entirely fictitious. Sleator's did exist in the 1930s, but I have modified it to suit my purposes.

As with all my novels I try to be accurate about both the social and the economic situation in which my characters find themselves, together with the actual geographical settings where they live and work. While the city and countryside of Armagh is very familiar to me, I could not have been as confident about Peterborough, Ontario, had it not been for the Canadian Library and Archives Service.

For an extremely modest fee they provided me with a ship's manifest which allowed me to locate the family of my great-uncle, who went away and never came back. With the help of a childhood friend, my cousins were contacted and my questions about Peterborough answered with documents, photographs, old books and a bicycle ride round Quaker Oats.

Here in Belfast, I must thank the television company, now resident in my great-aunt's tall, terrace house who let me stand on a chair among their computers so I could look out the attic window and refreshed my memory of the Antrim Hills and the view over Moonstone Street.

Ellie Scott is the gentlest of my protagonists, but she is typical of many Irish country girls. They have little formal education, but possess tenacity and common sense, virtues which stand to them whether they help to open up the Canadian forest at Scott's Plains or make a life and a home in the difficult 1930s in a country town like Armagh.

Finishing this novel in the autumn of 2008 with the dark shadows of recession and unemployment making daily headlines, I hope this fiction may bring comfort to all those women who will do what Ellie does and make the best of all their capabilities at a difficult time.

Anne Doughty
Belfast
November, 2008

One

Robert Scott drained his mug of tea, retrieved his cap from the fender, pushed back his chair from the table and headed for the open door of the kitchen. Once outside, in the freshness of a fine May morning, he paused under the wrought-iron arch that framed the solid front door of his long, low dwelling. Though his eyes were dazzled by the light and still watering from the shimmer of fat smoking in the heavy pan his wife, Ellen, had used to fry soda bread for his breakfast, he gazed down the path to the forge, along the lane beyond, across the main road and up the sloping fields on the far side to where a clear, blue sky rested easily on the low, green hills he'd known throughout his fifty-odd years.

All was quiet. As so often at this early hour, no vehicle moved on the county road, no cattle lowed in the cool of morning, no friend or neighbour came tramping up the short lane to his workplace.

He took a deep breath, drew in the familiar scent of hawthorn and glanced across the front of the house. The windows reflected the almost cloudless sky except where they were dappled by the flutter of leaves on the flourishing climb-

9

ing rose. There were tiny splashes of colour on the windowsills where his youngest daughter, Ellie, had lined up a row of pots, the slips of geranium she'd cared for indoors over the winter.

He smiled to himself. She was taking no chances with them. If there'd been a thought of a frost at bedtime last night, she'd have had them into the kitchen should she have gone out in her nightdress to get them.

In the broad open space beyond the windows, the hens paused in their scratching and gave him quick, darting looks. It took but a flick of their bright eyes for them to see he was not the bearer of food. They returned at once to their random movement backwards and forwards across the stony area between the remains of the old ruined house where Ellie had her small garden and the well-tramped area beside the water barrel. Round this ran a path that passed under the gable and in to the largest of the handful of orchards surrounding both the forge house and the neighbouring farm.

Having surveyed his territory, he limped quickly down the path, the surviving sign of his old injury so long forgotten he rarely noticed it.

The lower half of the forge door was closed, but the upper half stood open. He leaned inside, silently withdrew the bolt and stepped quietly over to his anvil, his eyes screwed up in the darkness as he peered towards a small space above the low lintel under which he had just entered.

Before he'd even had time to listen for the tiny

10

seep, seep of the fledglings, a wren flew past him, inches from his face. She shot back out into the light, as indifferent to his presence as if he were a piece of machinery or the handle of the bellows.

All well there too, he said to himself. He raked out the cinders and added small pieces of coal to the smoored fire, till a thick, white rope twisted its way up from the hearth. It gathered in the broad chimney and then rose straight into the still air above the trees and bushes that enfolded his small parcel of land.

'Cheerio, Da. See you tonight.'

He paused, turned from the hearth and saw his daughter standing outside his open door, the sun glinting from her hair and reflecting off a spotless white blouse.

'Yer in good time the mornin', Ellie,' he said, surprised to see her, setting down the tongs he'd only just picked up. He wiped his sleeve across his forehead, the sweat already breaking from the heat of the fire.

'Delivery,' she said, laughing at his puzzlement and patting a large, brown paper parcel laid across the basket of her bicycle. 'Drumsollen,' she explained. 'The dressmaker's coming to make new maid's uniforms.'

'Wou'd it not a been easier to drop it off last night on yer way home?'

She laughed again and threw out a hand in a light gesture.

'Of course it would, Da. But nothing's as easy as that with Missus Senator Richardson. There's people coming over from London. I don't know

11

if it's young Missus Edward's family or Parliament people. She said *she specifically did not want a delivery in the early evening when they'd be arriving.*' She shook her head, mimicking perfectly the haughty tone of the command.

Robert nodded and raised his eyebrows. The Senator's wife was well known for making her wishes clear. A different woman entirely from her new daughter-in-law. Young Missus Richardson was a favourite of his. She loved horses and understood them and unlike some of the local gentry who'd barely bid him the time of day when they came to have their horses shod, she'd stand and talk to him while he worked, never getting in his way while she made sure the animal was easy.

'Must go, Da. Have to be at Drumsollen before eight. If she complains to the boss, I'll get my head chopped off.'

'Good customer, is she?' he asked, stepping out into the sunlight to see her off.

'The best. Pays cash. Boss loves to see her coming,' she added over her shoulder, as she wheeled her bicycle carefully beyond the reapers and harrows awaiting repair, a sharp eye open for any bits of metal and rusty nails that might have found their way on to the short lane down to the road.

He stood watching her go, saw her wheel her bicycle to the far side of the road and catch up her dark skirt before she got on. As she took her weight off the ground, his heart was in his mouth, for the heavy parcel shifted under her restraining hand and the front wheel looked as if

12

it might turn below her. But it was a moment only. It wasn't the first time Ellie had delivered a bale of cloth to the big house and she was well used to coping with heavy loads on her bicycle. For her own sake and those she worked with, Robert hoped there'd be many more orders for Drumsollen.

He saw her pedal steadily down the slope and was about to go back to his work when her arm shot up in the air. She waved vigorously, though he knew rightly she didn't dare turn her head to see him wave back.

In his family of four girls and two boys, Ellie was the youngest, now just nineteen and the only one with fair hair. It was so pale it seemed to pick up every hint of sunshine, even on a dull day. In any crowd of young people, he could pick her out a mile away.

'There's no knowin' about these things,' he said to himself, the glints of her hair in the morning light still alive in his mind's eye. He laid a bar of one-inch iron on his workbench, picked up his chalk and callipers and began to measure the four pieces he'd need to make shoes for Robinson's big carthorse.

As far as he knew, there was no one in the Scott family with fair hair. His father had been dark before what little hair he'd had receded so fast and so thoroughly, he was seldom seen without a cap. As for his mother, he could hardly remember her, never mind her hair. Though his father said he was seven or eight when she died, it was only now and again some wee thing would even make him think of her.

If he saw a woman carrying a big Bible under her arm, or if he had to mend the metal straps on a horse collar, he would suddenly be aware of the smell of hard, yellow soap from her hands and her clothes. But the strange thing was he could never remember what she looked like. His stepmother, Selina, a woman he'd loved from the first day his father brought her home, had asked him sometimes about his own mother. Once, he'd told her about the way a horse collar would make him think of her and she'd said that in her young days women sometimes used a horse collar to keep a child from straying when they had their work to do. Maybe, she'd said, gently, his mother had put him in one sometimes when he was very small.

Even when he'd talked to Selina like this, no further memory had stirred. But the more he thought of it, the surer he was that his mother must have been dark like his sister, Annie, or his older brother, James. Of course, his mother's hair might have been thin and mousy like that of his own two sons, Bob and Johnny. He laughed shortly as another thought occurred to him. Wasn't it a good thing neither Polly, nor Mary, nor Florence, had inherited hair like that and them so particular about how they looked and what they wore. Especially Florence.

He peered down at the chalk marks on his piece of iron and shook his head. He could barely make them out. He'd have to go round the back of the forge and cut the cow parsley. He couldn't put it off any longer. It had grown waist high in the last weeks, the mass of feathery stems were topped with rich, creamy-white flowers. Ellie said it was a pretty sight all along the road into Armagh, but it was hard on the eyes, for it made the light penetrating through his rain-streaked windows even dimmer and turned it greenish into the bargain.

He reached up above the long bench and took down a sickle from a row of hooks between the two windows. He tested its edge cautiously with his thumb, hurried out round the tall gable, walked a few yards along the short cut to Robinson's farm, then turned aside to push his way through the rampant growth brought on by the first real warmth of the year.

The sun was well up now, the light glancing off the high-pitched roof above him, the heat shimmering over the hot surface of the felt, the dew already gone from the luxurious vegetation which fell below his hand. He was no great hand with a sickle, so he cut down only the stems that grew immediately in front of his windows. He knew from experience they were always tougher than they looked.

'God Bless the work.'

He looked up, startled, dazzled by the light. He'd been so absorbed in keeping his balance on the uneven ground he'd heard no step. The short, dark figure was blurred, but the slight sing-song note of the voice was quite unmistakable.

'Ach, Jamsey. How are ye?'

'I'm the best at all. I have sweet milk for herself. Is she up?'

'Aye, she is. She made m' breakfast the day.'

Without another word, Jamsey walked past

15

him and turned up the lane to the house, his total attention focused on the jug he carried, his thumbs jutting awkwardly as if they didn't fit properly with his hands. The unexpected, late son of an elderly mother, Jamsey was a biddable child, once one made due allowances, as Robert and his family always did. Sadly, however, there were those who treated the young man's abruptness and his frequent, sullen silences as if they were intended.

Robert dragged the cut stems away from the windows with the point of the sickle and left them to ret down where they lay, tramped back to his workbench and wiped his blade with an oily rag.

'That's a bit more like it,' he said, as he glanced down at his chalk marks and found he could now see them clearly.

As the sun rose higher and the shadow of the forge grew shorter, the air itself warmed up. A new and more delicate scent mingled with the familiar perfume of hawthorn. Before Robert had even stepped into the orchard behind his own house to refill the bucket of drinking water he carried to the forge every day, he knew what he would see.

Even so, it still amazed him, year after year, the way the fat pink and white buds of the apple blossom would linger and linger. Then, between one hour and the next on a warm afternoon, suddenly unfurl, the petals opening almost as you looked at them.

He paused only a moment to breathe the per-

16

fumed air, for even as he filled his bucket, he remembered yet another job he'd promised to have ready by the evening. How he was going to do it, he had yet to figure out.

He carried the white enamel bucket back to the forge and set it down beside the wooden seat just inside his door. From the embrasure of the window behind, he took up a shoebox and brought out a clean, delph mug. With it, he baled cool spring water into the soot-marked tin mug that sat all day on the hearth within reach of the anvil. He drank deep, throwing his head well back to let the water rinse the dust from his throat. Then he put the delph mug back in its box with its fellow and from a nail on the wall nearby unhooked a square of material, patterned with daisies and neatly hemmed on all four sides. He spread it carefully across the surface of the bucket and picked up his hammer again.

'Da, you can't offer your customers a drink of water out of that mug of yours,' Ellie had remonstrated. 'And look at all those bits of soot and the metal flakes in the bottom of your bucket.'

She'd laughed when he protested it wouldn't do them a bit of harm. They wouldn't see the bits down at the bottom. What the eye didn't see the heart didn't grieve.

'And what about the ladies?' she'd come back at him. 'What about the Misses Cope and young Missus Richardson,' she'd added slyly.

So she'd gone away and found a pair of decent-looking mugs, not china, but not tinker's delph either, and put them in one of the shoe-boxes Florence had left behind, with a couple of

17

pieces of tissue crumpled up in the bottom to keep them from chipping each other.

The cover she'd made was a remnant so small it had never sold in the shop. It was only just big enough to hang over the rim and cover the surface of the water, but it did keep out the soot and sparks that flew everywhere when he really started hammering.

As he shaped and curved metal the long, slow notes now echoing on the still air, carried as far as the parish church up on the hill, the small shop at Scott's Corner a mile away towards Loughgall and, on the Armagh side of Robinson's farm, as far as the stretch of bog that ended in a deep quarry and a projection of grey stone known as Reilly's Rocks. The lighter notes from the hammer's dance didn't carry beyond the forge itself, but they punctuated the long steady strokes, the balancing rhythm his father had taught him to help ease the pain of throbbing muscles and keep at bay the dull ache of fatigue.

He worked steadily and without apparent haste throughout the long hours of the day, the list of jobs diminishing and then increasing again with every dark figure who stood in the doorway and greeted him. Even before it was time to stop for the evening meal, he was tired and he knew it, but that was the way it was at this time of year. Like the farmers who would be on the land as long as there was light to see by, he'd work on till the shadows filled the forge or his own fatigue got the better of him.

'Is it not time you stopped, Da? It's near eight

o'clock and Ma says she's hardly laid eyes on you all day. You haven't even lain down for half an hour to give your head a rest.'

He glanced up at the sound of Ellie's voice.

'Ach, I'm all right,' he said dismissively, only now remembering what the doctor had said about the headaches.

'You look worn out,' she added, coming closer.

'Mind yerself now,' he added quickly as she moved towards him. 'You don't want a dirty mark on that nice wee dress of yours. Are you and George for the dance?'

'Aye, he's going to borrow his brother's motorcycle, so I'm meeting him down on the road,' she said, suddenly beaming at him.

'Is he a good dancer?'

'The best at all,' she laughed. 'I don't know where he gets the energy from and them so busy on the farm.'

'Ah, it's great to be young.'

Maybe it was just the tiredness getting into his voice, but the easy remark didn't come out as he'd meant it. He saw the change in her bright face, the light go from her eyes. She had opened her mouth to speak when they heard a vigorous tune on the horn of a motorcycle.

'Away now and enjoy yerself,' he said firmly. 'I've only one wee thing to finish, then I'm for soap an' water an' my pipe. I'll see ye in the mornin'. Run on now, ye can't keep your young man waitin'.'

It was only moments after the rapid sound of the bike died away in the direction of Loughgall that it was replaced by the throb of a much heavier engine. He shook his head. They must be getting a good crowd if there was a motor coming from Armagh direction, he thought to himself, as he began the last shoe of the day, for a child's pony he was expecting to shoe in the morning.

As he put his hammer down a few minutes later and turned to plunge the glowing metal into the water tank, he was surprised to see a tall figure standing in the doorway quietly watching him.

'God Bless the work.'

'Ach, Sam Hamilton,' he exclaimed above the cloud of steam and the noise of bubbling brown water. 'Man, how are ye? I haven't seen ye since you brought your mother over to Selina's funeral. That's near three years now,' he added, as he took the outstretched hand firmly without even wiping his own on the back of his trousers.

'Aye, an' the time before that when we met it was *my* father's funeral and you and Ellen and Selina came with Ned Wylie and Peggy over to Banbridge.'

'Dear aye. Isn't it a sad thing when we only see each other at funerals?'

'Or when misfortune brings me a beggar to your door,' Sam Hamilton replied promptly.

'Dear goodness, an' what would make a good man like you a beggar?' Robert replied, half amused, half curious.

'Did you hear the motor?'

'I did surely. Have *you* brought a motor?'

'No, Robert I have not,' he replied with a short

20

laugh. 'To tell you the truth, even if I had the money, I get enough of motors and lorries every day.'

Sam Hamilton was a broad-shouldered man in his fifties, his face brown from exposure, his wispy hair combed back from a high, broad forehead. He came in and settled himself easily on the visitor's bench. Robert set the shoe aside, leaned back against the shaft of the bellows and stretched his aching back.

'One of these days maybe I'll buy a pony and trap,' Sam went on thoughtfully. 'We had a wee mare called Dolly when I was a boy and I loved looking after her. I used to take Ma into Banbridge on a Saturday afternoon or maybe drive Sarah and Hannah out somewhere of a fine evening. We had some grand times with Dolly,' he added, a hint of wistfulness in his tone.

'Aye, we never know when we're well off,' Robert nodded. 'As the saying is, you never miss the water till the well runs dry.'

Sam Hamilton smiled his gentle, slow smile, collected himself and explained why he had his boss's car for the night and why he hadn't been able to finish the piece of work he was doing for him for want of oxygen in his acetylene welder.

'Well sure that problem's easy solved,' said Robert nodding, pleased enough to help his old friend. 'Work away there while I finish this wee shoe an' then I'll make us a pot of tea we can take outside till I hear all your news.'

The dusk was fading in tones of pink and grey, the air still warm, as they sat down on the grass

21

bank under the pear tree at the gable end of the forge, the county road visible at the end of the lane now deserted. Robert had fetched sweet milk from the silent house, for Ellen had gone to her bed, and the two men sat side-by-side, the two delph mugs filled full of a strong brew, and watched the light go.

'D'ye mind when the Hamiltons set off for Banbridge with their bits an' pieces on Sinton's dray?' Sam asked suddenly, his mind travelling back to a day when he and his brother and sisters had sat on this same grassy bank beside the pear tree waiting for the dray to come and collect them.

'Aye, that was the year of the terrible bad accident on the railway, wasn't it?'

Sam nodded, his mind still engaged with memories of the part of his childhood spent in the now ruined house across the lane. His family had lived there when his own father, John, had worked with Robert's father, Thomas, in the darkened forge behind him.

'There's some of us lucky to be here to remember it,' Sam said suddenly, realizing he'd not said a word for quite a while.

'I mind m'father comin' back from the railway banks with blood dried on his clothes an' didn't even know it was there,' said Robert abruptly.

It had only just occurred to him that his mother must have been there in the house when her husband and John Hamilton had come back from collecting up the dead and carrying them to be laid out in Armagh. But he still couldn't remember her. All he remembered of that night was his

22

father asking Annie was there anything you could use to get the stains out.

'Now then,' said Sam, drinking deep, 'tell us how all your ones are. Is Bob a Bank Manager yet?'

He settled back to listen to his friend and to take the good of the evening. It was a rare moment of rest at the end of a long day for which he would give thanks when he said his prayers.

No, Bob wasn't yet a manager, but it wouldn't be long till he was, for he was not only good with figures, he had a knack of sizing people up. Johnny wasn't as clever as his brother, Bob, but he'd served his time as a grocer and was up in Belfast now getting a bit more experience. Doing well. Polly was still in Toronto with Jimmy and the two boys and the wee one, though she was worried about Jimmy's job. Sure, wasn't that the way it was everywhere these days. Mary had taken a chance and gone out to her two years back and had got started in Eatons. Florence was up and away to London and knew not a soul there. She was working in the dress department of a big store. Right up her street and she loved it. Ellie had been walking out for two years now with George Robinson next door and they were expecting a wedding once the harvest was over.

Sam had to concentrate hard, for in the years since he'd last been to the forge itself the children he'd seen playing in the orchard had grown into young men and women. He could just remember Mary handing round sandwiches after Selina's funeral, but he couldn't call to

23

mind the youngest wee girl at all.

'And all well and healthy, thank God,' he said soberly, as Robert finished his tally.

To Robert's surprise, Sam Hamilton said less than he'd expected about his own large family. The two older boys were well settled, both in the police force, and Bobbie was now in Irish Road Motors. The eldest girl, Emily, had come home from New York with her husband, Kevin, and he was working with a man who'd started making bodywork for motors. They were just down the road in Richhill. Rosie and her husband, the doctor, had had a third child, the wee girl Richard had so wanted. Jack had got Emily's old job at Fruitfield, in the office doing the books. Dolly was the only one at home now. She'd become a dressmaker and was very good at it.

Robert threw the last dregs of his tea into the long grass and wondered if he'd missed something, for he was sure there were nine in Sam's family. He puzzled over it for a minute or two as they sat in silence, then he remembered one of the wee girls had gone and lived with her aunt who had no family. He couldn't remember her name and he thought it rude to ask about her without having her name.

'Martha well?' he asked shortly.

'Grand. Working away. And how's Ellen?'

'About the same. Good days and bad.'

There was a pause which began to lengthen as each man reflected on this ritual exchange about the well-being of their wives. Neither had made a happy marriage. Martha Hamilton was sharp and had little time for the father of her children.

Ellen Scott had little time for anyone but herself. She was one of those people who never found anything in life to be pleased about. She complained continually about her health and anything else that displeased her, so that Robert and those who knew her best had long since ceased to pay the slightest attention to anything she said.

'Sam, that's it.' He could not imagine how he could have forgotten his friend's namesake, the good-natured young man he'd met a couple of times now, most recently when he'd gone into Armagh to see about a more respectable bicycle for Ellie when she got her job in Freeburn's.

'An' what about *young* Sam?'

'Aye, I was coming to young Sam. Not good Robert, not good.'

'Ach, dear, is he poorly? And him such a fine lad.'

In the dim light, the whites of Robert's startled eyes stood out in sharp contrast to his dark and grimy face as he waited anxiously for a reply.

Sam Hamilton ran a hand over his thinning hair and shifted uneasily where he sat.

'Young Sam was to be married in June. A girl from Portadown. They've been going together three, maybe four years now. He's been working all the hours there are to save up for furnishing a house when they find one. He's even been cycling home of an evening to work with me for a few extra bob to add to his wages. It's a good, steady job he has at the cycle shop, but not great pay. An' you know yourself there's not much hope of betterment these days, there's so few

25

jobs going,' he said, shaking his head, and looking Robert in the eye.

'Well, about March time, Sammy ... Sam, I should say, for he doesn't like to be called Sammy now he's a man. Off he goes to Rountrees and buys a bedroom suite and a dining table and chairs with a sideboard to match, and a dresser and kitchen table and chairs to go with that. He paid cash for the whole lot and goes off in great glee to tell her what he's done. Well, she's not one bit pleased. She says he should have asked her to choose the furniture. He says he'd asked her what she'd like and they'd looked at stuff in the shop windows together. He'd picked out just what she'd admired. But that was only the start of it. She kept finding fault with him and he begins to get very uneasy.

'Well, at the heels of the hunt, it seems there was some other fellow had a fancy for her and the parents came in on his side and said what a good match it would be. The long and the short of it is, Robert, she jilted him, and I could hardly believe how badly he took it. Sure he cried like a child when he told me and I couldn't think of a word of comfort I could offer him. All I could do was get him to go over to see Rosie, for she and him were always very close. But our wee Sammy ... Sam, I should say, is a different man.'

'Ach, dear, that's a hard thing, and him a soft-natured man. Sure there's no badness in him. What did he do with the furniture?'

'Well, fair play to them, they gave him every penny of his money back, for the stuff had never left the showroom and he went straight out and

26

got drunk for the first time in his life. Then he bought a motorbike. A racing model, for he said he fancied entering the TT races. And I don't know which I'm more afeard of, him killing himself off the bike or him taking to the drink. I know I must put my faith in God, but I'm heart sore every time I look at him.'

'Aye you would be. Sure it's desperate to be young and feel that way about a woman,' said Robert in a tone that any other time would have made his friend sit up and take notice, but Sam Hamilton was thinking only of his son as he turned to Robert and finished his story.

'An' the worst of it is, Robert, he told me the other night that he thought he'd never marry now. That indeed he'd be unlikely even to look at a woman for many a long day.'

Two

The burst of applause and the roar of voices when the band stopped playing made it clear to Ellie and George that the small, wooden hall with its galvanized roof and peeling green paint-work, built some ten years earlier to accommodate a newly-formed Orange Lodge, was packed to capacity. Through the open door and the thrown-up sash windows, the beat of dance music throbbed out again into the evening quiet of the surrounding fields and lanes.

Close to the hall, against every convenient bush, tree and gatepost, bicycles were propped up. Released from the shafts of their traps, a few ponies tethered along the boundary hedge munched away quietly. At the entrance to the weed-grown and neglected field surrounding the hall itself, two motors were parked one behind the other almost blocking the narrow country lane.

Ellie had never been on a motorbike before and she'd caught her breath as the warm evening air raced past. It felt as chill as a winter gale, whipped her hair backwards and forwards across her face, gusted and swirled round her bare legs and plucked at the full skirt of her pretty, floral-patterned summer dress as George speeded along the twisty lanes through Ballybrannan, round the foot of Cannon Hill and on to Mullanisilla.

She'd clung tightly to his tweed jacket for warmth as well as safety, but when they came to a standstill and she climbed stiffly off the pillion and stepped on to the stony path leading away from the field-gate, she found she was shivering uncontrollably. As soon as she got her feet on the ground George left her and strode off, pushing, not his brother's borrowed bike, but his own new bike, his one thought the need to find a safe parking place.

Well at least it will be warm inside, she thought to herself, as she watched him go. She dabbed her dripping nose, ran her fingers through her tangled hair and shivered fiercely. *Well, you live and learn*, she said to herself, hearing her father's voice. She smiled ruefully, wrapped her arms round herself, covered up the expanse of goose-pimpled skin exposed by her scooped neckline and rubbed her arms vigorously to see if she could generate a little warmth in them while she waited.

Minutes passed. When George still failed to appear, she moved a little further in the direction he'd taken and found him eyeing a drainpipe at the side of the building. She watched as he took a chain from his pocket, attached one end to the drainpipe and fed the other through the spokes of the motorcycle before attaching a small padlock. He turned a key in the lock, tested it several times, then put the key carefully back in his top pocket. He stared all around him to see if there was any hazard he might have overlooked. Satisfied at last that no harm could come to his new possession he glanced towards her.

'That should be all right now,' he said, a bright smile on his face. 'Don't want anyone pinching *my* new bike.'

He took a final look over his shoulder as she came up to him, dropped an arm round her, marched her up to the door of the hall and produced his two half-crowns for the pair of men guarding it, so large they almost filled the entrance.

When they moved marginally apart to allow them to pass between them, she followed him as he elbowed his way towards the crowded dance floor, an indeterminate area between a deep line of girls on one side and a less deep line of men on the other. Here couples were entwined, if not

29

actually able to dance. He turned to her, put his arms round her and used his superior height and weight to propel them round the floor.

The band stopped. The applause was enthusiastic.

'Big crowd,' he said.

'Yes,' she agreed, fishing in her pocket for her hanky and dabbing her nose, now dripping even more vigorously than it had outside.

She was warming up now, for the atmosphere was like a warm blanket, but was much less pleasant. From somewhere nearby, there was an overpowering smell of cheap perfume and sweat. All around her, men with shiny foreheads were mopping their brows and girls with light dresses had patches of damp under each arm.

The floor was so packed, there was little opportunity for George to demonstrate his dancing skills. As the band grew more enthusiastic, encouraged no doubt by a crate of beer parked in the tiny kitchen behind their raised platform, Ellie gave up the attempt to make conversation and find out what George could possibly mean by talking about *his* new motorbike.

She exchanged smiles with girls she'd known only since working in Armagh. Others she'd known from childhood and the years they'd spent together in the schoolroom just inside the gates of the grey-towered parish church built on Church Hill. There was a new school now, down in Ballybrannan, which had only been open a year. It had a separate entrance for Boys and Girls and even separate flush toilets.

She smiled to herself. Very different from the

old schoolroom, where she and George were taught by Master Ebbitt and Miss Taylor. The visiting Inspector complained every year in his report that there was but one *office*, the earth privy used by both boys and girls. Probably it was the privy that had closed the school in the end. These days there were new regulations for shops and schools and places of work. Why, even her own boss, who paid as little attention as possible to such things, had had to provide seats for all his shop assistants even if they never had time to sit on them.

'Will we go out for a wee breath of air?' George asked, bending down to her ear to make himself heard.

She nodded and followed his tweed jacket as he carved his way back through the somewhat narrower lines of girls and out into the grassy area surrounding the hall. All around them couples were entwining their arms and setting off in search of a grassy bank or a low wall to sit on.

'There's a bench outside the smithy over there,' he said, pointing to a low, whitewashed building a couple of fields away. 'It's not far. I have something to tell you. It'll be worth the extra wee walk on up the lane,' he added, looking unusually pleased with himself.

George smiled a lot. He always had. Even when they were wee things together at school, he was known for his good nature. Nothing ever seemed to bother him. He was on good terms with everyone. He was two years older than she was and he'd had a notion of Ellie since she was twelve or thirteen. Given they lived next door to each other, it had always been assumed they'd make a match. As their teenage years passed neither of them had objected to this assumption. Their only problem was the one faced by all their contemporaries. Where were they to get the money to get married?

To be able to get married you needed a job that paid enough to rent a house and support a wife and family. Jobs that paid well were few and far between and houses were scarce even if you could afford the rent. It made no difference that George was the second son of Tom Robinson, a fair-sized farmer for these parts of North Armagh. Still in his late forties, Tom had no thought whatever of retiring and, even when he did, he'd made it clear he had no intention at all of splitting up the farm his father and grand-father had managed to put together. The land would pass intact to the eldest son, young Tommy.

Meantime, George was working on the land with his brother. He had his keep, his clothes and ten shillings a week in his pocket. The motorbike was a present from his Uncle George, the Direc-tor of a Canadian timber company, well enough off to come home every seven years or so to see his brother and his family. He'd been in resi-dence next door for nearly two weeks of his usual three-week visit.

Ellie and George walked along the lane swing-ing their clasped hands. The May evening was still warm. After the stuffiness and overpower-ing smells of the hall, Ellie was more than usually grateful for its freshness. There were wild roses in the hedge, pale pink petals freshly unfurled, the first she'd seen that year.

'Aye indeed, sure they're early enough,' he replied agreeably to her comment. 'It's an early season altogether. Ah hope to goodness we don't get frost.'

'So do I. I still have my geraniums on the windowsill. I'm waiting till after the full moon to plant them out.'

'Are ye now?'

He turned towards her for the first time that evening and looked her up and down, from the crown of her still-tousled fair hair to her neat little feet and the shoes with their latticework pattern her sister Florence had sent her from London.

They sat down together and he drew her into his arms, kissed her vigorously and then took her hand.

'I have some great news for you, Ellie,' he began. 'You know how we've been talkin' and plannin' and wonderin' how we could manage to find a wee house and get married. Well, *I* have the answer,' he announced, pausing for effect.

'My goodness, George, what's happened?' she cried, her grey eyes sparkling with excitement.

'I've been offered a great job. Ye'd hardly believe how much money I'll be earnin'. I'll have saved up for a house in no time an' I'll be able to send out for ye.'

Ellie's smile faded. Her mouth, half open to ask about the great new job, closed again as she put together the clues in what he'd said. There were no jobs with big money in Armagh or anywhere else in Ireland. Or if there were, they were not for the likes of George.

She could see he was waiting for her to tell him how pleased she was with his news. She pushed her unease to the back of her mind and asked the obvious question.

'Is it your Uncle George's business?'

'How did ye guess?'

Not exactly difficult, she thought to herself, when he'd talked about nothing but Uncle George for the last fortnight. Out loud she asked quietly what the job was and whereabouts in Canada it was.

Once started there was no stopping him. The words tripped over each other as he told her all the details he'd gleaned from his uncle since his arrival. She already knew Uncle George had a timber business. Now he told her its headquarters was in a place called Peterborough. Ellie had never heard of Peterborough and George himself seemed vague as to its whereabouts, but he was quite clear the timber came from some distance away. There were logging camps in the northern forest where men worked cutting timber till the snow fell. Then they used sledges to move it out to the bigger rivers and have it ready to float down to the sawmills in the spring. As Uncle George had said, you needed to be strong and very fit.

It wasn't hard to see why Uncle George had made his proposal, Ellie thought to herself. His nephew looked the part. Tall and broad, suntanned and easy-going. What she couldn't see was why George thought this plan would solve their problem. The more he talked about the camps, the chuck wagons that cooked their food and the paymasters who brought their dollars every week, the more she felt that something dreadful was happening. Instead of being pleased and happy, she grew more and more anxious.

'But where would we live George?' she broke in, unable to listen to any more of his excited account.

'Oh, we'd live in Peterborough,' he said firmly. 'Or one of the smaller places with a saw-mill. But that wouldn't be for a wee while. I'd have to learn the job out at the camps before I could be given a supervising job in one of the mills or an office job in one of the retail ware-houses.'

'And where would I be when you were up in the forest with the other men and the bears?' she asked, a tremor threatening to break up her carefully chosen words.

'Ach, ye needn't worry about me an' the bears. I shoulden have told ye about them at all,' he said, drawing her close and patting her bare arm. 'You'll be safe here till I've saved up to send for you. Sure we can get married out there as well as here,' he went on reassuringly.

Ellie shivered. Even this late in the evening, there was still no chill in the air, but the thought of going out to Canada to marry George was so different from anything they'd ever planned, she just didn't know where or how she'd find the courage to go through with it.

'How long do you think it might be before I

could come out to you?'

'Ach, not long. A couple of years or so. Sure you'll not know the time goin' an' you can go on savin' up a wee bit too,' he said encouragingly.

'What happens if you find someone else to marry, George?' she asked, determined to get him to focus his mind on them rather than on all the things his uncle had told him.

'Ach, sure there'll be no women up at the camps. Ye can rest easy there,' he said with a grin, as he pulled a strand of her long hair.

'And what happens if *I* find someone else that wants to marry me and stay here?' she asked quietly, looking him straight in the eye.

'Now don't be sayin' things like that, Ellie,' he replied quickly. 'Haven't you and I been goin' out together since the time you left school? Aren't we made for each other?' he went on, his deep voice rising somewhat as he made his point. 'Sure we can talk it all over next week. Our Tommy's startin' a man on the farm, so he won't be short-handed when I go, so I'll be able to take you out every evenin'. We could go to the pictures in Armagh one night and maybe the Friday dance in the City Hall. They say it has a great floor and it's never crowded like these wee places,' he added, nodding his dark head towards the distant sound of music.

'So when are you thinking of going?' she blurted out, as the implications of what he'd just said dawned upon her.

'Uncle wants me to travel back with him. It's too good an opportunity to miss havin' someone to go with that knows their way about,' he explained quickly. 'He's booked us on the Liver-pool boat for Sunday week and we'll pick up the Canadian Pacific ship on the Monday. It sails that evening for Quebec. So he says.'

As Ellie climbed into her large, cold bed a couple of hours later, she wondered how she'd ever managed to keep from crying through the rest of the long, long evening. Now she need try no more. Tears came instantly, running silently down her face, sinking into the crisp, white pillowcase with the decoration of pink daisies she'd embroidered in her last year at school.

She felt her head in such a turmoil, she didn't even know where to begin to make sense of things. Between the morning and the evening of an unexceptional day, her world had changed completely. George, who had been there all her life, her fiancé in all but name, was going away. In just over a week, he'd be setting off from Armagh Station and by this day fortnight he'd be on a ship on his way to Canada. He'd even told her the name of the vessel and how they'd get off at Quebec and not Montreal, because that was the quickest way to travel to Peterborough. And within the month he'd be up in his camp with the lumberjacks and the chuck wagon.

At the thought of the immense distance open-ing up between them, the tears flowed faster. For as long as she could remember, he'd been next door, a minute or two's walk down the short cut from her own house, past his father's barns, along the front of the substantial two-storey dwelling and into the farmyard. And if she couldn't see him anywhere, or hear his voice echoing from stable or byre, she'd only to go to his mother in the dairy or the scullery, or even in to old Granny Robinson sitting by the fire in the big kitchen and ask them where he was.

What *was* she going to do?

She turned restlessly in the large bed, big enough to have taken all four sisters together when they were still small. If only she wasn't on her own with all her brothers and sisters gone. Mary, it's true, was always so bound up in her own affairs, she'd seldom been any help, but Florence was only a little older than herself and always sorry if something had upset her little sister. Although she might not be very good at giving advice she would always listen. She'd try to encourage her and remind her things were never as bad as one thought and often she'd been right.

It was Polly she needed now, but her eldest and dearest sister was in Toronto with a husband, two small boys and a little one, and a load of worries of her own. Not that Polly would ever let her own problems get in the way. If you asked her something, you could always be sure she'd pay attention. She had a way of looking at you as if she was hearing more than you were telling her. When you'd finished, she'd say not what would comfort you, or what she thought you wanted to hear, and certainly not what she herself would do, but what might actually help you to see your way.

If only there were more time, she could write and ask her what she thought of George's plan and what she herself should do. But even though letters took only five or six days each way, there still wasn't time to get an answer back before he went. She'd just have to manage by herself.

Tired out, she fell asleep at last, her face wet with tears. It felt like only minutes later that she woke suddenly, her whole body rigid with tension. A large brown bear had been staring at her and as she wondered whatever she was going to do, it began to lumber towards her. Her eyes flew open in the dim room and the whole evening with George unrolled before her once again.

She knew he loved her and indeed she had loved him for as long as she could remember. He certainly wasn't the first young man to go away, work hard for a year or two and send for his sweetheart. It happened all the time. But the whole thing had been so sudden. They'd never even considered it themselves. Maybe if he'd told her what Uncle George was proposing, or asked her what she thought before everything was settled, it would be easier. But then, he was doing his best, thinking of how they might be together. If he was the one who had to go she could hardly say 'don't go' when going was to give them the future together they'd planned.

But all the time, she felt something was wrong. Try as she would, she couldn't see what it was, except that she just didn't know how she could go on living at home and working in Freeburn's with no George and no one but girlfriends to talk to. The very thought of it brought the tears streaming down her cheeks again until the pillow was so wet she had to turn it over before she made another attempt to go to sleep.

'Ellie, are ye up?'

She jerked awake at the sound of her father's voice.

Brilliant light was streaming through the dust-streaked windows and making bright patches on the linoleum. She knew without looking at her clock she'd overslept. She, who always woke early and lay, warm and comfortable, till she heard her father raking out the stove.

'Just coming,' she replied, jumping out of bed and pouring water from the jug into her wash basin.

The water was icy on her face and warm body but she moved so quickly she hardly noticed. Within minutes, she was dressed in her black skirt and white, shop-assistant's blouse. She brushed her hair while pushing her feet into her everyday shoes, closed her bedroom door firmly on the unmade bed and the chair with her floral dress still draped over it, and hurried across the small entrance hall to the open kitchen door.

Her father was frying soda bread in the heavy griddle, the smoke rising already from the over-hot fat, the smell of burning just beginning to taint the air.

'Can I do that for you, Da?'

'Aye. Yer a better han' at it than me. Yer Ma says she's not well.'

'Would she like a cup of tea?'

He flicked his eyes upwards and tightened his lips. He'd forgotten to ask and he knew as well

40

as Ellie neither of them would hear the end of it until the day was out or some better opportunity for complaint turned up.

'Will I away and see?'

'You'd better,' she replied, her back to him as she bent over the pan, drawing it away from the heat and tipping it gently to redistribute the melted suet.

It was only as she heard a muffled step behind her that the confused dark shadows she'd brought from sleep finally came together in her head. George was going to Canada. There'd be no wedding after the harvest, this year or next. She had no idea how she would tell either her father or the woman who now limped across the kitchen in her bare feet and subsided with a heavy sigh on the wooden settle by the fire.

'I was dying of thirst,' she said, addressing no one in particular. 'I just hadta make mysel' get up, I was that parched.'

'I could bring you some breakfast to bed if you want to go back,' said Ellie, knowing perfectly well the offer would be refused.

'Ach, I haven't the energy to walk that far without a bite in me.'

'Well it won't be long now,' Ellie responded, glancing round at her.

Her mother's hair had been grey for years, but now, though she was only in her early fifties, it had gone both thin and white. Once she had worn it in a plait, curved round and pinned up in a bun, but these days she let it hang lank and loose round her wrinkled face in a tattered curtain that brushed against her dull skin and her

41

too-bright, red cheeks.

'Ye'll have to bring me water from the well afore ye go to work, Ellie, for I'm not fit for it the day.'

'Sure I'll get the water. Hasn't Ellie to go to her work for half past eight?' Robert asked crossly.

'Sit over, Da, it's ready,' said Ellie, moving between them with the teapot in one hand and a dish of fried bread in the other. 'Will you have yours there, Ma?'

'Aye, if I can eat a bit at all. Sure I hardly slept a wink last night.'

Robert pulled his wooden armchair up to the table and sat with his eyes on his plate as he munched the crisp pieces of soda bread and drank deep from a large mug of tea. Ellie brought a plate and cup across to her mother where she sat round-shouldered and slack on the wooden settle, her pale, watery eyes peering at the tiny bright points of flame dancing and flickering beyond the open front of the stove.

She appeared not to notice the cup of tea and the plate of fried bread Ellie placed beside her, but that was nothing new. She would only eat if no one were looking at her, as if by avoiding their gaze she could pretend she hadn't eaten at all.

Ellie drew up her own chair to the table. She knew she was thirsty but eating was going to be an effort. She would have to do her best, for her father would notice if she left anything on her plate. She'd always been slim and sometimes when she was tired or very busy at work, she lost weight quite quickly. He always noticed and she knew it worried him. As if he didn't have worries enough.

He never knew what tale of woe he'd hear when he came up from the forge. Sometimes it was just a string of complaints about trivial things, so he'd just fetch water, or make tea, or see to the bread man. Other times, she was lying down. If she was on the settle in the big, dark kitchen, then it wasn't too bad. If she retired to the sofa in the sitting room, it meant he'd have to fend for himself and try to find out what she wanted. If she went back to bed, he'd have to decide if she really was ill this time and whether or not he ought to send for the doctor.

She had a chest complaint common to spinners, a legacy of the days before her marriage when she worked at Drumcairn Mill. She also had what she called 'bad legs', a rheumatic condition which varied with the season, usually made worse by cold and damp. But most of all, Ellen Scott suffered from a condition that lacked a medical name. She had neither hope, joy, nor enthusiasm. In their place, she put dissatisfaction, anxiety and despair. Nothing in her life was right. It never had been. It never would be.

Ellie had often puzzled over her mother's endless complaints and had come to the conclusion, many years ago, that the only thing her mother enjoyed was feeding her hens. Standing outside her front door, a dirty apron over her oldest dress, her carpet slippers still on her feet, she would chatter and call, laughing in a strange, high-pitched voice, addressing them by name, throwing pieces of broken bread to her favourites, crowing with pleasure as they argued and squabbled over the scraps.

That was the only time Ellie recalled ever seeing her mother smile. For her husband and family, there had never been a word of warmth or comfort.

Only the thought of wheeling her bicycle down the lane and leaving the dark, stuffy kitchen behind her helped her get through the morning routine. But not for one minute was she able to put out of mind that this kitchen and this woman would be her life for as long as it took for George to make his way in Canada and send for her.

If ever he did.

Three

The May morning was once again fresh and pleasant as Ellie pushed her bicycle along the bumpy lane to the main road, caught up her skirt and freewheeled down the slope to where the gradient levelled out and ran past the three separate entrances to Robinson's farm.

Pedalling slowly, she glanced at the silver-painted, decorative gates her father had made for the shrub-lined avenue. They were closed as they always were, the drive beyond rising sharply to the farmhouse itself. Standing squarely, surrounded by a low wall, pierced by a small garden gate, also of her father's making, the morning sun reflected from its blank windows. There was no one in sight.

She could hear the clatter of pails from the nearby byre, but was not really surprised there was no one to be seen either on the driveway or in front of the house itself. The front door was seldom used. Only the doctor or someone collecting for the Parish church would walk up the gravel path under the shadow of the monkey-puzzle to disturb the highly polished brass knocker.

She moved on and drew level with the wide entrance to the farmyard. The large, five-barred field gate was seldom closed but there was no sign of life there either and no familiar figure to greet her. As she paused to glance in, the only movement was a row of ducks crossing from their shallow pond behind the hedge to peck hopefully among the scattered residues on the floor of the hay shed.

She stared up and down the familiar cobbled yard, its surface now caked with dried mud after two days of warmth. The hay shed stood open to the mild breeze, its year's supply of fodder almost at an end. The tall ladders needed to stack the uppermost bales after the harvest were neatly laid to one side until the new crop came home and the solid battlements were rebuilt for another year.

Still she waited, but George was nowhere to be seen. Her heart sank, the pain of disappointment so sharp she felt angry with herself. She'd missed seeing him yesterday morning, because of setting out half an hour before her usual time, but surely he could have made a special effort to walk down the yard from the byre this morning. He knew exactly what time she left home and it would only take him a few minutes. She so needed to see him, just to exchange a few words, after the turbulence of the night.

She turned her eyes back reluctantly to the empty road and pedalled off vigorously. There was no use at all hoping she might see him at the third and final entrance to the farm. It would not be used till the milking was finished and the cows were herded along its rough, dung-splattered surface and back across the road into the largest of the Robinson meadows.

As she cycled the two miles into Armagh she barely saw the passing countryside. Yesterday, she'd had an eye for every bush and tree, for every sign of the approaching summer, and especially for the flowers of garden or hedgerow. Today, she spared not a thought to her surroundings. She could not get beyond the fact that George was going away. Going to Canada. And she was not going with him.

Without the slightest prompting on her part, the facts printed out like newspaper headlines. It felt as if she were having an argument with someone who kept asking the same things over and over again, because they either wouldn't listen to what she was saying or didn't accept the answers she gave.

'He never even thought of taking you.'

'But that's perfectly reasonable,' she retorted,

46

stung by the implicit criticism. 'He couldn't very well take me to a lumber camp.'

'He might just have asked you whether you thought it was worth the separation to be able to start your married life with a home in a new country.'

As she came alongside the railway bridge, she was so absorbed in arguing on George's behalf, she didn't even hear the approaching roar of the Portadown train. It steamed past in the direction from which she'd come, enveloping her in a cloud of smoke and steam, but she hardly noticed the sting in her eyes or the catch in her throat and gave not a thought to the daily threat of soot particles falling on her clean blouse.

Perhaps Uncle George didn't realize that his nephew was as good as engaged. Surely George would have told him the only reason it wasn't announced was a lack of means. Everyone agreed there was no point getting engaged when you had no immediate prospect of getting married.

She cycled past the newly-opened gates of Drumsollen without noticing the elegant motor that paused between them until she had gone by. Sitting behind the wheel, wearing his chauffeur's uniform, Ned Wylie watched her go and wondered what could be the matter with Ellie Scott that she didn't give him her usual cheery wave.

Had he but known it, she was far away, trying to imagine a life in Canada, the wife of a lumberman or a clerk in a timber-office in an unknown town called Peterborough. The more she considered the prospect the more the thought of going to Canada filled her with anxiety. Her distress was the greater because she couldn't imagine why she could possibly be anxious about anything, so long as she had George at her side.

She knew of lots of women who had emigrated. Indeed, that's what two of her own sisters had done. But things were different when Polly and Jimmy had gone off five years ago. In 1927, Jimmy had a good job in Toronto to go out to with a house available at a modest rent. Two years later, Polly's newly pregnant with her second child, house and job had disappeared. They'd had to sell their lovely new furniture and go into lodgings and Jimmy had been lucky even to find a labouring job.

Still, that wouldn't happen to her and George, surely. His uncle's was a well-established business, selling lumber in Canada and the States and exporting to Europe as well. So what was she worrying about?

Struggling and perspiring, she found herself almost at the top of Asylum Hill without having stopped and wheeled her bicycle up its steep slope. Gasping, she got off to catch her breath.

Quite suddenly and unexpectedly, she remembered something Polly had said quite recently. If she and George were thinking of Canada he had to have a job lined up and an employer's address to put on his papers before Immigration would consider them.

She always told George about what Polly said in her letters. When she went to meet him that

48

particular evening, she'd wondered how he'd react when she mentioned the fact that Polly thought they might be thinking of joining her and Jimmy. But George had just listened to Polly's news, laughed and said Canada wasn't for him. He was a *home bird* and so was she. Something would turn up for them soon to let them get settled.

Some months later Polly had written to say the Canadian Government had begun to encourage immigrants who'd not become Canadian citizens to go back home. They were even handing out one-way tickets to speed up the process. With times as hard in Canada now as they were at home, there wasn't much point either of them thinking any more about it whether they were *home birds* or not, so she hadn't even mentioned it to George.

She wondered if this was why she felt so upset and so confused. She'd completely accepted that they were home birds. Some people were like that. She'd heard many a person say, for better or worse, they wanted to stay where they were, her father for one.

Many times he'd told the story of having the chance to go out to Alberta. His much older half-brother, Charley, had a successful clothing business and wrote home to his mother and told her anyone in the family, brothers or sisters, or even friends, would be welcome. He'd pay their fare, fill in their papers, have a job for them and find them somewhere to live until they got settled. But her father had said no. Charley was a good-hearted man and it was generous of him to make

49

the offer. It wasn't that he didn't appreciate it, but this was his place and here he intended to stay.

She sighed. Perhaps she had thought George was a man like her father, but clearly she'd been wrong.

The outskirts of the city were always quiet on a Saturday morning. As most of the goods arriving by rail came on weekdays, neither the jingle of harness nor the oppressive grinding of wheels on the cobbles outside the station gates interrupted her thoughts. Peddling on up Railway Street, she didn't have to pull in and stop if two Wordie carts met each other head on, one with a projecting load, the other empty, the carters shouting to each other as they edged past in the confined space.

Later, it would be busy enough as farmers and their wives came in to do the weekly shopping. But they would not appear till the morning jobs were done in byre and dairy and the mare brought up from some nearby field to be put between the shafts of the trap.

As the sun moved higher and cleared the rooftops in English Street, she pedalled on, perspiring now, her thoughts exhausted for the moment. She slowed to a crawl behind a hay float laden with wooden crates on its way to the egg packing station in Dobbin Street and scanned the frontage of the local newspaper office. Attached to the walls between the windows of the densely-packed shop were bright and bold posters. She loved their colour and pattern and their

50

striking images, but this morning she couldn't bear to look again at the familiar images displaying the ships of the Canadian Pacific Line.

They had been advertising cruises and holidays for weeks now. She loved the white ships on the blue water, the sharp line of the hull contrasted with the smooth rounded curves of the clouds of steam set against a perfect summer sky. There was one of the Rockies as well, high and jagged with patches of snow in dazzling sunshine. Superimposed upon them was a train steaming across the prairies, a smiling couple, arms entwined, in the observation car just like those she'd seen on the screen at the Ritz cinema, the man pointing into the distance with a long, suntanned arm.

Perhaps George had something like that in mind, she said to herself, suddenly glancing back at the smiling couple. She would come out to join him. He would meet her in Quebec and they would travel on to their new home, wherever that might be. Distances were so vast in Canada. Instead of an hour on the train to Belfast, you might say a day to Toronto, or two days to Alberta. George's geography wasn't any better than her own, but he'd made the point last evening about the size of the country, the huge, wide-open spaces. So different from the place they lived where nothing of any importance to you was more than a few miles away, and a hundred miles in almost any direction would take you to the sea.

Just as she was beginning to worry about being late for work, the float pulled off unexpectedly to one side of Market Place where the nursery-men were laying out their wares in front of the Technical College. As she set off again she saw a young man emerge from behind the egg boxes and begin unloading bundles of cabbages and a couple of young trees wrapped in sacking.

Though not the main one of the week, the Saturday market was already crowded and busy. Women were examining trays of bedding plants laid out on trestle tables and well-wrapped shrub roses parked against them. She glanced across at the splashes of colour, an equal and opposite grey sadness clutching at her. How often had she gone to walk among those same trestle tables in her lunch hour, looking at similar wee plants and just occasionally allowing herself to buy one she could slip for cuttings, growing them on in her own garden till such time as she and George would make their garden together. She couldn't take wee plants to Canada, so there'd be no point in making any more.

She edged her way through the market and was just rounding the corner into Scotch Street when she heard the clatter of hooves. She stopped and waited while three heavy Shire horses pulling grocery vans emerged one by one from the yard behind the tall, red-brick frontage of the Co-op. They blocked her path till there was a gap in the traffic coming up Scotch Street and they were able to turn right down Thomas Street on their way to begin their morning rounds in the vil-lages to the west of the city.

She freewheeled the remaining short distance to Freeburn's High Class Drapers, its wide, plate glass windows dazzling now in the morning light. She wheeled her bicycle up a narrow entry between high brick walls, pushed open the door into a crowded yard and parked it against a mangle left to rust beside the door of what had once been the privy. She had barely crossed the stone floor of the maid's scullery and set foot on the servant's staircase when a familiar voice echoed from the floor above.

'Ah, Miss Scott, you *have* arrived.'

'Good morning, Miss Walker,' she replied politely, as she climbed the narrow stair, perfectly aware of the older woman's half-concealed glance at the fob watch pinned to the ample bosom of her severe black dress.

Ellie did not possess a watch, but she knew the cathedral clock had not yet struck the half-hour. She followed the dark figure across a landing stacked to the ceiling with cardboard boxes and into a small, congested room, known as 'the staffroom' which served as an additional store for bales of cloth and yet more boxes of extra stock. She hung up her bag on the hook provided, took out her comb, ran it quickly through her hair and straightened her blouse and skirt.

Now in her sixties, Miss Walker was a tall, unbending woman with steel-grey hair and eyes so pale they seemed to lack any colour at all. She had been senior assistant at Freeburn's for the last thirty-five years. Her greatest virtue was the meticulous attention she gave to any piece of information that passed before her eyes, accompanied by an enormous memory for detail. Her greatest vice was a complete lack of forgiveness

53

for anyone not similarly gifted.

She stared at Ellie as if unwilling to accept, for the moment, the girl was presenting no opportunity for the sharp comments she felt entitled, and indeed required, to make on any aspect of her punctuality, appearance or demeanour. She compensated herself for this lost opportunity by a quite unnecessary asperity in conveying her instructions.

'I've made a list of replacement stock, Miss Scott. As soon as Miss Hutchinson favours us with her presence, I want you to collect the boxes and take them downstairs. You will need to do them one at a time behind the counter so that there are no boxes sitting on the floor when customers are...'

Though Ellie had heard the instruction a hundred times before, she assumed a gravely attentive expression, but this time Miss Walker was forced to break off as the door flew open. A tall, round-faced girl burst into the room, dark curls sticking damply to her flushed cheeks. From the floor below, the former kitchen clock ran through its preliminary wheezings. After a moment of complete silence, its tinny notes rose up through the stairwell. Though muffled by the barricades of cardboard boxes piled high on the landing outside, its message was clear enough. Eight thirty. They listened in silence as it struck the half-hour.

'You may indeed be *in time* for work, Miss Hutchinson, but I hardly think by any stretch of the imagination one could say you were *ready for* work.'

'I'm sorry, Miss Walker. Scotch Street is desperate busy. There was a Crossley tender tryin' to get down the street through the carts comin' up for the market an' I coulden get through.'

'Perhaps if you'd left home somewhat earlier the necessary activities of our Police force would not have inconvenienced you,' the older woman replied sarcastically. 'Tidy yourself up and when you're fit to be seen come and take over from me in the Ladies' Department. Miss Scott has her duties already.'

Her lips snapped shut on the last word like a vice and she sailed out with as much dignity as the congested area permitted.

'The old cow!'

'Shh, Daisy, she'll hear you,' said Ellie softly, as she took out her comb and pushed her friend gently down on to a bentwood chair. 'Let me do it, I'm quicker than you.'

One look at Daisy's crumpled face told Ellie that things were bad. It wasn't just the effort of getting up early and cycling the three miles from her home on the other side of the city, it was the burden she'd been carrying since her father had died suddenly, two years ago, leaving his small farm in debt.

For some time now her mother had been poorly. The doctor didn't seem to know what was wrong. That meant the only labour they had was Daisy herself and her two younger brothers, Bill and Johnny, who were both still at school. Their only regular income was Daisy's meagre pay. However much she hated Miss Walker, she just could not afford to upset her. Getting the sack would be a disaster.

'What's happened, Daisy? Something's wrong,' Ellie whispered as she undid the black ribbon, caught up the dark curls and repinned them into a neat chignon.

'We've had a notice from the landlord. He says he'll put the bailiffs in if we don't pay up,' she said gasping, her eyes wide, her lips trembling on the verge of tears. 'What am I goin' to do Ellie? What am I goin' to do?'

'I don't know, Daisy, but we'll think of something,' she replied, giving her a little kiss on the cheek. 'Tuck your blouse in, it's out at the back. We'll go and have an ice cream after work. My treat,' she added hastily, as she saw the look of anxiety in her friend's eyes. 'Now away down as quick as you can. Give her no excuse to pull you up. We'll manage something. We really will.'

Ellie took a deep breath, put her comb away and consulted Miss Walker's list, but the beautifully written copperplate suddenly blurred before her eyes as the thought came back to her yet again that George was going away and she was going to have to remain. Here, in this cramped and confined room. Here, in the more spacious but equally confining Ladies' Department. Here, being polite and courteous and helpful to people who were seldom polite to her in return, seldom courteous and rarely helpful.

But she had a home to go to, a roof over her head, and was short of money only because she'd been saving every penny she could, whereas poor Daisy had to spend every penny she earned on food for the family and meal for

56

the hens. She hadn't even been able to afford a new blouse in all of the two years she'd been at Freeburn's and her shoes had pieces of cardboard in them, because she couldn't afford the cobbler in Jenny's Row.

The box of *Ladies Knickers, Large* she needed was at the bottom of the pile stacked on the landing. She reached up, tugged at a box labelled *Leather Gloves, Black* which was pressed against the low ceiling, managed to slow its fall as it tipped towards her and dragged it to one side. A further struggle with *Aprons and Overalls, Assorted* enabled her to reach the one she needed. She had just finished rebuilding the column of boxes and was about to pick up *Ladies Knickers, Large* when from below she thought she heard her name.

Yes, someone was calling her. For a moment, she didn't recognize the speaker. She picked up her box and staggered down the steep stairs. The voice called again and she realized who it was. Miss Walker, of course. Who else? She was in the shop and the voice was her shop voice, so there must be a customer present.

'Miss Scott. Do come down please. Mrs Richardson is here and she would like your assistance with some of our new material.'

Miss Walker beamed at her as she stepped into the well-lit rear of the shop and looked around the cardboard shield of *Ladies Knickers, Large*.

'Oh Miss Scott, do leave that box for one of the young gentlemen. Really, my dear, that's much too heavy for you,' she said, smiling across at Mrs Richardson as Ellie put it down

57

and came up to the counter already strewn around with swathes of fabric.

Ellie said, 'Good Morning', smiled politely and took a deep breath. The working day had begun in earnest. Whatever problems she or Daisy might have, there would be no rest or comfort for either of them till it had ended.

Four

Charlie Freeburn, the owner of Freeburn's High Class Drapery was an unprepossessing figure. Short, with a well-rounded stomach, a thick neck and bulging lens in his gold-framed spectacles, he closed his own front door firmly behind him on Saturday afternoon and set off across the wide tree-lined road outside. He took in his surroundings with a customary sideways glance which seemed to suggest that, by avoiding a too direct approach, he would see something other people would miss. However limiting his short-sightedness, Charlie missed nothing. That indeed was the secret of his remarkable success.

Left an orphan at the age of six when he was too unwell to join the rest of his family on the ill-fated Sunday School rail excursion to Warren-point in June 1889, he had been brought up by his aunt and uncle in the domestic part of the premises to which he now proceeded briskly on this pleasant afternoon. It had not been an easy childhood. Charlie preferred not to remember how difficult his aunt and uncle had found it to make a living despite his aunt's long hours making mourning clothes for their shop customers and providing for her lodgers, two young men from a rival drapery business who slept in the attic rooms and ate with the family.

As soon as he left school, Charlie went into the business and served his time. He hated the rudeness and arrogance of the customers, the confinement of living over the shop and even the smell of fabric. Having no other option, he began to plan for the day when his uncle would retire and he himself become the boss. The time passed slowly, his only pleasures the books he read and the activity of increasing his small resources by trading on the Stock Market. Then came the flu epidemic of 1919 and his uncle died suddenly. By then Charlie had equipped himself not only with a formidable financial knowledge and a respectable amount of capital, but over the years had privately conducted a survey of all the other drapery establishments in his native city.

Along with thirteen churches and thirty-nine public houses, the number of these establishments in Armagh appeared out of proportion for a city of only some eleven thousand inhabitants. Unlike his rivals, Charlie did not wonder where all the customers came from, he made it his business to find out. And find out he did, from his aunt's former lodgers, or the young men who lived over Lennox's shop, or the many relatives of his wife, the former Mary Hutchinson, a Richhill girl from a large family whose prolific offspring and matrimonial links put him in touch with the senior servants, the housekeepers and the dressmakers of the local gentry and aristocracy.

Within the space of five years, Charlie had bought the adjoining property and doubled the size of the ground floor shop. In the next five, he increased his staff and removed his wife and daughters to a handsome, brick-built house overlooking The Mall, a pleasant, tree-lined, green space, which had once been a race track until the fulminations of the local clergy had put an end to this activity. Since then, it had become a place for ladies to walk, nursemaids to push perambulators and the local cricket team to display their skills on Saturday afternoons.

Now, in May 1932, Charlie knew he had more regular customers and more monthly orders for cloth and clothing than any of his rivals. His elder daughter had married into a prosperous, old farming family in County Antrim and his younger daughter, though not as likely as her sister to acquire a title when her father-in-law died, had ensured her future comfort by marrying the son of the motor company in English Street where he had bought his newest vehicle. The lack of a son of his own was a matter of regret, but, as he reminded himself regularly, what he lacked in sons to carry on the business, he most certainly made up for in grandsons and nephews. At least he would have plenty of choice.

By four thirty, as he made his way along Barrack Street and slowed somewhat on the steepest part of Scotch Street, he observed that the traffic had cleared. The pavements were much less crowded than when he'd made his usual mid-morning visit to the shop. Another hour and all would be quiet, the empty streets foreshadowing something of the complete silence of Sunday.

He congratulated himself on the wisdom of closing at five-thirty on a Saturday. Other drapers might remain open until six o'clock, but what was the point? Given that most of their customers had come a distance, many from farms as much as eight miles away where there were cattle waiting to be milked and an evening meal to be cooked, the women were unlikely to linger. In his experience, men seldom shopped for clothes without a female companion. Well, if his rivals wanted to waste gas or electric to light empty premises, let them. Attention to detail was a critical element in financial success and his success had proved it.

As if to confirm the rightness of his judge-ment, he found only one customer in the Ladies' Department. Miss Hutchinson was laying out black gloves for a pale-faced woman, a regular customer to whom he courteously touched his hat. Miss Scott was sorting a box of ribbon, re-rolling the disordered lengths with deft fingers.

In accordance with his instructions, the lights had been dimmed in the empty Gentlemen's Department which occupied the opposite side of the wide ground floor. Two of his male assistants were refolding garments, another was replacing bales of cloth in the central display units while the senior man was already making up the tak-

61

ings at the furthest end of the long wooden counter. Miss Walker would be writing up the account ledgers while awaiting his arrival in his office.

'Good, good,' he said, to no one in particular, his glance moving backwards and forwards, carefully avoiding Miss Hutchinson and her customer. A bereavement, of course, he thought to himself. People didn't often go for full mourning these days, though Freeburn's could provide it if required. But why else would you buy black gloves in summer?

He paused, made up his mind and set off down the length of the shop to where Miss Scott was working. Perfectly aware of his presence, but absorbed in her own thoughts and the job in hand, Ellie kept her head bent over the ribbons.

'An order, Miss Scott?' he asked genially.

'No, Mr Freeburn, just routine tidying,' she replied. 'Ribbon seems to have such a knack of unrolling, even when we use rubber bands over the spools.'

He nodded agreeably. The girl was good at her job. The customers liked her and often asked especially for her. Even Miss Walker couldn't find much to complain about. Miss Hutchinson was another matter. He sighed. She was one of his wife's innumerable cousins. One couldn't *always* pick and choose. Not a bad girl, but a little lacking in style. One had to be very particular about that sort of thing in the high-class trade.

'Miss Scott, I wonder if I could ask a little favour?'

Ellie looked up at him and smiled. She noticed

he was carrying a parcel carefully wrapped in tissue paper.

'Mrs Freeburn has asked me to deliver this to young Mrs Sleator. I'm told it's any day now,' he added confidingly. 'I wonder if you would be so good as to deliver it to the showroom. Mr Wright can carry on with any other tidying here that you think necessary.'

Ellie took the parcel and patted it gently.

'Has Mrs Freeburn been crocheting for the little one?'

'I expect so,' he replied, beaming at her. 'I am a mere messenger,' he added, laughing at his own joke.

The heat struck up at her from the pavement as she closed the heavy glass door behind her and moved beyond the shade of the awnings, but she was delighted to be outside in the warmth and light. She walked briskly towards the market-place and found the market itself had vanished as if it had never been. From all the morning's bustle and activity, neither a fallen bloom nor a stray cabbage leaf remained. Beyond the broad open space itself, the main street was almost empty of people. A scatter of confetti outside the Beresford Arms told her why there were so many motors parked along the street.

She moved on, the warmth on her shoulders easing the ache of the day's lifting and carrying. Just beyond the newspaper office she could see two brand-new motors parked in front of Slea-tor's showroom. She did her best to keep her eyes firmly fixed on them and on the frontage behind as she hurried past the Canadian Pacific posters, but for all her effort and resolution her heart still sank. She could hardly avoid seeing them when from the pavement they were close enough to touch.

All was quiet at Sleator's. No one was looking at the new models, their gleaming bodywork reflecting her image briefly as she moved towards the entrance. She could smell the leather, warm from the sun, as she stopped, looked around and wondered where to go. There was a small office inside the showroom door but there was no one perched on the high stool. She walked on into the showroom itself. Suddenly she heard a high-pitched whine and saw a flicker of light from the workshop beyond.

Acetylene welder, she thought, as she tramped between two much less well-polished second-hand vehicles and found herself outdoors in a vast work area protected from the weather only by a high glass roof.

The noise had stopped and for a moment she thought there was no one there after all. Startled by a sudden loud bang, she turned and saw two well-polished boots and a pair of legs clad in brown dungarees sticking out from under a battered blue vehicle raised up on a jack.

She gazed at the boots and hesitated. No man ever wants to be interrupted when he's in the middle of a job like that, but there wasn't much point seeking out the person doing the welding. He'd probably not see her through his goggles and he certainly wouldn't hear her if she spoke. On the other hand she couldn't just leave the parcel unattended in the office.

Before she had quite made up her mind to speak, the boots moved towards her, pulling themselves along the hard concrete surface, until a tall young man, his face streaked with oil, caught sight of her and lay staring up at her, a spanner in one hand and an oil can in the other.

'I'm sorry to trouble you,' she said quickly, catching the strange expression that crossed his face. 'I was looking for someone to leave this parcel with. It's for young Mrs Sleator,' she added, as he levered himself into a sitting position and continued to stare at her.

She found it impossible to tell from the piercing gaze of his startling blue eyes whether he was actually angry at being interrupted or simply surprised at seeing her standing there.

'Is Peggy not in the office?'

'No, she's not. That's why I came out here.'

He climbed to his feet and stood looking down at her, his eyes moving to the prettily wrapped parcel.

'I daren't take that off you,' he said solemnly, glancing at his oil-streaked hands.

'Of course you can't. How silly of me,' she said catching a hand to her mouth and laughing easily. 'And your friend on the acetylene welder wouldn't be able to help me either,' she added, smiling up at him.

'What do you know about acetylene welders?' he demanded brusquely, as he collected himself and studied her neat blouse and plain dark skirt.

She shook her head and laughed again, relieved to find he no longer looked so cross.

65

'My Da's a blacksmith. His hands are dirty even when he washes them. Could I fetch you a bit of cotton waste?' she asked hopefully, glancing at the nearest workbench.

As he seemed completely taken aback by this simple suggestion, she waited to see what he might suggest himself.

'We'll see if Peggy's back,' he said quickly. 'She can run up to Abbey Street with it. It'll only take her a minute or two.'

He strode off, pushing his large frame between the two second-hand cars.

'And if she's not?' she asked, slipping through behind him.

'There'll be a piece of brown paper somewhere an' you can wrap it up so it'll come to no harm an' I'll take it m'self. I know the house.'

'But can you just go off like that? Will no one mind? What about the boss?' she said anxiously, not wanting to get him into trouble now he was trying to help her.

'Ach, sure the boss is that pleased about the we'an, he notices nothin' these days. He's dyin' to be a Granda.'

'Just like my boss, Charlie Freeburn,' she responded happily, as they arrived outside the office and found it still untenanted.

'Ach aye, I'd forgot yer man Freeburn was Missus Sleator's father. Is that where you work?' he asked abruptly.

She nodded at him and bent down to search under the desk for a piece of brown paper. 'I could take it myself if you tell me which house.'

'Aye, you could, if I could tell you the number,

but I only know it by going there,' he admitted sheepishly.

'Here we are,' she replied, turning to face him. She smoothed out some saved brown paper, trimmed its torn edges, made a new parcel and tied it neatly from a large roll of fine string sitting on the desk.

'Ye've done that before,' he said, smiling at her for the first time.

'Like the fortieth horseshoe, as my father says.'

'What d'ye mean?'

'If you do a thing often enough you get good at it.'

'Ahhh ... I'm with you now.'

She held the parcel out towards him and tried not to smile as she watched him wipe his hands vigorously on the seat of his dungarees before he took it from her.

'I'd better hurry back,' she said quickly. 'It's getting on for closing time and Mr Freeburn likes to have a word with the whole staff about Monday morning. Thank you very much for helping me out.'

'Ach, not at all. Not at all.'

She turned quickly, stepped lightly past the new Austin and crossed to the other side of the street, a small, trim figure, the sun striking gold from her hair.

Sam Hamilton watched her go, the parcel held in his large hands. Even when she was out of sight, he still stood gazing up English Street after her. He was a right fool. He'd never even asked her name.

He turned away abruptly, strode along the front of the Post Office and turned into Abbey Street. It took him only moments to find the small stone house on the steep slope just below the City Hospital. A woman he didn't know, with rolled up sleeves and a white cap, took the parcel from him.

As he made his way back down the hill, he wondered if she was the midwife. Then another thought struck him, much more important than the impending birth. It occurred to him that the next time he and his father went up to visit his mother's cousin and give the two boys a bit of a hand on the farm, he could just ask Daisy Hutchinson who was her friend with the fair hair, the one that worked with her in Freeburn's.

Ellie was tired. As she approached the low hill that ran up past the entrance to her own lane, she found she was pedalling more and more slowly. It even struck her that perhaps it was no bad thing George was otherwise occupied this evening, accompanying his uncle on a visit to some relatives in Portadown. She'd been upset about it last night, but then, last night she'd been upset about everything.

Sometimes she got off her bicycle and wheeled it up the steepest part of the hill, other times she made the extra effort and stayed on till she turned into the lane and had to give way to the sharp stones and random fragments of metal created by the traffic to and from the forge. Tonight, she had no option. She got off much sooner than usual, perspiration breaking on her forehead.

Before she reached the lane end, she caught the familiar smell of smoke moving on the slight evening breeze. She glanced across at the forge, half-hidden behind the massive pear tree at its gable end. The smoke was the smoke from a fresh fire. Her father was back at work. She hoped he'd had some dinner and that a covered plate would await her in the oven or on the back of the stove. She was very hungry, the hastily made sandwich she'd eaten amid the cardboard boxes of the staffroom at midday seemed a long, long way away.

'Ach, hello. Yer late the night. Are ye not goin' out with George?'

Despite the bright sunlight outside, the forge was beginning to grow shadowy. Robert Scott had to peer at her when she'd propped her bicycle outside and came to sit down gratefully on the bench opposite his anvil. He was not happy with what he saw. Although she looked up at him and smiled, he knew she was more than just tired out. Something was wrong and George the most likely source. The trouble was that he never knew what to say, or what to ask her. It was one thing when she was a wee girl and fell down and hurt herself and he could lift her up and set her on his knee, but she was a young woman now, about to be married. She'd have we'ans of her own before long.

'Did yer man keep you late?'

'No, Da. I had an ice cream with Daisy. She's in a bad way. They're so far behind with the rent, they've had a letter about the bailiffs.'

'An' her mother still poorly?'

She nodded miserably, too tired to explain the details any further.

'Sure I thought puttin' people out was a thing o' the past. The las' time I heerd tell of people put out was when my friend Sam Hamilton was a wee boy and his mother and father brought the four we'ans into the old house that was over the way. John Hamilton, the father, wrought here with my father in them days an' the place was derelict even then, but they'd nowhere else to go.'

'You mean where our hen house is?' asked Ellie, a look of amazement on her face.

'Aye, an' where ye have your wee garden,' he said, nodding vigorously. 'That bit of a gable wall with the climbing rose up it, wouda been their kitchen,' he explained, 'and our hen house was their wash house, but after the roof fell in one of the landlord's men came an' took away a couple of loads a' stone from the walls for somethin' or other they were building on the estate. That's a brave few years ago now.'

'So that's how you know the Mr Hamilton of Liskeyborough that came to Granny's funeral.'

'Aye, he was reared in that house with his brother James and the two sisters, Hannah and the wee one. I fergit her name now.'

'I never knew that,' she replied, a flicker of pleasure lighting up her grey eyes.

'Ach, it's many a long day since I thought about it but Sam Hamilton called last night after ye went off with George and that put it in m' mind. Ye'd hardly credit his mother managin' to

70

make a home outa that house if ye'd seen the state of it. So Sam said. Ah hope you an' George'll have a better start than that, though I know things is not goin' well fer you at the moment findin' a place.'

Ellie dropped her eyes and said nothing. She'd been thinking all the way back from Armagh how she would break her news at home, whether to face them both or to make sure she told her father first. But now at the mention of George and a place to start, any sensible plan she'd made had flown away.

'Da, George is goin' back to Canada with his uncle. He's leaving on Sunday week,' she began quickly. 'He says he'll send me my ticket or come back for me when he's saved up enough for a house.'

She only just managed to get the words out before she burst into tears.

Five

When Ellie Scott looked back on that last week before George's departure for Canada she could not believe how quickly the time had gone. One Sunday afternoon they were taking their usual walk down the narrow road past her great-aunt's house in Ballybrannan and round to Cannon Hill, climbing the steep slope and gazing out over the surrounding countryside, the very next they were catching a last, brief half-hour in the lane that ran up between the orchards to emerge on Church Hill.

With all the visiting and activity of the week, George said he still had to finish his packing before the taxi came to take them to the Belfast train in time to catch the Liverpool boat.

'You could come to the train with us, if you like, Ellie,' he offered, glancing at the new watch his parents had bought him as a going-away present.

'No, George, I couldn't do that. It would only make it worse,' she just managed to say, shaking her head and trying not to cry. But the tears came unbidden, running down her cheeks, splashing unheeded to disappear amidst the pattern of small flowers on her best dress.

'Sure I'll be back in no time at all. Ye won't notice the time goin'. Ye'll be sewin' dresses for your trousseau an' puttin' stuff away in your bottom drawer for settin' us up,' he said, taking her in his arms.

He kissed her vigorously, then hurried her back down the bumpy lane, his arm tightly round her waist lest she should trip and delay them further when he was late already.

With a hasty kiss and squeeze, he left her standing beside the horse trough at the foot of the lane, the mid-point between their two front doors, the place they'd met since they'd been children going up the lane to school beside the church. She stood and watched him as he strode away, but he moved so quickly he'd disappeared into the farmyard before she'd collected herself enough to respond to his parting wave.

An hour later, sitting by the well in the orchard, she heard the taxi come up the drive and stop in the wide, bare space outside the garden gate. From where she sat, she could hear voices on the clear air, hear the throb of an engine running, hear a crescendo of shouted Goodbyes. Then the usual Sunday quiet flowed back as if it had never been disrupted.

She looked down into the sunlit waters of the well, saw her own pale face reflected against a background of cloud and blue sky. She dipped her hand into the cool water and saw the picture shimmer and disappear as she splashed her tear-stained face and dried it with her handkerchief. It would never do to show a tear-stained face.

She got to her feet, took a deep breath, and began to walk back through the long grass. The pink and white petals of the apple blossom fell like confetti all around her. Despite all her effort, such an aching space opened in front of her, she wondered how she would ever fill it.

The kitchen was dark and stuffy as she stepped through the propped open door. Her mother was nowhere to be seen. Her father sat at his usual place at the table, the *News of the World* spread out to catch the light from the small back window.

'Is he away?' he asked, his eyes flickering anxiously towards her as she sat down on the settle.

'Yes, he's away,' she said steadily. 'He'll be in Liverpool in the morning and off on the *Minne-*

dosa tomorrow night. Quebec in six days and then Peterborough.'

'Whereabouts would that be?'

Ellie could hear the note of relief in his voice. She stood up and pulled the kettle forward on the stove.

'I didn't know either,' she said, smiling at him as she reached up to the mantelpiece for the tea-caddy. 'I went into the Guardian office and asked Miss Trimble. She's always very helpful and I was sure she'd have an atlas.'

'Aye, she'd need one in her job, wi' people goin' for cruises and the like. Them that has the money, that is.'

'She got it out for me and the shop was quiet so we had a good look at a whole lot of places I'd only heard of from Polly. You know Toronto is on Lake Erie. Well, if you come a bit to the right of that and go inland away from the lake, that's where Peterborough is. It's about eighty miles from Toronto on the train.'

'That's a brave bit, isn't it?' he said, a startled look flickering across his face as he closed his newspaper. 'An' is that the same Peterborough that Polly mentioned in *her* letter?'

'Yes, it is. A real coincidence isn't it? But she didn't say if Jimmy was goin' to take the job there or not. The cost of moving might leave them worse off than they are, unless Quaker Oats are offering him more money.'

He shook his head sadly.

'I've seen so many go off, Canada or the USA, an' they all think they're goin' to make their fortunes. Aye an' a few do, ah have to admit, but

74

there's more doesn't. It's hard being poor in yer own country among yer own family an' friends, but it's harder still I wou'd think in some of these places away. D'ye think our Polly's all right, or does she just tell us the best of it an' leave the rest to one side?'

The kettle boiled and Ellie was glad of the brief diversion to collect her thoughts. She knew how her father turned things over in his mind in the long hours working in the forge and he often read and re-read the letters that came from her sisters, but she seldom had much idea as to what he thought about their news, he said so little most of the time and almost never asked her a question.

'I think Polly herself always makes the best of things whatever's happening to her,' she said carefully, as she poured him a mug of tea and fetched the milk and sugar from the corner cupboard. 'But she'd never *not* tell us if things were bad. She told us when they had to give up the house and go into digs, didn't she?'

'Aye, she did,' he said, nodding and drinking gratefully.

'I'm sure she'll tell us if Jimmy does take this new job. I know she likes Toronto and has lots of friends there, but Polly could make friends wherever she went. She might even be able to see George when he's down in Peterborough staying with his uncle.'

'Indeed now, she might,' he said quickly, getting up to go and visit the privy in the orchard.

Ellie smiled to herself. She'd managed it. She had mentioned George's name to her father

75

without crying and the look of relief on his face made it well worth the effort it had cost her.

To Ellie's amazement, she slept peacefully that night, neither brown bears nor falling trees troubling her rest. When she woke at her usual time, it was Daisy Hutchinson who immediately came into her mind, though she did a quick calculation to work out exactly where George would be at this early hour and what he and Uncle George planned to do during the time in Liverpool before the Minnedosa sailed on the high tide.

Poor Daisy. She'd had to work through a long, hard week without any respite from the worry of that letter sitting on the mantelpiece behind the clock. Each day, they'd spoken in whatever quiet moments they could find, Ellie encouraging her to be sure they'd think of something. Twice, when Miss Walker was up in Belfast inspecting stock for the July Sales, they'd risked having their lunch break at the same time, leaving Harry, the youngest and most good-natured of the young men, to stand in for half an hour. Harry Wright would do anything for Ellie, Daisy declared. He'd been sweet on her since his very first day when she had been so kind to him. 'I'll even sell a pair of knickers for you,' he'd said, grinning broadly, as they slipped out the back door.

They'd hurried down to The Mall and sat side-by-side on a stone bench under the trees eating their sandwiches and watching the well-dressed ladies go by accompanied by equally well-dress-

76

ed children or well-groomed little dogs. Much of the time they sat in silence, for Daisy had no more to tell and try as she might Ellie could think of nothing new to suggest. She'd offered Daisy her own small savings. The idea that Ellie should offer without telling George had really upset her. Besides, the sum itself didn't go far enough towards the arrears to be worth arguing over.

But now on this bright, May morning, Ellie had made up her mind. She had come to the conclusion there was only one person with the necessary knowledge and experience to help Daisy and although she was very anxious indeed about approaching him, she knew she had to try.

A few minutes after ten o'clock, when Mr Freeburn said 'Good morning' to each of his staff in turn, she took a deep breath, replied to his greeting and asked if she might have a private word when it was convenient. He'd looked so startled by her polite request it made her even more anxious. Nor did it help that, rather than ask her to follow him to his office, he suggested she come to his office at eleven fifty. An interminable two hours followed before she could go up and knock on his door, as firmly as her shaking hands would allow.

'Come in, Miss Scott,' he said briskly.

She stepped into the large, light room, its three tall windows framing the bustle of activity in the street below. Once the family sitting room, but now piled with stock along two of its walls, it still had an air of elegance about it. The ceiling was high and decorated with a large plasterwork

77

rose. A delicate chandelier hung from its centre.

She walked across the worn carpet and stood in front of the huge mahogany desk, its polished surface gleaming except where neat piles of papers were lined up and held secure with equally well-polished brass paperweights.

Mr Freeburn himself, his dark figure silhouetted against the central window, appeared even darker and more solid against the light and movement outside. He appeared to be absorbed in watching the traffic in Thomas Street. She followed his gaze. In the right-hand window, she could see the front of the Co-op and the gleam of the three gold balls on the pawnbrokers next door. In the left-hand window, the darkened upper windows of the large public house stared blankly back across the street.

'What can I do for you, Miss Scott,' he asked, turning towards her, his tone not unfriendly, but distinctly crisp.

'I wanted to ask your advice, Mr Freeburn.'

This was not at all what Charlie Freeburn had expected. A request for a private word from a female member of staff inevitably meant she was giving notice. In the case of some, he'd known before they spoke it would mean no more than the obligatory week. He would expect Miss Scott to be more considerate, but nevertheless the immediate thought of losing her had quite spoilt the morning and the good spirits with which he had greeted the week, the grandfather of one more flourishing grandchild in Abbey Street.

'Do please sit down,' he said, so taken aback

he could hardly contain his relief.

'I have a dear friend, Mr Freeburn, who is in danger of losing her home because of debts which she cannot pay,' she said, as soon as she had lowered herself into the chair he had placed for her. 'The debts are not her fault,' she went on quickly, seeing the look on his face, 'but there is no one else to pay them.'

'And how can I advise you?'

'Well, I've thought and thought about what one could do, but I have only a very little money myself, not nearly enough to be useful, and I can't think of anything else one could do.' She paused and smiled suddenly. 'It's all very well in stories. Someone always has some old piece of jewellery or some family heirloom they can sell when their friend is in difficulties, but apart from a Coronation teaspoon my great-aunt gave me as a christening present I don't have *anything* like that.'

'And do you think I might have the equivalent of some saleable object? Something that would provide for the financial needs of this young woman?' he asked, wondering what she would reply.

He had a good idea the girl in question must be Daisy Hutchinson. He'd noted how well the two of them got on and how often he'd seen Miss Scott helping her out when she was in difficulties in the shop.

'No, I didn't think that,' Ellie replied honestly. 'People must often ask for financial help, because they know you have a profitable business. I expect you have to say 'No' to many requests, but I wondered if you could use your influence with the landlord. Perhaps if Dais ... my friend's family had a little time, they could get back on their feet again. Something might come to help them.'

'I take it we are talking about Miss Hutchinson?'

Ellie nodded sadly.

'What makes you think anything ever comes to help us except the effort we make for ourselves?'

It was not said unkindly, but Ellie felt discouraged. Most people said that Freeburn was mean. That he gave nothing away. He was a self-made man and being what other people could only see as mean was what had made him so successful. But he had asked a question and she must try to reply. It wouldn't help Daisy much if she just gave up now.

'I don't know,' she said honestly. 'I suppose I think that while there's life, there's hope. It's something my father often says when people are poorly. Losing a home and a farm is just like losing a person. If it goes it might as well be dead. You can't get it back again even if later on you *do* have money.'

'You could buy a better one.'

'Yes, you could,' she agreed.

She wondered why he was watching her so patiently, waiting for her to say something more. She'd no idea what he might want her to say and even less of what she could say herself.

'It's *now* that matters,' she said suddenly. 'In a few months her brother might be able to find

80

work when he leaves school, or her mother might improve and be able to do more to help on the farm. Or Daisy might marry someone with a lot of money. There is *some* hope, if only there were a little time.'

'If Miss Hutchinson were to marry then I would have to train up a new assistant and I assume I shall be losing you in the not too distant future,' he said matter-of-factly.

'Oh no, Mr Freeburn,' she said quickly, shaking her head. 'It will be at least two years now before I can be married. My young man has gone to Canada with his uncle. He hopes to send for me when he has somewhere for us to live.'

'Ah, I see,' he said, nodding to himself, a small smile moving across his face.

'And when does the landlord foreclose?' he continued abruptly.

'He said he was sending in the bailiffs at the end of the month.'

'And how much are the arrears outstanding?'

Ellie was quite taken aback by his change in tone, but she answered his stream of questions as clearly as she could. It wasn't that she didn't have the answers, for she and Daisy had been back and forth over the figures and the money needed a hundred times, but she couldn't understand why he wanted to know all these details when he hadn't said anything whatever about helping her.

'I've been considering adding to my staff, Miss Scott,' he said amiably, to Ellie's further confusion. 'Another young woman. I have someone in mind. But she will need training and

I think you will be the best person to do that. Perhaps if you could undertake this task *for me*, I could negotiate with Mr Ruddell *for you* on behalf of Miss Hutchinson. I think you can take it that I shall be successful and we can review our arrangement in six months' time. If *you* are agreeable, that is,' he concluded, standing up and inclining his head slightly towards her.

'Yes, of course, Mr Freeburn,' she replied, not quite sure what she had actually agreed to.

'There is only one small condition. You may reassure Miss Hutchinson that all will be well, at least for six months, but she may *not at any time mention my name* to her mother or anyone else. This arrangement between us must remain completely private. I'm sure I can rely on you. I'm depending on you to explain to Miss Hutchinson. Is that quite clear?'

It was only as she was stepping cautiously down the highly polished front stairs that led directly into the shop that Ellie finally grasped something good most certainly had happened. She couldn't follow his thinking at all, but she was quite sure he had said *six months*. And Mr Freeburn always meant what he said. That was also something everyone said about him. *If yer man says a thing, then he means it and there's no shiftin' him.*

Alone in his office, Charlie Freeburn smiled and rubbed his hands together in pleasure. It was worth what it might cost him for the farm itself to have Miss Scott for another two years. She brought a great deal of trade to the shop, though she was quite unaware of the fact. She saved him pounds in wasted fabric by her skill in cutting and even if he eventually had to raise her pay when she became Senior Assistant, he'd saved himself that for six months.

It was always a good thing to avoid such increases for as long as possible, but if the other part of his plan went as he hoped, he'd make that up to her. When she left in two years' time, or whenever, he would certainly see she carried away something more substantial than the traditional gift of a silver cake stand.

He looked at his watch, decided there was no time like the present and lifted the large black receiver of the telephone standing on his desk. As yet another of his wife's relatives worked at the Exchange in English Street, he could say nothing whatever on the telephone, but he could make an appointment at Munroe and Anderson for this afternoon.

'Thank you. Three o'clock will be quite convenient,' he said, placing the instrument carefully back in its cradle.

He smiled and breathed deeply. He had never liked James Ruddell, a boy some years older and many inches taller than himself when they were in the same class at the school on The Mall. It would give him the greatest pleasure to make him an offer for the farm that he couldn't refuse.

Given he read neither book nor paper, nor took the slightest interest in the meetings of the Rural District Council, what James Ruddell would not know was the decision to proceed with the new Portadown Road would require the purchase of at least half the large meadow, and one of the three oddly shaped fields that made up the grazing on Hutchinson's farm.

'This ought to be *my* treat,' said Daisy wryly, as the dark-eyed Italian boy slid dishes of ice cream along the marble-topped table between them. 'After all you've done for me.'

'Not a bit of it,' laughed Ellie. 'Sure George is going to earn so much money we'll hardly need my savings. Anyway, *this* is a celebration. We've never had a North Pole before.'

'Isn't it lovely?'

Ellie looked at her friend and thought it wasn't just the ice cream that was lovely. She'd almost forgotten what a pretty girl Daisy was. She'd undone the tight pleat she normally wore for work and her dark wavy hair fell around her pleasant, rounded face. But it was her eyes that said so much. Freed of the anxiety of the last week, there was a sparkle, a look of mischief almost that made Ellie feel happy just to look at her.

'Why do you think we're not to let on?' she asked, spreading the chocolate dressing over another spoonful of ice cream and pausing before putting it into her small, mobile mouth.

'I've no idea. But you *will* be careful won't you, Daisy? Even with your mother...'

'You mean my big mouth,' she replied, giggling.

'No, I did not.'

'I'll behave myself. Honest. Brownie's honour.'

'Were you ever a Brownie?'

'No, but I *can* keep a promise.'

Yes, that was true. Daisy was always as good as her word. Whatever she offered to do, however difficult the task, she'd do what she said she would do. But hadn't they all been taught at school how important it was to keep promises.

She thought suddenly of their copy books with their beautifully written copperplate sentences. A whole collection of sayings about keeping one's word and not telling tales ran through her head. She remembered Master Ebbitt getting them to repeat something from a book he set great store by. *'A promise made is a debt unpaid.'*

She could still recall every detail of the hot afternoon, the smell of chalk and old floorboards and the chant of children's voices. Over and over again. No wonder she could still repeat it. There were other similar sayings they had also to learn by heart, like *'Be always loyal. To your family, your country and your King.'*

'Now, tell me all about George,' Daisy began, licking her spoon. 'It's been all about me this last week, more's the pity. Did ye get engaged? I looked for the ring when ye came in this mornin' an' then I thought, they'll hardly have had time, or maybe he hadn't enough after paying his fare, or maybe she doesn't want to wear it at work. Now c'mon I'm dyin' to know. Tell me what ye's did.'

As she paused, waiting, her eyes bright, Ellie felt her heart sink. Daisy saw George's departure as great news, something to be excited about, full of hope for the future, but somehow she herself didn't seem to be as happy about it as she

85

thought she should be.

'You're right, there wasn't much time,' she said, as she scraped up the very last smear of the delicious ice cream. 'We wouldn't have had time to buy a ring, even if George had any money. But you don't really need a ring. A promise is a promise,' she added firmly.

Daisy Hutchinson didn't agree. Some promises needed more than just words. Like a ring. But she didn't say so. Ellie Scott was the kindest person she had ever met, but she didn't think enough of herself. After all this time George could have done better. He could at least have bought her a little piece of jewellery, a brooch, or a bracelet. When they'd been walking out for years now, surely he could see the need for some wee token.

'Have you thought how you'll tell your Ma, Daisy?' Ellie asked, as she counted out coins from her small purse.

'Aye, I have. And not a word about yer man. That's a promise.'

As the two girls walked out of Caffola's Ice Cream Parlour, it suddenly struck Ellie that George had not said anything that sounded like a proper promise. But, really, he didn't need to. Everyone had always known they'd get married as soon as they could find a place to live. That wasn't changed by his going. It was just that he'd be looking for a home for them in Peterborough.

They said goodbye and see you in the morning, and set off in opposite directions through the empty streets of the city, happier than they had been in the morning. Still, Ellie was very thoughtful as she cycled quietly out to the Grange, thoughtful about the ship preparing to cast off from the Liverpool Dock en route for Quebec. About the young man it would carry away and what he might be thinking as it slowly moved down the Mersey towards the open sea.

Six

The fine weather which had begun early in May, Ellie's favourite month, continued as the apple blossom faded and the more striking colours of garden flowers began to catch her eye on her daily journeys back and forth to work.

On the south-facing side of the old stone gable, opposite the forge, her own small garden flourished. The tiny slips from Charlie Running's rich, red geranium he'd left for her at the forge on one of his regular visits, were now vigorous plants, already coming into bloom. They made a brilliant contrast with a purple clematis she'd found herself one Sunday afternoon out walking with George.

In a lane beyond Annacramp, she'd caught sight of a startling carpet of colour spreading over tall weeds, tangled briars and fallen stones in the ruins of an old house. He'd tramped a path for her to let her get a closer look, then he'd cut down some of the more rampant weeds that threatened to choke the roots. She'd laid down pieces of stone to protect them, then left the plant to go on blooming undisturbed. When they visited the old house again, she found some aquilegia and wallflowers as well, but they did not return with a spade to lift the clematis till all its flowers had gone and only their silvery seed heads and her marker stones showed them where to dig.

Cycling home in the evenings, she thought longingly of walking the lanes, hand in hand, talking about the events of the day, or their plans for the future, before finding a quiet field entrance with a stone pillar to lean against, their arms round each other, kissing. She'd known she would miss him, but the emptiness created by his absence was even worse than she'd expected.

Worse still was the feeling that grew on her every Friday and Saturday night when she came home to spend the evening reading by the stove instead of getting dressed to go to a dance or to the Ritz Cinema. She was amazed how sad she could feel hearing a snatch of dance music on the wireless, flowing out into the street from café or ice cream parlour.

Some evenings, when she could bear the dark kitchen and her mother's continuous monologue no longer, she'd walk down to the forge. There was almost always someone there sitting on the bench inside the door watching her father work. She never felt unwelcome, but unless it was a friend, or a neighbour she knew well, like Charlie Running, or Ned Wylie, she seldom stayed long, aware that her presence might limit the talk of the older men. She knew too that should she appear too often her father would see she was lonely and she didn't want to add another burden to the cares of his work, heavy and long at this busiest time of year.

She knew it would be almost two weeks before a letter could possibly arrive. Until he docked in Quebec he couldn't post what he'd written on the voyage. It would then take at least five or six days to reach Tom McQuaid's postbag. She probably ought to allow for a Sunday as well. Each night, when she came in from work, she looked up at the mantelpiece, but there was no brightly-stamped envelope poking out from behind the clock.

After two long weeks had slowly passed, only a card of Liverpool Cathedral with a hasty message on the back stood propped up against the mirror on top of the chest of drawers that served as her dressing table. Daisy had begun by asking each morning if she'd heard from George, but as day followed day, and still there was no letter, she'd stopped asking.

'Ah see yer man's written at last,' her mother greeted her one evening at the very end of the month. 'I'm sure you thought he'd fell and forgot, he's been that long. Sure maybe he's enjoyin' himself so much he'll not come back atall...'

Ellie was too overjoyed by the sight of the airmail letter to pay any attention to her mother's comments. She reached up to the mantelpiece and clutched the envelope, but before the smile had even spread across her face, it faded like snow off a ditch. The letter was indeed the familiar Canadian airmail, but it was from her sister Mary in Toronto, addressed to both her parents.

Later that evening, when her father had peered at the letter through his Woolworth's reading glasses, he handed it over to his wife. Both he and Ellie knew what she would say when he passed it to her, but they also knew what she would say if he didn't.

'Ach, sure ye know my eyes are bad. Let Ellie read it out loud.'

She collected herself as best she could, for her hands had begun to feel damp the minute she'd touched the flimsy blue pages, and began:

Dear Ma and Da,

I'm writing to tell you some good news. I am going to be married in the Fall. That's what we call the autumn at home, but my husband-to-be is from the States so I suppose I'll have to get used to their different way of talking.

I have known Franklin, (Frank for short), for over a year now. I met him at a dance held in the Eaton's Social Club and we've been going out a lot. He's a bit older than I am and he's been working in the Bank of Canada for a long time, but he says he's only done it so he can save up to buy a farm. We plan to be married here in Toronto where we both have lots of friends but we will be having a reception for his family in Indiana when we get back there. He lives near a place called Fort Wayne and he has cousins there who are farmers.

Frank also has a sister called Cherry, but it is spelt Cherie. She is much younger, about my own age. It will be nice to have someone for a girlfriend until we get settled.

I will not be giving up my job till the very last minute. As you know the pay is very good and I got a bonus as well last month. I am busy sewing for my trousseau as I expect Ellie is too.

I've not been in touch with Polly for some weeks now. I did ring her lodgings but got no reply. Her landlady must have been out. I will try again soon. The last I heard was that she and Jimmy were going to go to Peterborough because there was a house at a low rent with the job, though the pay's not great. I think it's a factory that makes break-fast cereal but I don't know exactly what sort of job Jimmy's got there.

The weather here has become very hot and humid. Too hot for comfort but Frank says that's nothing to Indiana. Hopefully it will be cooler living on a farm than in a city like Toronto.

That's all for now. I hope you are both keeping well and all the family too. I heard there'd been more trouble in Belfast but I know Aunt Annie and her family are well away from all that so you needn't worry about them. Bye-bye for now.

Your loving daughter,
Mary.

When it finally arrived four days later, George's missive brought Ellie little joy. Despite its generous array of stamps and formidable thickness, which for a few moments she'd thought might explain the weeks of delay, from the firmness of the package she quickly guessed that it contained a pack of postcards. And indeed, as soon as she cut carefully along the top of the envelope with her best sewing scissors, she saw he'd sent a complete set of views of Peterborough.

She took them out, turned them over and found to her amazement there was nothing at all written on the back. What he had written was on both sides of the two small sheets of paper in which he'd wrapped them. As she searched in vain for something to set against the anxiety of the last long weeks, her heart sank further and she was glad she'd found the letter on an evening when her mother had retired to bed.

Dear Ellie,

You'll know by now from Uncle George's letter home that we had a good trip across, great weather and good company and we arrived safely in Quebec. It is a very nice place. Jimmy and I had time to look around as Uncle George had some business there for a couple of days.

I wanted to send you a card from there but unfortunately everywhere I went people were speaking French and I couldn't find what stamps to use. Uncle George said I was unlucky, most people in Quebec speak some

92

English, but that he should have warned me.

Anyway we are now settled in Peterborough and as you can see it is very up-to-date. The Quaker Oats factory on the Otonabee is one of the biggest in the world. I have marked with a cross the house in George Street where Uncle George lives. That's a coincidence, isn't it? But I can go one better than that. Peterborough was founded by people from two families called Robinson and Scott. (That's us!) I've been reading up all the history of Peterborough as Uncle George is back at work.

He has shown Jimmy and I round the saw mills and the warehouses but I am really looking forward to going north tomorrow with some other young men that have just arrived from Scotland. Did I tell you or did I forget to say that my cousin Jimmy from Portadown did decide at the last minute to take up Uncle's offer. He was waiting for our train at Portadown Station and was able to get across to Liverpool on deck. There was no difficulty with his passage to Canada. The ship was not very full except First Class where the cruise passengers go.

Now I must stop and get ready for tomorrow. I hope you are well and not working too hard in the shop. I'll write again when we get settled at camp. Give my best regards to your mother and father but keep all my love for you.

A large, swirling signature took up most of the

final quarter of the fourth side of paper. The remaining space he had filled with kisses.

'Ah don't care what ye say, Ellie, yer not right atall,' Daisy announced, as they sat down together on their usual bench under the trees. 'There's somethin' wrong forby George bein' away and you bein' lonely.'

Ellie shook her head. 'I'm just tired, Daisy, that's all. I've been cutting remnants all morning and you know how it gets your back.'

'I might know if I ever had to do it, but you're so good at it yer man never let's me near it,' Daisy retorted sharply.

Ellie smiled, amused by her friend's vehemence, but she had to admit that Daisy was probably not far wrong. Try as she might, she couldn't seem to lift her spirits.

'Why d'ye think it took George so long to write? Why didn't he write on the boat an' post it first thing when they landed?'

'I think maybe it just didn't occur to him.'

'Well, maybe you should tell him that it shou'd have. Have you written to him yet?'

'Do you mean a reply to his, or the other letters I wrote before it came?'

'Before it came? You mean you'd already written to him for when he arrived?' Daisy paused dramatically. 'One letter or more?'

'Three,' she admitted sheepishly.

'Ellie Scott, *you* are *far too* good-natured. You're not fit to be let out on your own...'

Daisy waved her half-eaten sandwich so vigorously that a piece of cheese fell out, dropped to the ground and was promptly swallowed by one of the sparrows keeping a watchful eye on them.

They both burst out laughing.

'That's about the first time I've heard ye laugh in weeks,' Daisy declared, when they'd recovered themselves. 'Now you listen to me. You helped me when I was in a bad way. I know this is different, but yer not goin' the right way about it. If he's not thinkin' about you here at home missin' him, then you hafta tell him. An' if he's not much good at writin' letters, then he'll just hafta learn, won't he? He's not the first man went to Canada to make his money. And if he doesn't catch on, then there's still a few men left around here, though not that many I hafta admit.'

'Oh Daisy, now don't say that. I love George. I don't want anyone else.'

'Wou'd ye have gone out with him if he'd asked you?'

'Yes, of course. But he couldn't ask me, could he, given where he's going to get started?'

'And did he ask you was him goin' away what *you* wanted?'

'He didn't have much choice, Daisy. It was a good offer. He was only doing what he thought best for us.'

'Aye, well,' said Daisy doubtfully, polishing off the last of her sandwich. 'What happened about the motorbike? Did he sell it?'

'Yes, he must have done. I didn't ask him.'

'That money'd buy a quare nice ring and have plenty left over.'

'Oh Daisy, he couldn't do that. He probably

95

gave the money back to his uncle.'

'Well, we'll see,' the younger girl said dubiously. 'But you write an' tell him he'll have to do better than this, or I'll start lookin' for a man for ye here. I could do with one fer me'self as well so it'll be no extra bother.' With that, she stood up and swept the crumbs from her dark skirt to the waiting sparrows.

Whatever Daisy Hutchinson's weaknesses might have been, and Charlie Freeburn could certainly have listed some, Ellie Scott knew that she was no fool. Without her practical approach when her mother was so poorly the family would have been split up long ago. True, she'd not seen a way through the problem with the landlord, but that didn't mean she wasn't shrewd about other matters where she had some experience.

She thought over all that Daisy had said and made up her mind she'd have to say something to George. Quite what, she'd not decided when a letter arrived from Polly responding to her own in which she'd poured out all her distress.

Thankfully, Ellie closed her bedroom door behind her. No one would interrupt her now she'd said her goodnights. She sat on the edge of the bed and took out Polly's letter. The June nights were so long, the sky so clear, she could still see to read it yet again, even though it was after ten o'clock and the window was half-masked by heavy sprays of pink, climbing rose.

My dearest Ellie,

I'm so sorry you're so worried about George. I'd have thought you would have heard by now indeed, but remember *no news is good news*. If anything had happened to the ship it would have been all over the newspapers. If anything had happened to George himself then his uncle would have cabled right away to his parents. He's maybe a bit through himself with all the excitement of going away from home and him never been further than Warrenpoint before. I'm sure you'll have heard by the time you get this.

Well, we are settled at our new address. The house is very small but there is a garden (a yard, they call it here) at the back, and just down the road there's an enormous park with a lake and trees. I have never seen so many trees in my life as I did on the train journey here. No wonder Peterborough is one of the biggest lumbering centres in Canada. No doubt George will tell you all about that.

There is some furniture here in the house which belongs to the company, but it's all a bit bare. I have to confess I shed the odd tear when I remember the lovely new furniture we had when we first came out, but there's many much, much worse off than us.

Davy and Eddie are well but they are naturally a bit upset with the move. Davy has a bad habit of throwing stones when he finds them and I keep scolding him. Of course, Eddie copies everything Davy does. I hope it will help when Davy goes to school and perhaps I can get back to my sewing again. The money would be a great help. Ronnie is fine and is no trouble at all. I can't understand how this child is so different from the other two!

Jimmy is so glad to have a job. It's not what he wants but he says it's a foot in the door. It's just maintenance which is a bit of a comedown for a skilled mechanic, but we mustn't complain.

What has been quite lovely though is the welcome we've had from the Quaker Oats Social Club. There are an awful lot of people from home, North and South, and Scotland as well. The day we arrived there was a wee basket of cake and biscuits and a bunch of flowers on the table waiting for us, and a whole folder of information about Peterborough. It really is a very go-ahead place, but I had to laugh when I got the boys to bed and Jimmy and I sat down to read all the history and the details of the way the industry has come on.

It seems that the place used to be called Scott's Plains and the very first wee girl born there that wasn't native was a Scott. This was in 1820, three years before our house at home was built ... that's according to Charlie Running who is well up in these things as you know! Then apparently in the Potato Famine a man called Peter Robinson sent for people to come from Ireland. There was 50,000 wanted to come but he could only

98

take 2,024. I could hardly believe what I read about those families arriving with nothing. But according to the leaflet each family was given a cow, eight quarts of Indian corn, five bushels of seed potatoes, a hammer, hand-saw, a hundred nails, three hoes, a kettle, frying pan and an iron pot. I wondered what they lay on at night, no blankets or work clothes. They hadn't a table or a chair. They must have cooked on a campfire and ate sitting on the ground. Children and all.

But what was wonderful, Ellie, was what they managed. Good, brave people they must have been. In eighteen months they had cleared 1300 acres with those trees that grow all over the place. I've never been quite sure what an acre looks like but Da once said Robinson's biggest field in front of us on the far side of the road is five acres and you could get lost in it!

It makes me so grateful for a wee house and beds with mattresses and a table and chairs and a stove to cook on. I have bed linen and clothes and one or two precious things from home, wedding presents that were small enough to bring. I think Jimmy has a hammer and a few nails. But after I read that, Ellie, I just couldn't feel sorry for myself.

Apparently it was to honour Peter Robinson that the name was changed from Scott's Plains to *Peter*borough. And quite right too. That's something really worth doing. Isn't it amazing?

Now, my dear wee sister, this letter has taken three days to write in bits and pieces and I'm sure I've repeated myself or forgotten half of what I was going to say but I do want to post it today. I promise I will write again soon. Your letters are so welcome. Jimmy reads them over and over again. I think by now he knows the friends and neighbours round home near as well as I do and he asks after you.

Give all the family and friends our love and tell them we never forget them. Maybe it won't be too long before you and I are able to go for a walk together again. It won't be Annacramp or Church Hill but this is a lovely place in its own very different way.

With love and kisses from your big sister, Polly.

Ellie folded the pages carefully, slipped them back in their envelope, put the letter down on her chest of drawers and started undressing. She shook out her skirt and brushed it, hung it over the back of the chair for the morning, then examined her blouse. She noted the dried out marks of perspiration under her arms and caught the stale odour. It would have to be yet *another* clean blouse tomorrow.

It was always like this before the July sale. The top back room at the shop got the sun in the afternoon and that was where she prepared stock for the sale, labelling garments with reductions and cutting and folding remnants of the fabric brought in especially. The room got so hot, she could often smell her own perspiration, but she couldn't open the window because the sash cords had long since perished.

She didn't think she'd like the heat in Indiana. She wasn't sure she'd even like the heat in Toronto or Peterborough, but she was sure she'd get used to it if that's where she and George were to make their home.

She felt steadier now. She hadn't realized how much she'd come to rely on Polly's letters. It was just a stroke of bad luck she'd been too busy with the move to manage more than a few lines in the very weeks she'd been waiting for George to write.

For five years now they'd been writing to each other almost every week. They'd always been open with each other even when Ellie was a little girl and her big sister really did seem so *very* much older. But the gap between them had shrunk to nothing over the years and though Polly was a married woman with children, only a month ago it seemed Ellie would soon be married too and the first wee one on the way. Now all that had changed so rapidly she still couldn't take it in.

But what hadn't changed was that Ellie did have someone she could talk to. She gave thanks yet again that she had someone with more experience than her dear Daisy. Polly wasn't all that good at sorting out her own problems and Ellie had long thought she just wasn't firm enough with her two little boys, but that didn't stop Polly seeing someone else's problem quite clearly.

101

Ellie unhooked her bodice, slipped off her knickers, stepped out of her slippers and walked up and down the tiny space between the chest of drawers and her wash stand. She stretched her weary body from side to side and rubbed the marks the waistband of her skirt had left behind. She smiled to herself as she slipped on her nightdress. It wasn't often you could stand naked in this room. For most of the year she tried to get into bed quickly before she got cold, or frozen.

She pulled the curtains back before she got into bed. There was not a wisp of cloud in the clear sky, the air perfectly still. It would be fine again tomorrow. She had always hated dark rooms, waking in the night and not knowing where she was or what time of night it might be. She climbed into bed, stretched out between the cool sheets and lay on her back looking up at the pale, whitewashed ceiling, every knot and vein in each individual board familiar, all twenty-nine and a half of them.

Polly, Mary, Florence. They had all gone away and none of them ever spoke of coming back. To see new places, find out about a whole different world. Was that what she wanted too? She'd never really thought about it before. She'd just assumed that a woman went where her husband could find work, enough to support her and their children and keep a roof over their heads. Just like Polly, she assumed wherever it was she would make the best of it.

How many hoes was it Peter Robinson gave to each family? Three. One each for a man and his wife and perhaps the oldest child. Or perhaps the man worked on the land alone, so hard he'd wear out one hoe after another. Grain and seed. But what would they eat until the crops grew and they had a harvest? Birds and wild animals. Rabbits, perhaps. Wasn't it turkeys the Americans found when they first came to North America and now ate for that very reason at Thanksgiving?

Back and forth her mind moved in the gathering dusk. Polly walking along by a lake under trees with Davy and Eddy and little Ronnie in the pushchair. Perhaps she would walk there too with *her* children and George and Jimmy would talk together about their work and their bosses ... all the things men talked about...

She'd read Polly's letter again in the morning and tell Daisy about Scott's Plains and *Peter*borough. She'd enjoy that. It would make up to her for the letter from George where there was really nothing very much to share with anyone.

She turned on her side, her arms folded across her chest, the way she'd slept since she was a little girl. And tonight she slept peacefully, some deep anxiety resolved though she had no idea at all what it had been and what had resolved it.

Seven

'Rich! Ri-ii-itch.'

When the familiar, high-pitched voice finally got through to him, Sam Hamilton raised his head from the collection of small parts he'd laid out on a square of tarpaulin underneath the elderly Austin. Not an attractive voice by any means, he thought, but it certainly did the job.

Although the June morning was fine and dry, the sun glancing off the white-painted walls of the work area, Peggy stood peering out of the showroom door as if the rain were teeming down and one step further might find her soaked to the skin. But it wasn't the weather Peggy feared, he knew that by now, it was the prospect of getting even a speck of oil on her smart new shoes.

'Aye,' he shouted, peering round the offside of the motor jacked up in front of him.

'Boss wants ye,' she called. 'Ten minutes, he sez. Test drive.'

'Right,' he replied, lifting a hand in acknowledgement, a small smile touching his lips and adding a sparkle to his bright blue eyes.

He glanced down again at the pieces in front of him, picked up two that bore signs of rust and put them in the right-hand pocket of his dungarees. He'd leave them in stripper while he cleaned himself up and did his demonstration run to Richhill and back. He wondered if it would be the new model Austin or the Lagonda. He knew which he'd prefer.

'Row, Ro-oooo-ooh.'

Peggy was in such good voice that Sam Keenan, sanding a piece of metal at the workbench behind him, had jumped a couple of inches when he'd heard his call.

My goodness, we're busy this mornin', he thought, as he scrambled quickly to his feet and made sure he'd left nothing, neither parts nor tools, where anyone could trip over them.

Sam smiled wryly to himself as he recalled the March day he'd come to Sleator's to be interviewed for the job. Senior mechanic. A step up and quite a bit more money. It was Harry Mitchell's suggestion he try for it. He didn't want to lose him from his own cycle and motorcycle business, he'd said, but in fairness he was worth more than he could pay him at the moment, and after all these years it wasn't right to stand in his way when the job at Sleator's would add to his experience.

Harry's encouragement couldn't have come at a better time with him getting married as soon as he and Marion could find somewhere to live. If he got the new job, they might think of a place in Armagh. Marion said she wanted to be near her parents, who lived on the Portadown side of Richhill, but so far they hadn't been able to find anything in Portadown that she liked at a rent they could afford. Armagh might be better.

Sam remembered climbing the stairs to the

large, untidy office on the first floor. The door was open and John Sleator was sitting behind a dust-covered desk piled high with invoices and receipts, his back to the uncurtained windows that looked out over the showroom's narrow forecourt and across the road to the handsome, stone-built terrace known as The Seven Houses. To his amazement the owner of Sleator and Son, Motors, was wearing a pair of dungarees.

Admittedly they were a very clean pair of dungarees, but for Sam it was a great encouragement. He'd taken a real liking to the short, grey-haired man who came barely up to his shoulder when they stood side-by-side at the window working their way along the vehicles lined up outside on the forecourt below, sizing them up and sharing their experience of their weaknesses.

It was not very surprising Sam should take to John Sleator. He and Harry Mitchell had been friends since their schooldays and Sam had served his apprenticeship with Harry Mitchell in Scotch Street. Later, when he was more experienced and could have made a move, he'd stayed with Harry and taken the place he'd offered him on his support team when he raced in the Isle of Man.

Sam thought he remembered meeting John Sleator in the pits at the TT race some years earlier. And so indeed he had. The older man recalled that particularly hot summer and his friend Harry's near-miss on one of the notorious bends. One reminiscence led to another and Sam's interview had ended up being a long discussion of bikes and riders. If Sam had paused to wonder why John Sleator didn't ask him about his qualifications, he might well have realized that Harry Mitchell would already have told his friend all he needed to know, for Harry had never made a secret of how much he valued Sam. *'A wee puncture, or stripping down a whole engine, its all the same to Sam. He'll never be satisfied with anything other than a good job,'* was what he used to say.

Once they'd agreed wages and hours, holidays and overtime, John Sleator held out his hand.

'Well, Sam,' he said, as he shook the young man's hand firmly, 'you're welcome to Sleator's and I hope you'll be happy with us. I have only one difficulty with you,' he went on, smiling broadly.

'An' what's that, sir?' asked Sam, smiling himself, pleased he'd got the job and pleased that his new boss was the sort of man you could talk to, as easily as you could talk to Harry.

'Well, I thought I had a problem having two men called Sam in my workshop, Sam Deisley and Sam Keenan, but what are we going to do with *three of you*?'

Sam laughed aloud and went on smiling as the older man continued: 'Mind you, my father was John and his father before him. And my eldest son is John, as you know, and if the wee one on the way in Abbey Street is a boy there'll not be much doubt about what *his* name will be.'

'I think there's a lot of families like that in this part of the world,' Sam replied easily. 'My father is Sam too, though my grandfather was John, but

107

I remember Granny telling me that when her family was young *they* had two Sams, one was her brother, the other my father. Apparently my youngest aunt, Sarah, christened her uncle, *Uncle Sam, America*. And that was all very well. But then he came home and bought a wee farm in Donegal.'

John Sleator laughed heartily and shook his head. 'Ach dear, you'd think we could organize ourselves better than causing all this confusion. But the three of you may sort it out between yourselves. If I have to call someone in a hurry, I can't afford for all three of you to come running.'

He'd taken him back downstairs, asked Peggy to make them all a mug of tea and led the way out to the yard and workshops to show him round and introduce him to his new colleagues.

'Sam, this is Sam Deisley and this is Sam Keenan,' he began, his face perfectly straight, though his pale eyes were twinkling. 'This is *Sam* Hamilton.'

'Dear aye, what are we goin' to do now, boss?' demanded Sam Deisley, the older of the two men.

Short and plump with huge, hairy forearms projecting from rolled up sleeves, he crushed Sam's hand in his own, looked up at him, took in his broad shoulders and then directed his gaze to Sam Keenan, the apprentice, a young man of barely medium height, lightly-built, with pale skin and deep, dark eyes that dropped shyly when the older man looked towards him.

'Where are ye from, Sam?' the older man

108

demanded, turning back to the newcomer.

'Liskeyborough.'

'Well that's no good,' he said dismissively. 'That's near Richhill, isn't it?'

'Aye it is, near enough.'

'An' this good-looking lad here is from Mill Row,' Sam Deisley continued, to the great embarrassment of Sam Keenan, who blushed furiously and studied the ground at his feet as if he had lost a nut or a washer.

'So what are you going to come up with, Sam?' John Sleator asked, a broad grin beginning to spread across his face. He looked from one to another in the small group as Peggy appeared, carrying a tray with four mugs of tea and picking her steps with great care.

'Sam Richhill and Sam Mill Row,' he replied. *'Rich* and *Row* for short. Wouldn't that do rightly?'

'It would indeed, Sam, but what about yourself? You live on Workhouse Hill, don't you?' John Sleator asked, a mischievous twinkle in his eye.

'I was christened Sam a brave while ago,' Diesley replied firmly, ignoring the smiles of his namesakes. 'Before either of these two were born or thought off. They'll need to show a bit of respect,' he said severely. 'If I catch either of them callin' me Wee Sam there'll be trouble.'

Sam Hamilton never knew whether Sam Deisley really meant it, or whether it was part of the joke, but from that day forward Wee Sam was exactly what everyone called him. But not to his face.

* * *

'Rich' he'd been nicknamed and rich he felt as he walked briskly down Scotch Street to tell Harry Mitchell that he'd got the job. As he climbed back into his dungarees, with Harry's congratulations and good wishes still echoing in his ears, he felt that something great had happened. He hadn't felt like this since he'd had the chance to test out the timing on Harry's motorbike the night before the big race, two years ago, and had come within a few minutes of the lap record itself.

It wasn't just getting near the record, though he'd been excited enough over that, it was the feeling of freedom, of moving effortlessly through the air. It was almost as if he were flying, swooping along the winding course he'd got to know over the previous years, using all his skill and memory to keep up speed even on the notorious hairpin where Harry had skidded on the dangerous right-hander.

He was going to be married to the girl he'd loved and had courted for over four years now. With the bigger pay, they'd be able to find a house she liked and soon there'd be a wee girl or a wee boy. Maybe one day his own son might be able to race, if that was what he wanted to do. It wasn't just the money you needed to race. Even if you did have the right temperament, you had to have someone behind you, someone to encourage you.

He thought of his sister Rose over in Banbridge and how happy she and Richard were with their little family. Two lively boys and now

110

the baby, the wee girl Richard had wanted so much. It was not that his brother-in-law didn't love his two sons, but when he'd gone over to see the new baby, Richard had told him that he'd been an only child himself. Never having had a brother or a sister, he wanted a real family. Now his boys had what he'd have so loved for himself. And the wee girl would have brothers to depend on, just as his beloved Rose had her Emily and Sam.

It was two weeks later, at the beginning of April, that Marion had given him back the ring. At first he simply couldn't believe it. She didn't give him any reason and he tried desperately to see what might have gone wrong. Could it be the nerves one was supposed to have before a wedding? But then, the date of the wedding wasn't yet settled so it could hardly be that. There were Canadian cousins coming over in the summer and Marion wanted them to be there, so they must wait till they heard when it would be. That was perfectly reasonable. But now she told him they weren't coming after all.

He hadn't grasped what was happening until in despair he decided to call and talk to Marion's mother, a woman who'd always made him welcome whenever he went to the house. From the minute she opened the door, he could see she didn't want to talk to him. She wouldn't answer any of his questions and she kept referring to what Marion's father said and what he thought. She'd even tried to tell him that perhaps Marion was a bit young to be settling down. He could hardly believe his ears. His birthday was in

August and Marion's in December. They'd both be twenty-seven before the year was out. You could hardly call that young, could you?

Things had been bad for a week or more. She'd said she didn't want to see him, but he couldn't let it rest. He'd called at the house each evening after work and asked to see her. Her mother had said she was out and closed the door firmly in his face.

Finally, he could stick it no longer. He asked for a day off, got up at his usual time and cycled through Richhill and out the Portadown road early on a bright April morning. As he'd expected, this time Marion herself opened the door. She hadn't wanted to let him in, but he'd insisted she owed him that much. He'd asked her again what was wrong. Was it really about him buying the furniture when he only wanted to surprise her? Did she think she didn't love him enough? Or did she think he didn't love her enough? What was it had come between them after all this time?

She wouldn't give him a proper answer to any of his questions and in the end she'd lost her temper. She told him bluntly she'd made up her mind she didn't want to marry him. She never wanted to see him again. If he came bothering her or her mother any more she'd have to speak to her father.

She was so vehement, he could barely believe what he was hearing, for this was the girl he'd loved for so long, the girl he'd worked so hard for, so that he could give her the very best effort could buy. Her face contorted with anger, she

112

was now looking at him as if she hated him. He'd turned away and stumbled from the house, the tears tripping him, not knowing where to go, or what to do.

The road outside the smart new bungalow was busy with people going to work, but he wasn't fit to be seen at the garage in this state. If he went back home, there'd be no sympathy at all from his mother. She'd told him often enough he was far too generous with Marion, giving her presents as well as taking her out, when he was paying so little at home for his bed and board. His father would be at Irish Road Motors. He couldn't face the thought of the empty workshop in the barn or going upstairs to sit on his own bed waiting for him to come home.

In the end he'd gone over to his sister Emily. He knew it was Rosie he needed, but she'd only just had the wee baby and Emily was nearer, just outside Richhill itself. He'd found her baking bread and she'd come and put her arms round him before he said a word. She'd got flour all over his best jacket though he never noticed at the time. That night, he went out with his brother-in-law, Kevin, and got so drunk in Lavery's that Kevin had to ask a neighbour to drive him home to the farm by Richhill Station because he couldn't even walk.

Sam wiped his hands on a piece of cotton waste and headed briskly for the wash-room. He scooped cleanser from the tin, rubbed his hands vigorously, examined his nails and picked up the stiff brush. Some lubricating oils were harder to

113

get off than others, but you couldn't drive a brand-new motor and get oil on the steering wheel. The boss was very particular about that. Rightly so, he thought to himself, as he went on scrubbing. It was several minutes before he was able to reach for the clean towel.

He glanced anxiously at his watch, untwisted the legs of his dungarees, straightened his tie and ran his pocket comb through his dark hair, sweeping it back from his broad, high forehead. He brushed his shoulders with a quick, practised flick of the hand.

As he bent down to look in the mirror, he smiled. The mirror was large and new and always kept spotlessly clean, but it had been adjusted to suit Wee Sam. Everyone else in the workshop had to bend their knees to see anything in it at all.

He removed the grease streak he spotted on his cheek with a corner of his handkerchief. As he hurried out across the yard and into the showroom, the thought came to him quite unbidden that the face he'd seen in the mirror looked a bit happier than it had done a couple of months back.

'Ah, good man, Sam,' the boss said briskly, waving one hand to the Lagonda before turning back to a small, smartly-dressed gentleman with a neat toothbrush moustache and a soft black hat.

Army man, perhaps, thought Sam, noting the upright bearing as his passenger climbed briskly into the front seat beside him.

'General Slessinger was interested in the *per-*

formance of this model, Sam. Take your time and find a quiet bit of road.'

Sam nodded and caught his boss's eye. As Wee Sam had commented the other day, *It's amazin' what ye can say without sayin' anythin'*. Clearly what the General wanted was a turn of speed. Well, he'd see what could be done.

Given that he rode the six miles between Armagh and Richhill back and forth every day on his recently acquired motorbike, there wasn't much about the road he didn't know. There were a few bad patches where the surface needed attention and a couple of sections where the camber, or lack of it, meant you had to keep a very steady eye on the verges. The worst bend on the whole road was the left-hander just past the Post Office at Woodview.

His father knew the woman who lived in the small house with a high-pitched roof just before the bend itself, one of the gate-lodges to the Leader estate. She'd told him that the family got Christmas cards from young men they'd pulled out of the hedge and the deep ditch beyond. They made tea regularly and phoned for the doctor from the Post Office. For the lucky ones, that was. She admitted that over the years there'd been just a few who wouldn't be drinking any more tea.

The June morning was fine, the air so clear the stone steps and pillars of the Courthouse looked as if they'd been freshly cleaned, so brightly did they gleam in the sunshine. He took it easy till they were beyond the Royal School and the busy junction at the Dean's Bridge, then he allowed the speed to rise in a slow curve. Even on the bad bits of road he had to watch for on the bike, the Lagonda sailed smoothly on as if the surface were perfect.

By great good luck, the last stretch of road into the village was empty so it was not until they reached the main square that he had to reduce speed. He went up the left-hand side past his uncle's shop, turned right across the front of Richhill Castle and stopped halfway down the far side of the square, the bonnet pointing back towards Armagh.

Throughout the drive his passenger had not uttered a word.

'You enjoy driving, young man?'

The tone was short, almost brusque, but the look on the General's face was not unfriendly.

'Yes, sir,' he replied honestly. 'Particularly this model.'

'D'you have a vehicle?'

'No, sir. Motorbike,' he replied, adding the make and model.

'Had an early one of those myself. Nearly broke my neck once,' he said matter-of-factly. 'Too old for that sort of thing now, more's the pity.'

'Would you like to take her back yourself, sir, and see how she handles?'

'No, no. No need for that. You've convinced me,' he said with a short laugh. 'D'you get commission on sales?'

'No, sir,' said Sam, smiling. 'But I've a good boss. He's very fair.'

The General grunted and looked him up and
116

down.

'What's he pay you then?'

Sam told him.

'I need a young man like you. My chauffeur's getting past it. Time he retired,' he went on. 'I live in County Down, visit a lot, both parts of Ireland. I've a house in London. Keep a Bentley there. Like to get about. Daughters, you know, since my wife died,' he explained abruptly. 'I'll double your salary. Good time off when I'm visiting them. Use of the motors now and again. What d'you say?'

For one moment, Sam thought he was dreaming. Here he was sitting in the middle of Richhill almost outside Lizzie and Hugh Loney's new shop and he was being offered a job that would take him all over Ireland and across to London as well. Driving a Lagonda *and* a Bentley. What an offer. He could hardly believe his ears.

'Thank you, sir,' he said slowly, his mind still dazed. 'I can think of nothing I would enjoy more, but I've only been three months with Mr Sleator. He's been very good to me when I had a ... wee bit of a personal problem. I couldn't let him down now I'm over it.'

'So the answer is no?'

'I'm afraid it is. But I'm most grateful to you for asking me, sir.'

'Pity. Great pity,' said the older man sharply. 'You've a great feel for a motor. But loyalty is an important thing too. Not much of it about these days,' he said, nodding to himself. 'Lucky man, Sleator. Do you think we can do it faster on the way back?'

'We can try, sir,' Sam replied, beaming.

He was just about to start the engine when he saw the sun glance off metal. Almost on the edge of vision, a mile or more away on the road leading into the village, he saw the glitter of a black, highly polished motor. Seconds later he saw that there was a second vehicle behind the first. Unusual. Not one, but two, and both Rolls-Royces. Not motors he knew of belonging to any of the local gentry or landowners.

They could be bringing visitors to the Castle, but hired vehicles were more likely, perhaps a funeral, but surely he wouldn't have missed seeing the hearse turning across the foot of the square towards the Presbyterian churchyard or the Quaker burying-ground.

'I'll just let those motors through, sir. It's rather narrow on Red Row,' he explained. He leaned forward to get a better look at them as they swung into the square.

Moments later, all his speculation was resolved. The Rolls were two he'd seen often enough parked outside Loudan's in the Seven Houses. Father and son were driving, but this was no funeral. Sitting in the first car were two bridesmaids, the pink tulle of their dresses matched by ribbons in their piled-up hair. He didn't recognise either of them but the figure in the second vehicle was unmistakable. Sitting in solitary state on the back seat, looking somewhat uncomfortable in a very large hat, heavy with artificial flowers, was Marion's mother, the woman who had shut the door in his face only three months ago.

118

He took a deep breath, put the car in gear and let in the clutch. Accompanied by her father, the bride herself would be following. The thought of seeing her in all her wedding finery was more than he could bear.

He slipped the Lagonda neatly out of the square and accelerated down Red Row to the junction with the Armagh road. The briefest glance towards Portadown revealed the third vehicle approaching. Instantly, he spun the wheel, turned out in front of it and accelerated so fast the driver had neither time nor necessity to modify his own speed.

To the obvious delight of the General, the journey back to Armagh was achieved in an appreciably shorter time than the outward journey had taken.

Sam had a bad afternoon. Whatever job he put his hand to managed to produce some complication or other and he blamed himself for his poor concentration. Had his father been there to observe his work, he could have comforted him. There were times when problems clustered. It was mysterious, but it happened to everyone, no matter how good they were nor how long they'd been doing the job.

As it was, Sam was puzzled as well as upset. Even in the dreadful weeks after Marion had first broken it off, he'd been able to do his work quite normally. If his colleagues knew he was in a bad way, as he now suspected they did, it was probably only the fact that they couldn't make him laugh that had given him away.

The afternoon wore on and Sam spoke to himself severely. His mother had told him there was someone else. He hadn't wanted to believe it, so he'd put it down to rumour and the gossip of neighbours. His mother brought home all the gossip there was to be had and you couldn't believe the half of it, but he remembered now that one evening in the workshop his father had asked very quietly if he thought there might be someone else involved. He'd denied it vigorously. Whatever he might feel about Marion and what she'd done, he'd never think that of her. If there'd been someone else, surely she'd at least have had the courage to tell him.

His father had just nodded to himself and said that maybe however bad it was just now, it was better now than later. There was many a man had married with the greatest of hope, thinking he knew the woman he'd chosen, and then found out she wasn't at all the woman he'd imagined.

He hadn't paid much attention at the time, but now he knew for sure. Well, whoever it was she'd lined up for the June wedding she'd always wanted, he'd a lot more money than he had. Marion's father had made it clear when they'd told him of their engagement that their wedding would be 'a family affair'. There'd have been no wedding cars from Loudan's if it had been him and Marion. No doubt his mother would be able to provide the details of the day even before it went into the newspapers. Bride's dress, bridesmaids, number of guests, reception and *honeymoon venue*, as the Portadown Times always called it.

Hardly a week in Newcastle, or Portrush after all that style, he said to himself bitterly, as the bell rang in the yard for quitting time.

'Boss sez to call upstairs afore you go,' Peggy informed him, as she collected the keys of the Austin he was working on and put them back in the safe.

'D'ye know what he wants?' he asked abruptly, a sudden wave of anxiety sweeping over him.

'Maybe yer for the sack,' she said pertly, as she closed her handbag and waited for him to remove his large frame from the entrance to her small office.

'Ach, I was only foolin' ye,' she added, relenting, when she saw the look on his face.

Nevertheless, Sam felt anxious as he tramped upstairs. The only time any of them ever went to the boss's office was to collect their pay packets on a Thursday.

'Sam, come in. Sit down a minute till I finish this receipt, will you.'

Sam settled himself, looked out the window, and waited patiently while the older man carefully transferred the Lagonda's details from its logbook to the bill of sale. It took him a good five minutes and when he finally applied the sheet of blotter to the completed document, he shook his head wearily.

'Every job has things you dread. I can't stand filling in receipts,' he admitted, 'despite the fact that that's what keeps me in business,' he added, smiling for the first time and handing Sam a brown envelope across the desk. 'Go on, open it,' he said. 'I think I know what's in it, but I want to see your face,' he went on, grinning at him.

Sam's large fingers caught at the sealed envelope, managed to tear off a small corner and finally ripped it apart. As he pulled out a large, white banknote, a small card fell from the envelope and dropped on the threadbare carpet at his feet. He picked it up and looked at John Sleator in amazement.

'Is it a fiver?'

Sam nodded and stared at the flowing italic script on the banknote and the fine silver line running through it. Then he focused his attention on the business card. There was something written on the back.

'If you change your mind in the next year, let me know. Thank you for the drive.' There was a squiggle by way of signature, but the author's full name, rank and addresses were clearly laid out on the other side.

'It seems I might have lost you,' John Sleator began. 'He told me he made you an offer. Do you not think it was a good chance?'

'Oh yes, it was a great offer,' Sam replied, his face lighting up. 'He has a Bentley forby the new Lagonda.'

'But you said no?'

'I did,' Sam said, nodding. 'If I'd been here a couple of years, or if you hadn't given me time off I wasn't entitled to, I might have said yes.'

'I appreciate that, Sam. I know from Harry it's not been a good time for you, but you've kept up your work and never let your workmates down on the job. The General was right. He told me I

122

was lucky to have you,' he said firmly. 'Now what are you going to do with your fiver? Something for the bike or something for yourself?'

Sam smiled and shook his head.

'No, I think what I'll do is take my colleagues out for a meal and maybe the pictures. A night out for the boys and Peggy and the two young lads. Sure I mightn't have another fiver dropping into my lap for many a long day.'

Eight

Along with all the other young shop assistants in Armagh, Ellie looked forward to the extra day's holiday July always brought. On Tuesday, the Twelfth, she would spend the day with Daisy going to the demonstration field just outside Armagh to hear the bands and watch the annual Orange procession. But apart from this brief day's respite from the Great Summer Sale, there was little to recommend the month of July. As she admitted to Daisy, while drying their hair one morning before work after cycling through a cloudburst, it was her least favourite in the whole year.

To begin with, Freeburn's itself was hot and airless. The extra bales of cloth and piled up garments for the sale made the narrow aisles even narrower and closed up completely any unused space. Even with the front and back doors propped open and all the upstairs windows thrown wide in the hope of creating a through draught, it was stuffy as well as claustrophobic. The assorted fabrics gave off a strange musty odour, not exactly unpleasant, but pervasive. At times Ellie felt desperate for fresh air, but even when she managed to get away from the shop in her short lunch break, she found the air so warm and humid outdoors there was no freshness to be had.

Half a dozen times in the course of the month, setting out from home under an overcast sky, she'd watched the heavy clouds darken as she cycled along. Large, sixpenny-sized spots of warm rain would drop on her shoulders so suddenly, she'd have barely a minute to find shelter before the clouds opened and cast their burden in dancing spires on the road in front of her. More than once she'd been caught in just that part of her daily journey where there were neither trees in the hedgerow nor a neighbour's house near enough for her to drop her bicycle by the front gate and run for the shelter of the porch.

On the third Monday of the month, standing under a large chestnut in the line of dark-canopied trees that overhung the footpath on the edge of the Asylum grounds, she watched the sudden downpour blank out the small houses in Mill Row and the tall, brick mass of Drumcairn Mill beyond. Within moments of leaning her bicycle against the hedge, she watched sheets of water pouring off the surface of the road and filling up the gutter. Little fragments of torn leaf, brown sepals and tiny twigs were swept along in the sudden flood. Immediately, she thought of the rivers in the Canadian forests where the logs jostled and rolled on their way down to the saw-mills, tossed by the churning flow as easily as these little fragments.

As suddenly as it had begun, the rain stopped. The sun appeared and within minutes the road began to steam, swirling around her like a November mist as she pedalled faster to make up for the time she'd lost. However damp and sticky she might feel, she could hardly complain when she thought how much worse it must be for George.

His letters now arrived more regularly, although she had to admit they were still short nor did they tell her very much. In most of them, he simply said there wasn't any news, because every day was like every other day and it was only once a fortnight they had a break when they went north for two nights to a mining camp, so much larger than their own modest lumber camp it had a saloon and a boarding house.

It did sound a bit like the Wild West, the sort of thing they'd seen together in the Ritz Cinema, with cowboys and gunslingers and battles with the Indians. She'd asked him if there were Indians in his part of Canada or if that was only in the States. He'd said he hadn't noticed any and then went on to tell her about the heat and the insects.

She felt she could hardly complain about the Armagh temperature being in the seventies when George said where he was it was in the nineties or even more. He hadn't told her exactly *where* he was though she'd asked several times, nor was the address any help. All it said was: Box 32, Lot 7, Peterborough Lumbering Company and added the number and street of the Head Office in Peterborough, a street not very far from where Polly and Jimmy lived.

As she pedalled on feeling sticky and uncomfortable she wondered anxiously how she would cope with the temperatures he talked about when she found the summer heat difficult enough here at home. She'd told Polly about her worry in a recent letter, and Polly had been a comfort, explaining that Peterborough itself wasn't as humid as it would be in the forest where George was working. Polly admitted she herself had found the higher humidity difficult to begin with, but she said you did get used to it. Sometimes you felt washed out when it got really bad, but then so did everybody else. It wouldn't just be you.

As she made her way into the city, Ellie reminded herself that one of the good things about the month was that Miss Walker took her annual leave during the second fortnight. It made such a difference knowing there was no one watching the clock to see if you were even a moment late, delayed by rain or traffic. Harry, Stanley and Joe, the three young men in the Gentlemen's Department all had digs in a boarding house only two doors down from the shop while Mr Maginnis, the senior man, lived in Ogle Street, a short walk away. They knew Ellie had to cycle two miles and Daisy more like three to get to work. None of them ever minded if they weren't there on the dot of eight thirty to share the jobs in the early morning routine.

'Hello, Ellie. How did *you* miss it? I got wet *again*,' Daisy greeted her cheerfully, as she emerged from a towel, wisps of hair sticking to her damp cheeks.

'I was quick on the draw,' Ellie replied promptly. 'Saw it coming and got under a tree. We've had plenty of practice this month, haven't we?'

'Sure have, pardner,' Daisy replied, laughing.

Daisy loved the cinema, Westerns in particular, and often lapsed into a very good mimicry of the minimal exchanges between her heroes, even though she'd seldom been able to go to the Ritz in the last two years.

She dropped the towel over the back of a chair, took out her comb and swept her damp hair away from her face. It was when she turned back from the mirror that Ellie saw her smile, her brown eyes sparkling, her pleasant face transformed to prettiness.

'Something's happened. Something good has happened, Daisy. Tell me. Tell me quickly before we go down.'

'Sure there's no hurry. Doesn't Harry just love doing your jobs?' she said, teasing.

'Go on, Daisy.'

'Well, I told you Uncle Sam knew this doctor over Banbridge way. He's married to one of m'cousins. Anyway, Uncle Sam said he was goin' to ask him to come and see Ma. Dr Stewart. D'you mind?'

'Yes, of course I do. You said your uncle thought a younger man might be able to help

127

more. Anyway, he thought Dr Stewart was a very good doctor. Has he been?'

'Aye, he came on Sunday of last week, but I wasn't sayin' anythin' till I saw if there was any improvement. The doctor we have kept givin' her different things and said they'd do the job, but they never made a bit of difference. I can't believe it, Ellie,' she said with a great sigh as she dropped down on the chair, knocking the towel unheeded to the floor. 'He talked to Ma for an awful long time an' then left her some wee pills and a bottle of tonic. She's took them three times a day for the week and on Saturday mornin' she's out feedin' the hens. She looks about ten years younger. She says it's a miracle, all that sick feeling that made her so miserable has gone. She was complainin' yesterday that there was no flour. She was lookin' for it to bake. Sure we haven't tasted anythin' other than baker's bread since Da died.'

'Have you any idea what was wrong?'

'Apparently he said there were two things, one makin' the other worse. One was simple enough, the other was more difficult, but he hoped what he was going to prescribe might help. Well it did. An' that's not all,' Daisy went on, pausing as she bent down and rubbed fiercely at her wet shoes with a piece of rag.

Ellie waited impatiently until Daisy straightened up again and caught her breath.

'Uncle Sam came over again yesterday to see us. He works for Irish Road Motors in Portadown and he's got a place as an apprentice for Jimmy ... and him only out of school two weeks.

He won't earn very much, but they give their apprentices a bicycle and a midday meal and work clothes and that's worth a queer bit.'

'Oh Daisy, Daisy, I'm so *very* glad,' said Ellie, as Daisy stood up and hugged her.

Ellie felt her eyes misting over when she looked at her friend and saw her eyes shining, her shoulders and the whole set of her body full of a lightness she'd quite forgotten. She would not have minded how often she'd got wet if she could have brought about this amazing change herself.

Although preparations for the sale made a lot of extra work in June, the sale itself did not make the shop any busier. People came knowing what they wanted, especially bed linen and towels, and although the day's takings regularly made Mr Freeburn nod with gentle satisfaction, there were quite long periods when there were no customers in the shop at all. It was the one time in the year when the assistants could be sure of catching up on everyone's news and sharing whatever jokes were being passed around.

In fact, so lively were the days that followed Daisy's good news and the absence of Miss Walker that Ellie almost forgot her dislike of the month. Though he seldom took part himself in the talk and banter, Mr Maginnis had no objections to the young people chatting to each other when there was no work they could usefully do. Indeed, he made no secret of the fact that he thought Miss Walker created quite unnecessary tasks for Ellie and Daisy, just to keep them busy.

It was Harry, a tall, pale-faced young man with a flame of red hair, who announced one morning when mugs of tea were being circulated at the back of the empty shop that he had some good news for Ellie and Daisy.

'Are ye gettin' married then, Harry?' demanded Daisy. 'Someone rich I hope, so you won't have to work here and bother us any more?' she continued, as Harry pulled faces at her and pretended to be annoyed.

Seventeen years old, Harry was from a large family in County Tyrone and was one of those young men who had a genuine good nature about him. He appeared incapable of being unpleasant and even the most difficult of customers usually capitulated to his easy manner and ended up saying 'Thank you', and smiling at him. His regard for Ellie was obvious to everyone. Being teased about it was a pleasure to him, a small comfort for knowing that not only was she spoken for, but, being younger and poor, he could never hope to pay court to her anyway.

For her part, Ellie was fond of the young man and never minded the teasing. Unlike her brothers, who had never had much time for her, Harry would talk to her about his family, the long walks he did on Sundays with friends from the boarding house and his hopes for the future. Had it not been for Miss Walker's disapproving eye, Harry would have ensured that Ellie never again lifted anything heavier than a box of silk stockings.

'As I said, I have great news for you two

ladies,' Harry repeated, as he and Stanley propped themselves against the back door leaving the folding chairs for Ellie and Daisy.

'Stanley and I joined the RUC Tennis Club this year,' he began, nodding to his friend, 'and we've had a great time. Met a lot of nice people. A few girls, though not as nice as present company,' he added bowing to them, 'forby the tennis. They've a lovely court with big stone walls around it so you don't keep losing the tennis balls like some places I've heard of.'

'Aye,' said Daisy, raising an eyebrow. 'Are ye for Wimbledon then?'

'I think I'll wait till next year, Daisy. My backhand needs just a bit more work.'

'His front hand's not great either,' Stanley added soberly, 'but he can fairly put away the sandwiches when there's a match.'

Undeterred by interruptions and his friend's comments, Harry went on to explain that the club wanted to recruit new members. Particularly lady members. Given that the season was so far advanced, the evenings dropping down already, they were offering free membership for the rest of the year, with a special session on early closing day for newcomers.

'Now what about you two ladies coming with Stanley and me on Wednesday. We'll see you're properly looked after and introduced to everyone. I'm sure you'd both be very good,' he said encouragingly.

'Given I've never had a racquet in m'hand in m'life I'm sure you're absolutely right,' Daisy commented cheerfully.

131

'Did you ever play rounders at school?'

'Aye.'

'With a bat or with your hand?'

'Both.'

'Well, sure it's the same thing. It's only keeping your eye on the ball, like cutting a length of cloth and keeping the line straight,' said Harry persuasively.

'Ellie's the one for that,' commented Stanley abruptly.

'Why don't you *both* come on Wednesday. There's spare racquets for those who haven't their own and you only need shoes that are flat and kinda soft.'

'You mean we don't have to wear whites? Oh dear, an' I fancied myself in whites.'

At that point the shop bell sounded and they dispersed with practised ease without another word being spoken.

'I think we *should* go, Ellie,' Daisy said firmly, as they sat under the trees on The Mall some two hours later. 'My Ma said las' night that I never went anywhere but work an' it wasn't right at all. I'd had a lot to put up with when she wasn't well, but I should be gettin' out an' enjoyin' myself now that she was better. An' sure you're just the same. You go nowhere either. An' don't be tellin' me that George thinks you should sit at home. Doesn't he go with his friends to this saloon you were tellin' me about? Joinin' a tennis club isn't like goin' out with some other fella.'

Ellie had to agree there was no harm in it, but she confessed she was afraid she'd be no good at

132

tennis and would be embarrassed in front of people she didn't know.

'But that's the whole point. If we go with Harry and Stanley on Wednesday, we can have a bit of a laugh, an' if we're hopeless there's no harm done. Ach, Ellie, I promised Ma I'd start goin' out, but I don't want to go somewhere on m'own. Don't let me down.'

'All right. I'll come.'

Ellie wasn't at all happy about the decision she'd made, but when she'd thought how little pleasure there'd been for Daisy in recent years she just couldn't say no. Had things been the other way round, she knew Daisy would never have said no to her.

Cycling home that evening she made up her mind that whatever happened and however uneasy she might be with the tennis itself and the meeting of the members of the Tennis Club, she'd stick it out for a couple of weeks at least. Knowing Daisy, she'd have made friends by then and it wouldn't matter at all if she didn't go again herself.

The Royal Ulster Constabulary Tennis Club had originally been set up to provide recreation for policemen and their wives, but at some point it was recognized that policemen and their wives might well wish to make friends beyond their immediate colleagues. For some years, however, the membership of the club had been dominated by young men. Despite the great popularity of the RUC Annual Tennis Club Dance with the young women of Armagh, there were so few

133

women in the club that Harry and Stanley had never yet managed a set of mixed doubles.

'It's really very handy,' said Harry, as they prepared to close the shop on Wednesday afternoon. 'It's only about ten minutes walk, but I expect you'll both want to bring your bicycles for going home. Stanley and I will go on ahead when we've had our lunch and we'll be waiting for you when you get there.'

Thomas Street and Dobbin Street were familiar enough to both Ellie and Daisy, but when they turned right as instructed between the back of Hillock's large hardware business and the new fire station, they found themselves in quite unfamiliar territory. After a few moments they identified the overgrown ruins of an old building, a Franciscan Friary according to Joe, the third and quietest of their male colleagues.

A short distance beyond the remaining walls stood a pair of handsome houses. That told them they were now in the grounds of the Archbishop's Palace and somewhere nearby on the left was the path they were looking for. It led to what had once been an old, walled garden, the pleasure and delight of Lady Anne, sister of one of the former Archbishops.

They got off their bicycles and stood peering beyond the ruins at the luxuriant growth of grasses and wild flowers densely shaded by mature trees.

'Look, there's Harry!' Daisy cried.

They both laughed as Harry came towards them, his arms held high above his sides, the seeding grasses clinging to his shirt and trousers.

'How in the name of goodness did ye expect us to find that wee path?'

'It's easy once you know where it is,' he grinned, brushing at balls of robin-run-the-hedge firmly lodged on his clothes. 'You can leave your bikes behind this tree. No one will see them. And there's plenty of policemen about anyway. I'll go first and collect up the rest of this stuff,' he said laughing, as he pulled a length of clinging green vegetation from his shirt and led the way back through the thick grass.

Ellie was sorry it wasn't very far. The day was hot, the sky brilliant but under the trees in the cool, dappled shade, pencils of light were picking out the remaining pink blooms on some tall wild flowers just beginning to seed. Clusters of white fibres spun and shimmered on the light breeze, floating over the sea of grasses, broken only by some elderflower bushes, whose faint perfume floated across to them from broad, creamy blooms.

The path curved and ahead of them rose high walls. From niches and crevices where the mortar had been eroded, ivy-leaved toadflax and Herb Robert hung in delicate fronds against the pale-grey stone. To Ellie's amazement she found the broken top of the wall supported large branching wallflowers brilliantly in bloom. They *were* called wallflowers but this was hardly the season for them to be in flower.

Painted dark green and fitted closely into the wall was a metal door. Harry pushed it open and waited for them to go through.

'Good gracious,' Ellie burst out, amazed at the

contrast it revealed.

After the richness and wildness of the approach, an immaculate and verdant green court, freshly marked and showing very little wear after a summer's use occupied only the centre of a much larger, perfectly kept enclosure. Sunlight spilled into the open space and caught the bright stripes of a small pavilion outside which a collection of young people sat or lay, some watching the four men playing from the base line, the resonance of ball on racquet beating a strong rhythm on the warm air.

'It's lovely, isn't it?' whispered Daisy.

'Yes, it is,' Ellie agreed, gazing round.

She didn't say it, for Harry was leading them over to the pavilion where Stanley was already talking to some other young men, but what Ellie was thinking was how much she would have loved to have seen this place when it was a garden. She gazed round the inside of the lovely old walls, thought of the shelter they'd give in winter and the support they'd provide in summer. Roses and clematis and all sorts of other climbing plants she didn't even know the names of, plants that Lady Anne's skill and money would have been able to provide.

It was no surprise to Harry or Stanley that Ellie and Daisy made a good hand of playing tennis. They learnt quickly. Within a couple of weeks they were perfectly at home on the court. Ellie was the steadier of the two, often winning points by moving up to the net and cutting off a strong return. Daisy found serving difficult, but once started she had a fierce return and could drive from the back line as strongly as either of the two young men.

At first they played every Wednesday afternoon, but then they decided they could have a game after work on Mondays and Fridays as well. Daisy was thoroughly enjoying herself and after the first uneasy week, Ellie never seriously considered giving it up once her friend was settled.

'Well, we've done well getting new lady members,' said Harry, early one Thursday morning in the middle of August. 'It seems we're short of men now.'

'Have we chased them all away?' demanded Daisy.

She glanced round the empty shop, finished pouring bags of small change into the compartments of the till and closed it firmly.

Ellie was puzzled. Even though they seldom saw the same players every time they went to the club, she certainly hadn't noticed any lack of men. All those young men they'd met on that first afternoon still turned up regularly. When they did meet someone new, it was simply a member who'd been away or not free on the evenings when they themselves played.

'Postings,' said Harry, with a wry look as Stanley walked over to join them at the back of the shop. 'All this trouble in Belfast. They need more police. They haven't gone yet, but they know they'll be going. The word is they'll be needed by the end of the month. It doesn't matter all that much for this season, it's only got five or six weeks to go, but if they're posted, then we'll not get them back and we'll be short next year.'

'Ach dear, that's a pity. D'you know whose goin'?'

Harry listed the names and Ellie too felt sad. They were all young men they'd partnered at some time or other and had got to know. One of them had fallen for Daisy and had asked her out, but she'd said no, much to Ellie's surprise.

'What about your brothers, Ellie?'

'Sorry, no good. Bob's in Belfast himself for the next year and Johnny's in Cookstown. Anyway, they're both going strong. From what I hear I doubt if their lady friends would let them join anything.'

'I might try Sammy,' said Daisy abruptly. 'He's mad about motor racing though he can't afford it, I'm sure he could well afford to play tennis. He's a bit like I was, all work and no play.'

'Is that your older brother, Daisy?' Stanley asked.

'Ach, no. Our Bill's only left school. Sammy's m'cousin from Richhill, but he's a motorbike so he can go where he likes. I'll ask *him*.'

Ellie smiled to herself. Another young man mad about motorbikes.

She thought back to her one brief experience of riding pillion behind George and wondered what it was that so appealed to them. For herself, all she remembered was the chill of the wind on her bare arms and her heart in her mouth as they leaned over on every bend. It was an experience she'd much rather forget.

Nine

August of 1932 began with an unwelcome continuation of the warm and very wet conditions of July. Then came a sudden change. In the middle of the month, between one day and the next, the weather settled. To the great delight of the four young people from Freeburns's High Class Drapery, day after day now turned out fine and warm. It was such an encouragement to come to work on a Club day and know that their pleasure was unlikely to be spoilt either by the continuous rain which made it pointless even to go to the court or by the kind of sudden downpour that drove them to shelter in the pavilion in the middle of a game knowing the grass would be dangerous and unplayable after it passed.

As she cycled slowly home one Friday evening after a particularly happy couple of hours on the court, the sky already paling to gold in the west, Ellie admitted to herself that she would miss the club badly over the winter months. Although it barely affected her or Daisy, who both left early to cycle home, she'd heard Harry and Stanley complain their final set had to be played in the gathering dusk. Earlier in the week, Harry made them laugh when he told them how his partner the previous evening proposed dipping the

139

tennis balls in the whitener used for marking the court, so they could see them well enough to finish their set.

'That wou'd do the racquets a lot of good, wou'den it?' Daisy had commented sharply, ever the most practical of the four. It was she who had found proper tennis shoes for herself and Ellie at half price in a shoe shop in Thomas Street and insisted they bought them. Then she started them saving up for next year's subscription and racquets of their own. Being the quicker of the two at figures, she'd counted up the weeks till the club reopened at the end of April, added the cost of the racquets and provided two clean jam pots with lids to keep in the cupboard in the staffroom along with the tea and sugar. Each pay day, she had ensured that the relevant coins were added to each of them. She'd left a double payment in her jar before she took her holiday and warned Ellie that she'd have to do the same before she went off at the beginning of October.

It wasn't a huge sum, but it did mean that what she put in her Post Office book each week was smaller than before. She'd felt uneasy and wondered if she should tell George, but she knew perfectly well what Daisy would say if she mentioned it. She'd told George about joining the Tennis Club, but he'd made no comment, just said that there wasn't anything to do in the camp in the evenings except get cleaned up or play cards. Then, to her surprise, just as she'd finally made up her mind to tell him that she wasn't able to save as much as usual, he mentioned the subject of saving up himself.

He said he was a bit disappointed with the way things were working out from a money point of view. The pay was great, just as he'd told her, but they had to pay for their food, which wasn't cheap, and their share of the cook's wages as well. Also, they had to pay for their own board and lodging whenever they had a weekend off. Besides that, they'd had to fork out for special work clothes and safety equipment as well as laundry every fortnight. Added to all of that, his uncle hadn't mentioned they were laid off in the winter months, receiving only a small retainer and cheap board if they needed it in a hostel in Peterborough until the work started again when the ice melted. Some of the lads went down to the States to look for winter work but apparently it was hard to get.

She might not be as quick at mental arithmetic as Daisy was, but what he was saying could only mean one thing. It was going to take much longer than he'd thought to save up enough money to get them started. Unless something came to help, a different job or a legacy, or something totally unexpected. It might take years.

'Hello, Ellie, how are you? You're surely not working as late as this?'

Ellie leaned her bicycle against the entrance to the shoeing shed as a familiar voice hailed her from the bench inside the forge. She said hello to her father and smiled down at Charlie Running as he moved promptly along the bench to leave room for her.

'No, Charlie. Pleasure tonight,' she replied, dropping gratefully down beside him. 'Daisy and I've joined the RUC Tennis Club and we go a couple of nights a week.'

'My goodness, it's great to be young,' declared Charlie, looking across at Robert, a distinct twinkle in his eye.

'It'll be a day or two before ye draw yer pension yet, Charlie,' Robert replied tartly.

Ellie laughed. That was one up to her father. She leaned back comfortably against the well-polished piece of wall behind the bench and looked from one to the other. She'd never quite been able to work out the friendship between Charlie and her father. Charlie was ten years younger, a senior clerk with Armagh Council, a man passionate about books and learning. Yet he sought out her father regularly and never took offence at the uncharacteristically sharp comments his presence always produced.

'What about your holiday, Ellie? Are ye going up to see Aunt Annie and the family? I thought you'd have been away before this. Would your man not spare you till the sale was well over?'

'No, to be fair he would have let me go before Daisy went,' Ellie began, knowing Charlie rarely had a good word to say about Freeburn or any of the other employers in Armagh. 'But Ruth won't get any holiday till October,' she went on. 'She started a new job in May so she's not due any time off till then. She'll get a few days the week I'm there and I'll amuse myself, or help Auntie, for the rest of it.'

'I'm not sure Belfast is the best place to be going just at the moment,' said Charlie slowly. 'I think there's going to be trouble there before

142

very long. What do you think, Robert?'

Robert glanced across at him and hammered vigorously at a piece of metal before plunging it into the water tank.

'You're better up with these things than I am, Charlie. Is it the Socialists or the Communists stirrin' up trouble this time?'

'Man dear, d'ye not see the difference between troublemakers and the organizers of downtrodden labour?' Charlie asked vigorously. 'Have ye no idea of the poverty in that city? One and a quarter million in this little piece of Ireland and one hundred thousand of them unemployed and most of those in Belfast. And how many of those do you think get even a pittance by way of benefit? Less than half. Thirty-seven per cent of working class families are living in absolute poverty. Nearly half those who die between fifteen and twenty-five are dying of TB...'

Robert drew the dripping metal out of the tank, plunged it into the fire, leaned on the bellows and pumped them gently till the fire glowed red and gold. Charlie paused, but did not stop. As soon as the roar of the fire quietened he returned to his bitter charge.

'There's people starving, Robert, as surely as they starved in the Famine. Catholics and Protestants alike. Their only hope of survival is a change in the rate of Outdoor Relief.'

'Sure haven't they the Workhouse if they're beat?' Robert asked sheepishly, pausing with his hand on the metal bar, its further end now glowing like gold in the heart of the fire.

'Aye, there's the Workhouse, if you'd wish that

on any decent soul, but have you not heard of the means test? Sure you have to be destitute altogether for them to let you in and what man wouldn't try to keep his family out? How can you feed a wife and children on a few shillings a week?'

Robert drew the bar from the fire and hammered the glowing tip so vigorously that bright sparks traced minute arcs of light into the now dark corners of the shadowy forge before they disappeared entirely.

Ellie glanced quickly from one face to the other. Her father's was streaked with soot and sweat and lined with fatigue, Charlie's clean and rounded, but so pale it might have been the face of someone shut up where they never even glimpsed the summer sun. In his eyes was a look of such pain as she'd never seen before.

She'd read in the local paper about disturbances in Belfast and there'd been some talk at the Club among the young men being posted there, but it hadn't been clear to her either from what she read or heard exactly what the causes of the disturbances were. Everyone knew about the unemployment, how bad things were in the shipyards and in the mills, but her only contact with the city was the tall brick house on the Lisburn Road where her aunt and uncle lived and the area round Royal Avenue where she and her cousin, Ruth, went to gaze at the latest fashion in the shop windows.

The hammering had stopped, the metal thrust back in the fire. Before either man could speak again, they heard a rustle and a shadow fell

144

across the door.

'There's not a drop of water in the house an' I'm parched.'

Ellen Scott stood in the doorway, an empty pail in her hand. She looked at none of them, neither her husband standing by the hearth, nor her daughter seated on the bench, nor one of their closest neighbours sitting beside her. In a thin, wavering voice she told them she wasn't fit to carry buckets from the well.

Charlie and Ellie rose at the same moment, both speaking at the same time.

'No, Ellie, I'll go,' Charlie said firmly, laying a hand on her arm. 'You go back to the house with your mother and I'll bring the water to you.'

He strode off up the path and disappeared round the gable into the orchard.

'Isn't it great to have someone to help you,' Ellen said, as she stumbled back towards the house. 'Kate Running doesn't know she's alive, has a man to fetch and carry for her,' she began.

Ellie had heard it all before. There was no point whatever making any reply, so she counted ten and said nothing.

The third week in August brought the arrival of the new assistant Charlie Freeburn had 'had his eye on'. She turned out to be the fourteen-year-old sister of young John Sleator of Abbey Street and the youngest aunt of the most recent addition to the line of John Sleators, the robust baby born in May and mercifully known as 'wee Johnny'.

A pretty, likeable, dark-haired girl, Susie had been sent to the local Grammar School but apart from a talent for playing games she'd shown none of the ability that had produced a series of successful businessmen from the male side of the family.

Not of sufficient social standing to be sent to finishing school to be groomed for a good marriage, but too lively and energetic to sit around at home fulfilling the dubious role of her mother's little helper, or even acting part-time nursemaid to the newest Sleator, Susie had jumped at the chance of working in Uncle Charlie's shop.

Technically, of course, Charlie Freeburn, was *not* her uncle. He was her older brother's father-in-law, a point which he made to her very tactfully before she took up her appointment. At the same interview, Charlie told her that though she must at all times be polite to Miss Walker, it was to Miss Scott she was directly responsible. Miss Walker no longer supervised the female staff. Purchasing stock in Belfast and Manchester and ensuring the inventories and accounts were up to date was now her sole responsibility. Whatever problems Miss Sleator might have were to be referred to Miss Scott, who was now Senior Assistant.

Ellie had given no thought at all to the change in status which Charlie Freeburn had hinted at some months earlier when she'd approached him about Daisy's problems, but a significant change in his behaviour made her suddenly sharply aware of it.

While he had always been courteous towards

her and had often asked to 'have a word' about stock, or customers, he would now ask her to come to his office *when it was convenient*. His questions were not very different from the ones he'd put to her before, but now there were many more of them and much more detailed. Sometimes indeed she had to admit she hadn't got an answer, but he appeared to be quite satisfied when she told him she would think about it and come back to see him when she'd found out what he wanted to know.

He never forgot anything he'd asked her, even though she never saw him make a note of what he'd said, but nor did Ellie forget what he had asked. She would set her mind to the problem, consider it patiently until she was satisfied she had an answer, then she'd knock on his door, ask him if it was convenient to have a word and give him her conclusions.

There was another significant change too, though it was some time before she realised it. The stock being bought in by Miss Walker was of a kind and quality which she herself had recommended to her boss.

As for Susie, Ellie found the girl a delight. It was true you had to tell her everything at least five times, but when she grasped something new she was so pleased with herself, one couldn't help smiling and sharing in her pleasure. Daisy was amazed at how slow Susie could be, but, instead of being irritated by her slowness, Daisy showed a quite surprising patience with her. She'd go as far as trying to find ways to help her remember how many inches there were in a yard and a quarter or how to use the ready-reckoner without having to ask for help in front of a customer.

It seemed to Ellie that Daisy was happier than she'd ever seen her, helped by a new measure of confidence which grew out of helping Susie. Then it came to her there was something else as well. There was no longer Miss Walker looming over her all day, giving expression to a disapproval poor Daisy could never hope to modify because the cause of it was the very nature of the person she was. Of her own growing confidence, however, she was quite unaware.

The very last opening of the dark-green gate into the RUC court was planned for Wednesday 7th September at 2.00 p.m. If rain were to interrupt or even prevent play the Club would still be meeting thanks to a marquee provided by the Committee from funds raised at the Annual Dance in the City Hall. All members were urged to attend for as much of the event as possible.

If the weather was fine there would be a knockout tournament, names to be drawn for mixed doubles at two o'clock and at six o'clock. Tea would be served from five thirty onwards and play would go on as long as the light lasted, or until the winning couple had been found. Dancing would follow in the marquee.

Daisy could talk about nothing else and Ellie felt sorry for Susie. It was bad enough that she was already a good player but too young to join the club, but worse still, for a girl who so loved dancing, was the thought of missing this opportunity. However small and informal compared with the Annual Tennis Club Dance in the City Hall, a dance was a dance and not being there was almost more than she could bear.

There was little comfort in Daisy telling her she could join when she was seventeen and that she and Ellie would introduce her to everyone. But, to her great credit, Susie cheered up as the day approached and insisted on helping the two girls make the loaf of sandwiches they'd been asked to provide as their contribution towards the tea.

'Make sure one of you wins the prize,' Susie said, as they wrapped the sandwiches in a damp cloth and packed them carefully into a cardboard box.

'Depends who we draw, Susie,' explained Daisy. 'Can't do it without a good partner. If one of us draws Harry or Stanley we'd have a chance, they're among the best of the men, but it's a lucky dip. Two lucky dips actually. One for those who have the half day and one for those that haven't. There'll be a play off then between the winners.'

'Well, good luck to you both. I hope you have a *great* time. I'll want to hear *all* about it tomorrow,' she said, beaming at them both, as they changed their sensible shop footwear for something prettier they could dance in later and gathered up their bags and tennis shoes.

The three girls walked together down the dim, high-walled entry which led from the back of the shop and emerged into Scotch Street. Bright sunlight spilled down from a cloudless sky.

'Well, that's a good start,' said Susie enthusiastically, as she turned away. 'See you win.'

A few minutes later they were cycling into the Palace Grounds, the path to the left entirely visible, especially scythed for the occasion by the elderly groundsman who mowed the court and marked out the white lines. As well as the bicycles parked against convenient trees, they spotted a couple of motorbikes pushed into the thicker undergrowth. On the narrow road that ran in front of the two estate houses and led up to the Palace itself, three motors and a police tender were lined up neatly one behind the other.

The familiar dark-green door was propped open and all around the still-empty court people moved backwards and forwards, some of the men in whites, girls in summer dresses, some delivering baskets and boxes of food to the back of the marquee, others joining the queue at the Secretary's table to write their names on slips of paper ready for the partner's draw.

'Here, I'll take the grub to the tea-ladies, you away and write our names down,' said Daisy, her face shining. 'There's Harry waving at you. You'd better away and say hello to him.'

Ellie filled in the two slips of paper, folded them as instructed, dropped them into a cardboard box covered with pink wallpaper and went over to tell Harry how smart he looked. Both he and Stanley had acquired new white flannels and she couldn't help noticing how dazzling their well-worn tennis shoes were. Even the laces had been carefully coated with whitener.

'Ladies and gentlemen...'

The Secretary, a non-playing member with a neat toothbrush moustache, small round spectacles and a balding head, raised his megaphone and requested their attention.

In the complete silence that followed, he repeated the details of the afternoon's arrangements most of which they were perfectly familiar with already. He then went on to explain how the draw for partners had been designed to incorporate the draw for opponents as well. The first pair drawn, one from each of the two boxes, pink and blue, would play the second pair drawn. Pair three would play pair four. And so on. The winner of each two pairs would play the next winning pair and so on in similar fashion. One set only and sudden death if it went to five games each. He would read out the names of players drawn together and then post a printed list on the side of the pavilion.

Ellie sat down in the deckchair Harry had been keeping for her and lay back briefly with her eyes shut, her face turned towards the sun.

'Wake me up if you need me,' she said laughing, just before the first names were announced.

'Daisy Hutchinson and...'

Ellie's eyes opened immediately. She sat up and they listened intently.

'Frank Armstrong.'

'Ohhhh. He is good,' said Harry quickly. 'That's the Sergeant Armstrong I told you about.'

'The one who wanted to paint the tennis balls?'

'The very one. But he was only fooling. He

151

plays a lot.'

They stopped talking and waited, their eyes on the woman who was picking out the slips of paper and handing them unopened to the Secretary.

'Adele Simpson and ... James Nethercott.'

'He's police as well. Not as good as Armstrong. Don't know her,' Harry whispered quickly, as a tall, blonde woman stood up just a few yards away.

'Sadie Ballantine and ... Stanley Orr. Dorothy Trimble and ... George Montgomery.'

Some minutes later Harry was drawn with one of the policemen's wives. Sitting some distance away, her small daughter parked in her pram beside her, she raised her hand in acknowledgement.

'Is she any good?' Ellie asked, sensing the young man's disappointment.

'Yes, better than you are, but guess who I'd like to have drawn,' he said, smiling down at her.

He walked away, spoke to Mrs Edwards, smiled and knelt down beside the pram to speak to her daughter. The little girl regarded him solemnly, then stuck out her hand and offered him her rather grubby stuffed rabbit.

Ellie watched them out of a corner of her eye as the remaining names were read out amid a chorus of comments, of delight, chagrin or amusement. Harry had such a gift for being easy with people. Old or young, titled lady or servant, it was all the same to him. Some girl would be fortunate in five or ten years' time if Harry were in a position to marry. But that was the problem,

152

wasn't it. Even when he was more experienced, what Harry could earn at Freeburn's might pay his keep, buy him a new suit for the shop every two years, pay his subscription to the club or replace his worn racquet, but it wouldn't look at supporting a wife and children.

Just like George had been. She sighed inwardly. Just like he still was, for the moment at least. She put the thought hastily out of mind as she saw the first two couples walk onto the court and toss for sides and service.

'Miss Ellie Scott?'

The Secretary stood in front of her looking apologetic.

'I'm afraid we were one man short for the afternoon draw. I'm so sorry, but I assure you, you'll have the first man out of the blue box at six o'clock.'

Ellie laughed and was pleased to see him looking relieved.

'I'm quite glad really,' she said to reassure him. 'Three of my friends will be playing each other and I'll be able to watch them all.'

'Good. Good,' he said. 'Enjoy your afternoon. You'll hear from me at six o'clock.'

The afternoon passed quickly, the couples urged to change over promptly at the end of each set. Daisy and her partner, a tall serious-looking young man took their opponents to five all and had Ellie sitting on the edge of her seat. She realized it was Daisy's service, her one weak spot. But Daisy was on form, not even a foot fault and once her service went over the net, both she and her partner, now well adjusted to each

153

other, slogged it out through one of the longest single games of the afternoon. In the end, they just made it, shook hands with their opponents and came off the court dripping with sweat, Frank's arm lightly around Daisy's shoulders as Ellie walked over to congratulate them.

By late afternoon, to the Secretary's great satisfaction, all the necessary matches had been played. There would be fewer couples arriving for the evening and as it was still fine and dry, he could be almost sure the light would last and he'd not have to declare a draw between the finalists, or even, as had happened in previous years, to ask the semi-finalists to share the honours as darkness fell.

Tea was very welcome and Ellie realized how hungry she was.

'Excitement, that's what does it,' Harry announced as he loaded up her plate from a passing tray of sandwiches.

'You played well, Harry. Sorry you didn't manage it. Richard Sleator is very good, isn't he?'

'I wish I'd a serve like his,' Harry replied ruefully between mouthfuls. 'I think Mrs Edwards was frightened of him. Though she did her best,' he added quickly. 'But we gave them a run for their money.'

'You did indeed,' she agreed vigorously. 'Have you seen Daisy anywhere?' she went on, looking around the moving figures in the marquee.

Harry smiled shyly.

'I think you'll find she's getting to know her partner better before they play in the finals.'

The megaphone was not working properly. Strange whining noises issued from it as the Secretary picked it up and looked at his watch. The newcomers had got as far as the cake, but were still munching when it was finally persuaded to work.

'Ellie Scott and ... Sam Hamilton.'

Oh goodness, Ellie thought, her heart leaping to her mouth. Someone I've never even met. He must be a policeman who's been on duty. She took a deep breath, stood up and walked slowly towards the Secretary's small table as he read out the next pair of names, their opponents in the first game of the evening.

'Ellie Scott?'

She looked up and saw a tall, broad-shouldered young man in white flannels gazing down at her, a strange look on his face she couldn't quite make out.

'Are *you* Sam Hamilton?'

'Yes, I am.'

He seemed to be about to say something else when the Secretary finished his much-shorter list of names and hurried them on to the court to shake hands with their opponents and toss for sides and service.

'Which side do you like?' he asked, turning to her, when he won the toss.

'The other side, please.'

He looked anxious and uncomfortable as they walked round the net together and headed for the baseline.

'Are they good?' he asked quietly.

'I've never seen *either* of them before,' she whispered back.

'Nor have I. What should we do?'

Suddenly Ellie thought of the day she'd gone to Sleator's to deliver the matinee coat for wee Johnnie and she'd had to search for brown paper in the receptionist's office. Now, perfectly clean, his face shining, not a trace of oil in sight, he looked just as awkward as he had in his dungarees.

She laughed up at him as they turned to face their opponents.

'We can only do our best. Sure, we delivered the parcel between us.'

'Aye, you're right there,' he said more cheerfully, as he caught the new balls deftly from the ball boy and asked her if she would like to serve.

They won the set with ease.

Ten

Ellie lay on her right side, her eyes closed, but aware of the dim moonlight that filtered into her bedroom through the rustling leaves and fading blooms of the climbing rose outside her window. In the deep silence of the late evening she could still hear the rhythm of the little three-piece band who appeared to enjoy playing as much as she and her friends had enjoyed dancing.

156

It had been a quite extraordinary day. She smiled as she stretched her weary body between the cool sheets, feeling the throb of music, the joy of dancing again after this long, long time. She thought of Susie and of how amazed she would be at the story they had to tell her in the morning. She still couldn't quite believe it herself.

For a start, she and Sam Hamilton had won the tournament. Between 6 p.m. and 7 p.m. they had beaten two couples, their first two opponents quite unknown, the next pair known only by sight. They had then met the winners from the afternoon in the final play-off, her dear friend Daisy with her partner Frank Armstrong.

They'd beaten them too, in a long, hard game, she and Daisy playing better than they'd ever played before. At the end of the set, instead of the customary handshake they'd hugged each other over the net. The applause of the rest of the Club, the cheers and whistles from Harry and Stanley, Richard Sleator and the other young men defeated in the earlier rounds, followed them all the way to the Secretary's table.

She and Sam had both won subscriptions for next season, Daisy and Frank tokens for sportswear, and the Secretary himself presented both her and Daisy with a bouquet of flowers from his own garden.

It was the Secretary who had insisted it should be the winning couple who led off the dancing. She had given her flowers to Daisy to hold, laid down her borrowed racquet, and turned towards her partner. She wondered if Daisy's cousin

'Sammy' could dance as well as he played.

With the same ease as he'd moved round the court, sure-footed and knowing exactly what he wanted to do, he held out his arms and swept her round the floor using every inch of its limited space. After two circuits, they were joined by Daisy and Frank and then, moments later, by the rest of the remaining players.

The first sequence of dances was a long one, but not long enough for Ellie. Tired as she was from the sustained effort of the winning set she could think of nothing nicer than to go on moving as easily together as they had on the court. But all too soon, the music stopped. They clapped enthusiastically.

'Next dance, please.'

'D'you think I might have another dance later on, if your boyfriend can spare you?' Sam asked quietly.

'Boyfriend?' she queried, puzzled by his manner.

'That nice-looking lad over there,' he said, nodding gently towards Harry. 'He never takes his eyes off you.'

She smiled up at him and shook her head.

'Harry's not my boyfriend. We work together at Freeburn's. My boyfriend is in Canada. He's working in a lumber camp. We're saving up to get married.'

It was fully dark outside now. The marquee was lit with Christmas tree lights and storm lanterns covered with red crepe paper, so she couldn't see his face properly. The only strong light played on the faces of the band, thrown up from two Tilley lamps placed so they could see their music.

'Aye, it takes a bit of saving up to put a home together these days,' he said quietly. 'I'll come and ask you again later,' he said, drawing her away from the floor and disappearing out into the darkness.

She'd danced with Harry and Stanley and Frank and Richard Sleator, who told her he was Susie's elder brother, so he'd heard all about her. She'd enjoyed herself so much, she couldn't believe it when they called the last dance. Before she'd even had time to think about Sam Hamilton, she felt his hand on her elbow. They had danced the long sequence of slow dances in silence and then spun round the less crowded floor in the final quickstep. *'Goodnight, sweetheart, goodnight.'*

For another moment they stood side by side as the band played *God Save the King* and then it was all over, the band already packing up, couples streaming out into the darkness.

'Thank you, Ellie, for a lovely evening,' he said quietly.

It sounded, she thought, like a well-brought-up child doing what it had been told. Doing it with a good grace, but not being quite sure of itself or the response it might meet.

'Thank you too, Sam. I haven't enjoyed myself so much for a very long time.'

As the strains of dance music began to fade and the warmth that precedes sleep began to creep over her, she wondered if perhaps she shouldn't have said that. But it was true. She hadn't. There couldn't be much harm in telling the truth, could there?

It was fortunate indeed that Miss Walker was absent on business the following morning when the young people arrived for work. Despite the fact that she was no longer required to oversee the female staff, that the morning jobs were done in record time and that the establishment was temporarily without customers, the poor woman would have been hard pressed to control her disapproval at the level of excitement. Even Joe, the eldest and most serious-minded of the young men, broke into a broad grin when Harry and Stanley relayed the news that *both* the girls had reached the final.

Susie hopped up and down and demanded that they all acknowledge the fact that *she had told them so*. With a solemn face and a mischievous look in her eye, Daisy assured them that her failure to win was entirely her own fault.

'How do you make that out, Daisy?' demanded Harry. 'You were in great form. I've never seen you play so well.'

'Well, ye see, if I hadn't nagged away at my big cousin, Sammy, when he and his Da came over to give us a hand on the farm, sure he would not have been there to give Ellie a hand to beat me and Frank.'

Even Charlie Freeburn was anxious to hear the outcome of the previous day's activities and he seemed genuinely pleased when he heard how both girls had distinguished themselves. When he requested a word with Ellie about their range

160

of autumn curtain fabric, later in the morning, he repeated his congratulations.

'I'm afraid my own youth did not provide the opportunity for much in the way of amusement,' he said unexpectedly, 'but unlike some I could name, I see no virtue in that whatever. "All work and no play makes Jack a dull boy".' He paused and smiled wryly. 'Are you old enough, Miss Scott, to have written that in your copy book?'

'Oh yes, Mr Freeburn. They were still using that one in the schoolroom up on Church Hill. I wouldn't be surprised if they're still using it at the new school down in Annacramp.'

'Some old techniques *do* serve us well. It's a mistake to think that everything new is always better. It's just as bad to move with the times without giving due thought to the changes as it is to cling to the old ways without review, don't you think?'

Ellie was quite taken aback. For a moment she could think of nothing to say, though this wasn't the first time he'd surprised her by saying something of so personal a nature. In fact, she'd decided he was a much more thoughtful man than people realized. They assumed he only thought about business, but she'd discovered there was this other and quite different side to his nature.

'My father often says that you can't mend new tools with old metal,' she began tentatively. 'He gets quite upset sometimes when he can't mend things at all, but if they've been made by machine they're designed to be thrown away.'

He nodded sharply.

'I fear our society is becoming steadily more

161

wasteful and nothing is more wasteful and degrading than unemployment.'

'A hundred thousand,' she murmured, the figure coming instantly to her lips without her having even considered it.

He looked at her closely for a moment, then cast his eyes around the room as if he had lost something.

'Changing the subject, Miss Scott, I was just wondering where Miss Hutchinson and her partner were going to exchange their sportswear tokens. Not in the city, I think.'

Ellie smiled, happy to be on firmer and less unhappy ground.

'No, there's nowhere in Armagh. The tokens are for the Athletic Stores in Belfast. I'm going to have a look at what they've got when I have my holiday.'

'You'll be going to your aunt again?'

Ellie said that she was. Knowing his keen interest in all aspects of the drapery trade, she told him of her cousin's new job at Robinson Cleavers. The biggest and most elegant store in Belfast, according to Ruth.

'Will you go and visit the store during your holiday?'

'Yes. I've never been in it before. Usually Ruth and I just window shop, but as Ruth works there now, I think we'll go in and have a good look round.'

He nodded and considered this new information.

'I wonder if you can you tell me, Miss Scott, if the RUC Club is the *only* tennis club in

Armagh?'

The question took her by surprise as she could see no connection to the conversation they'd been having.

'No, Mr Freeburn, it isn't. There's The Archery Club as well.'

'Archery?' he asked, raising an eyebrow.

Ellie laughed.

'I don't think there *is* archery any more, but the club was founded quite a long time ago when there was. It's the Armagh Archery and Lawn Tennis Club.'

'A somewhat lengthy name for everyday use,' he said smiling. 'And do they have many members?'

'I think they're bigger than the RUC.'

'And am I right in thinking some of the schools play tennis?'

'Oh yes, most certainly. Su ... Miss Sleator played at the High School and the Royal School have courts. I expect *all* the grammar schools in the area play tennis.'

'And all of them have to go to Belfast for the relevant clothing?'

Ellie smiled and nodded, the drift of the conversation now quite clear to her.

'I think, Miss Scott, we could look into this opportunity more closely. Perhaps you'd be so kind as to find out for me what your colleagues would consider appropriate dress, were they to be able to afford such a small luxury. We have the whole of the winter season to make our preparations, but it will be no harm to start immediately, if you have no objections,' he said, adding his customary little nod of dismissal.

'None at all, Mr Freeburn,' she replied, standing up. 'It will be nice to think ahead to whites and playing tennis in the sunshine during the dark winter months,' she said smiling back at him as she crossed the room and opened the door.

Thursday was pay day and even after all this time Ellie and Daisy still felt a sense of excitement and pleasure when Mr Maginnis came downstairs in the late afternoon to distribute the familiar little brown envelopes. For Susie, the novelty of having a pay packet completely outweighed the very small amount it contained. The look on her face as she transferred her coins to a very smart handbag made Ellie smile.

Watching Susie gave her one of the few times in her life when she felt old. Not old in years, like her mother, or her aunt, but old in experience. Susie was only fourteen, she had so much to learn, while she herself had now turned twenty. However much more there might be for her to learn, at least she'd made a start, she'd been finding out about work and the world she lived in since she'd left school.

To Ellie's great surprise she found her pay had been increased *with effect from September 1st.* There was no explanation of any kind, but she noticed that beside her name, a firm, familiar hand had written *Senior Assistant* in large letters. Even more surprising, Mr Maginnis had handed her a second envelope labelled *for the attention of Miss Scott.* Opening it discreetly at the back of the shop while Daisy and Susie were both busy with customers, Ellie found it contained a ten shilling note and a small slip of paper saying: *To celebrate your and Miss Hutchinson's achievement.*

'Well, wou'd ye believe it? I'd never thought Old ... Mr Freeburn had it in him,' said Daisy, suddenly remembering that Old Freeburn was Susie's uncle, more-or-less.

'It's a very nice gesture,' said Ellie honestly. 'What shall we do with it? Would you like us to split it between us, or could we take Susie out for an ice cream after work.'

'Oh lovely, lovely,' said Susie instantly. 'But it's really for you and Daisy,' she said, having second and more considerate thoughts rather more quickly than usual.

'I think that's a great idea,' said Daisy. 'But what about the boys? That'll stretch to five of those posh ice creams.'

'Six,' said Ellie. 'We mustn't leave out Joe.'

'Or we could *all* go to the pictures and have a bag of sweets,' said Daisy thoughtfully.

'Or we could have chips for tea and go downstairs?' suggested Ellie.

'No, that comes to thirteen and sixpence,' said Daisy briskly. 'We can't sit downstairs for a celebration night out.'

The bell over the shop entrance rang three times in quick succession and suddenly everyone was busy again. Ellie put all thought of celebration out of mind until the day ended and they were back upstairs in the staffroom.

'Right, fork out!' Daisy said, bringing the two

jam pots from out of the cupboard.

Susie giggled and watched first Ellie, then Daisy, count out their shillings and sixpences and drop them in. Susie already had a tennis racquet and were she seventeen, all she'd need to do to join the Tennis Club was ask her father or her mother for the money.

'Daisy, how much of this is sub money?' asked Ellie lifting up her jar.

'Five shillings, five weeks.'

'And I don't need sub money now. Only racquet money. Isn't that right?'

'Aye, we could reduce your weekly rate for the racquet.'

'No, Daisy. No need,' she replied, spilling out the coins on the table below the window and picking up four shillings and two sixpences.'

'Ahhhh ... I see what your at,' said Daisy beaming as Ellie put the rest of the money back in the jar. 'Fifteen shillings means we can have tea AND sit on the balcony.'

'What about it then?' Ellie asked, turning to them both.

'Lovely, Ellie. Yes, please. When?'

'Saturday night?'

Susie nodded vigorously

'I'm goin' to the pictures m'self that night, Frank Armstrong asked me to go,' Daisy said, blushing furiously. 'But sure he's only doin' it to be polite.'

'Then we can go one night next week,' Ellie said, trying not to smile, 'providing it suits the others,' she added and looked away quickly to avoid catching the twinkle in Susie's eye.

166

* * *

'Ach, come away on in chiledear. Come in. Isn't it great to see you. You're well on time, just what ye said in your letter. Isn't it handy that the driver stops for you outside the door instead of you havin' to go inta town and out again. Here, let young Bob take your case.'

Ellie hugged her aunt awkwardly in the narrow hallway as twelve-year-old Bob pulled her case from her hand.

'Bob, don't take it up,' she called after him, as she disentangled herself from her aunt's embrace and saw him heading for the equally narrow stairs. 'Take it into the kitchen, will you please?'

'It's powerful heavy, Ellie. Is it *all* dresses?' he asked, hauling it round the awkward corner where the staircase rose sharply just outside the kitchen door.

'No, it's *not*,' she said, pretending to be cross. 'It's Bramleys and butter from Robinson's and maybe the odd sweetie,' she called to him, as he humped the heavy case across the cold, tiled floor. 'And there are some eggs from Ma,' she said to her aunt as they followed him. 'But I thought they'd be safer in my shoulder bag,' she added, slipping it off gingerly and laying it on the bare boards of the well-scrubbed table.

'Ye never come empty-handed, do you, Ellie?'

'The Bramleys are only windfalls, but some of them are perfect. I think they just dropped with their own weight. It's a great crop this year.'

'Apple tart, Ma?'

'Aye, we might just manage that,' Annie Magowan said cheerfully as Ellie opened the

167

suitcase on the floor, picked out the Bramleys one by one, found the well-wrapped pound of butter and handed over a bag of toffees.

'Thanks, Ellie. Those are great. My favourites. Can I take the case up to the attic now?'

'Aye, away on,' Annie said abstractedly, a large, perfectly formed apple held to her nose. 'They're never the same from the shops, though I buy them sometimes,' she said, breathing in the fresh, autumn smell. 'I can niver get used to payin' money for what was always given free. Sure we had the run of all Robinson's orchards to take whatever we wanted, even if it hadn't fallen on the ground,' she said with a little laugh as she put the apple down and turned to fill the kettle at the sink.

'Sit down an' rest yerself while I make us a drop of tea. Yer Uncle John's listening to a programme on the wireless. He's stopped drinkin' tea in the evenin'. Cocoa is the *great* thing now. But it's too early for that yet.'

Ellie smiled to herself and watched her aunt light the gas. A thin, almost emaciated woman, she had the same narrow face as her brother Robert, but unlike his tanned and worn skin, hers was pale, creased and parchment-like.

Five years older than her father, Aunt Annie had married at the first possible opportunity, though by that time her own mother, Mary-Anne, was already dead and her stepmother, Selina, was trying to create a more kindly home for her three stepchildren.

Selina came too late. The harm was done, was what Annie had once told Ellie. The house by the

168

forge had nothing but unhappy memories for all three of Mary-Anne's children. Annie had married a farmer from Ballyards, Thomas had gone to Canada and never came back, and her father, the youngest of the three, always swore he couldn't remember his mother at all.

Annie's had been a reasonably happy marriage though not exactly a love match. John Magowan had something of the hypochondriac about him. He disliked the countryside and had never wanted to be a farmer, so Annie encouraged him to move to the city. He'd got a job as a milkman, looked about him and ended up using the money from the sale of the farm to buy a run-down corner shop on the Woodstock Road. They'd lived over the shop, stayed open from early morning till late at night, until three children and their savings made it necessary and possible to make a move.

By dint of letting out the best room to a lodger, they were able to afford the rent of both a tall, terrace house on the Lisburn Road as well as a less run-down grocer's shop a couple of minutes' walk away. Now that Ruth and her younger brother Tommy were both out at work, the lodger was no longer needed and Annie had more time to accommodate John's regular requests for changes in his diet, along with the newest in tonics and vitamins.

'Ye must be tired, an' you at your work this mornin',' said Annie, as she poured their tea. 'Ruth said she wouldn't be late, but this fella asked her to go to a dance.'

'The one she told me about? Norman?'

'Ach no, this is *another* one. You know Ruth,' her aunt said, shaking her head and passing over the milk jug. 'What about this man of *yours*? Any word of him sending your ticket yet?'

Ellie shook her head and drank her tea thirstily.

'He says the money's good, but he's had a lot of expense. I don't think he's been able to save much at all yet.'

'Ach, sure they all think America is made of money. But it's the same everywhere. There's some just puts their hands out and money drops into it and others could work till the cows come home and hardly buy enough to keep themselves fed. D'you fancy goin' to Canada?'

'I don't know, Auntie. I really don't know. I think of Polly and I'd love to be near her. And of course I want to marry George,' she added quickly. 'If his uncle produces a better job as he says he will, then Canada it has to be.'

'D'ye think Polly's happy out there?'

Ellie thought about it as her aunt offered her more tea. She'd never been quite able to make up her mind how Polly felt.

'Polly's always been good at making the best of anything. Even when she was a wee girl. I know she loves Jimmy, but it's been hard on her since he lost that good job in Toronto and they had to move,' she said sadly. 'I think she's too easy on the wee boys and they give her a bad time, which doesn't help. Sometimes I know she's tired out. But I can't make up my mind whether she's happy or not. I just know I miss her,' she added abruptly.

'You and her were always close. I still wonder

170

was I right at all to let her bring Jimmy here for his tea that week she was up and she'd only just met him. The next thing we knew they were getting married because he'd had the offer of a job out there better than he'd ever get here and he didn't want to go without her. She took a big chance there, didn't she?'

'How do you mean?'

'Ye meet a man at a dance and ye get on well together and the next thing it's down the aisle. Sure how can you know the half of it, just walkin' out and goin' to this dance or that picture? I walked round every inch of Salter's Grange with John, but I'd had no idea about him at all till we started workin' together in the shop. An' I'll say this for him, he always worked hard, but if I'd fallen on the floor in a dead faint, he'd never have said: "Are you tired?" Yet he'd go out and spend a shilling on a bunch of flowers for me,' she ended, with a wry laugh.

Ellie yawned and apologized.

'For goodness sake ye must be tired out. Why don't you go on up to bed? Ye'll see yer Uncle John and Ruth in the morning. And Tommy's coming home for the day. Either he wants to see you or he's bringin' me his washin',' she said laughing. 'I'll not come up with you if you don't mind. One flight up to the lavatory is one thing, but the other two I'll leave to you and Ruth.'

Tired as she was, Ellie felt better when she sat on the edge of the narrow single bed, took off her shoes and unbuttoned her dress. She took out her nightdress, but made no move to put it on.

Instead, she switched off the electric light, went to the window and looked out across the roofs of the houses below, towards the Bog Meadows and the slopes of the mountains beyond.

There were lights in all the little houses along Moonstone Street. In uncurtained kitchens women were making the last tea of the day. Behind pulled blinds or drawn curtains shadowy figures moved, bedspreads were being turned back, Sunday clothes laid out for the morning.

It was so strange to look out over row upon row of houses. All these people living side by side, unknown to her and as surely to each other. She raised her eyes again into the moonless night, seeking out the tiny sparks of light where small farms lay on the gentler slopes that ran up to the steep edge of the great escarpment towering over the city.

White Mountain, Black Mountain and Divis. Until she had come to Belfast, she'd never seen a mountain before. Tonight, it was the dark of the moon and she'd have to wait for morning to see that sharp edge she remembered so well between one visit and the next.

Such an excitement it had been when she'd first come with Polly. She discovered the city was never quiet. Even if she woke in the night, disturbed by some particularly sharp sound from the broad, metal acres of the railway sidings beyond Moonstone Street, she could still hear a quiet roar as if all the houses were breathing in their sleep. There were always lights on too all through the night.

Away to her right, she could see the regular

172

rows of bright patches marking the wards of the Royal Victoria Hospital, a huge building where once as a little girl they had gone to visit Uncle John, tramping through a maze of corridors that left her exhausted and confused.

Would it be like this in Canada? Looking out from a top window over some unknown city that never slept? Would it feel as strange and different standing there with George as once this city had felt when she'd first come to it from the little green hills with the sodden meadows between, the twisty lanes and the apple-orchards and everything around her known and familiar?

You got used to it, was what Polly had said. Yes, of course. She'd got used to working in the shop, become familiar with the till and counting out change and cutting fabric and knowing not to be upset with customers who were rude. That was just part of growing up and learning to do one's work. But something told her going to Canada would be different, very different. Somehow she couldn't see what the difference was. Yet she was sure there *was* a difference between the new experiences that had flowed into her life during her first twenty years and this new experience that lay ahead of her, in Canada, with George.

She left the window open as she undressed, the night warm and the small room stuffy. From the marshalling yards came the clank and groan of goods wagons being manoeuvred into sidings or coupled up for night journeys. She got into bed and lay in the darkness looking up at the dark sky. There were no stars in the city either.

173

Eleven

Sunday was a happy and lively day at 621, Lisburn Road. Despite a recurrence of his sciatica, Uncle John was able to walk as far as the newsagents for his usual Sunday paper. Tommy arrived late morning by train and tram from his living-over-the-shop employment in a men's outfitters in Bangor. Wearing a new sports coat and flannels, his woolly hair well slicked back with Brylcreem, he carried a small box of chocolates for his cousin and a bulging carrier bag for his mother.

'Ach, Tommy, a present for me, sure you shouldn't have troubled yourself. Will I open it now or later?' she asked effusively, as he handed it over.

Annie's teasing was as good-humoured as Tommy's when he proceeded to enquire after his 'wee cousin up from the country'. Bob wanted to know how many *more* dress patterns his big sister had bought since Ellie had been up last year, while Ruth had insisted that if it weren't for the dress patterns there'd be less chance of the odd threepence for him. There was much laughter throughout the morning and good appetites were displayed by all at the special meal Annie had prepared on the ancient gas cooker that

174

smelt of gas even when not in use.

'Will I give the rest of this to the birds?' asked Tommy soberly, as he carried the plate that had held the apple tart back into the kitchen.

'No don't do that,' said Ruth seriously. 'They might only fight over that one crumb.'

After Tommy and the two girls had done the washing up, Bob disappeared to meet a lad from Moonstone Street. John and Annie settled for a wee doze in their respective armchairs leaving the three young people to go for a walk. They made their leisurely way westwards along the leafy avenues and lanes till they came to the banks of the Lagan. Standing on the King's Bridge looking upriver towards the old brick-fields, they watched a flotilla of swans sailing towards them in perfect formation, their images reflected in the brown water.

The afternoon was warm and pleasant, only the chestnuts seriously marking the advancing season, their pink and gold leaves fluttering down to lie on the dry pavements as they passed. Late flowers still bloomed prolifically in the allotments that lined large parts of the avenues between the Lisburn and Malone roads, sweet peas clustered at the highest point of the pea sticks provided and the dahlias stood at attention, red and yellow, as bright as traffic lights.

Ellie enjoyed every moment of her unaccustomed leisure. She put out of mind the laundry that would be waiting till next Saturday afternoon, the blouses she would have to wash and iron for her return to work. Poor Da, she thought suddenly, as she eyed an impressive pair of wrought-iron gates he would most certainly have stopped to examine and admire. He'd said he could manage for a week and he always did, but unless her mother got tired of his hit-and-miss cooking, he'd not get a decent meal till she got back.

'I'm afraid I'll have to leave you beautiful ladies after tea,' said Tommy sadly, as they strolled down from Notting Hill, crossed the Malone Road and turned towards home.

'I take it there's an even *more* beautiful lady in Bangor,' said Ruth, laughing and tossing her dark curls.

She turned away from him and gazed across the road, taking in every detail of one of the handsome, double-fronted houses. Approached by short, gravelled drives, decorated with pillared porches and colourful flower beds and discreetly screened by flourishing shrubs and young trees, the comfortable residences of Cranmore Park looked out over the trees to the park itself. They stood solid and quiet in the sunshine of a peaceful Sunday afternoon.

'No, I fear not,' he said soberly. 'A much less happy reason. The boss's brother is on the Board of Guardians of the Workhouse. He says there's going to be trouble tomorrow. There's a strike of relief workers and he's not sure how it will affect the city. He's taking no chances, wants to make sure we're in the shop in Bangor at 8 a.m. so I was only let come home on condition I go back tonight,' he explained crisply.

Ellie thought of Charlie Running. She'd not spoken to him since that evening in the forge

176

when he'd sat on the bench inside the door and said there'd be trouble in the city. Now, as they strolled on in the sunshine, all he'd said to her about unemployment in the city came back to her. She made up her mind to ask Ruth and Tommy the questions she would have put to Charlie.

'We've a wee while yet to teatime,' said Tommy, as they approached one of the park gates. 'C'mon and we'll go and sit on a seat an' I'll tell ye all I've heard. Sure if we walk on down through the park, it's only a couple of minutes home.'

Ruth wasn't the slightest bit interested in the plight of the unemployed, so she left it to Tommy. It seemed they'd just put forward a new demand for an increase in payments to fifteen shillings for a man, eight shillings for a wife and two shillings for each child. Ellie listened, wide-eyed, wondering how you could feed a family even if they got the increase they were asking for.

But it wasn't just money for food. How could they pay their rent? And what about fuel? The afternoons were still warm but the nights had started to get cold. When the sky had cleared last evening and Uncle John had announced there'd be a frost before morning, she'd been glad of the extra blanket Ruth had brought her.

She shivered at the very thought of a family that couldn't afford a fire, of the men tramping through the city looking for work that was seldom to be found. According to Tommy, the shipyards had no orders, the linen mills were closing one by one as the depression bit deeper and other manufacturing companies were just as affected.

'But why, Tommy? Why are places closing like this, what's happening and why doesn't the government do something to help these poor people?'

'You're not the only one asking that, Ellie. It's not the government's fault there's a depression. It started in America and now it's spread across the world. As far as I can get the hang of things it's about money and powerful business interests and banks. You could hardly credit how wicked people can be when all they want is money.'

He paused, the look on his face more sombre than Ellie had ever seen it before, his dark eyes a confused mixture of anger and sadness.

'People say our government *could* do more, if they wanted to,' he continued. 'But they don't seem to care and that's what's making people so angry.'

Suddenly and quite unexpectedly, a small cloud, generated by the warmth of the afternoon, moved across the sun. It cast a chill shadow across the green-painted summer seat, where they sat side-by-side watching the well-dressed inhabitants of Marlborough and Cranmore taking their Sunday afternoon stroll. As if some-one had flicked the switch in her attic room, the light went out and all the colour was drained from trees and flowers and women's dresses.

'I think it's time we were going home for our tea,' said Ruth briskly, as she got to her feet. 'There's nothing any of us can do so there's no good talking about it,' she added, as Ellie and Tommy stood up. 'We just need to make sure we don't land up like that ourselves. Isn't that right, Ellie?'

Her tone was so sharp and dismissive, Ellie was shocked. She glanced at Tommy to see how he'd taken it. He shook his head sadly, but he said nothing. Suddenly, she was aware that the difference she had always sensed between herself and Ruth had grown much wider.

As they moved off down the path, they became aware of a pleasant-faced, elderly woman coming towards them, walking with the aid of a stick and holding the arm of a middle-aged man. The three young people stepped off the narrow path to let them pass and Ellie smiled and said a friendly 'Good Afternoon'. Both man and woman returned the greeting courteously as they drew level.

Ellie was glad of the slight diversion for it allowed her to avoid responding to Ruth's question. Clearly, the plight of the unemployed was not a subject Ruth wished to discuss.

'D'you think you're doing the right thing at all over George?' Ruth asked, as she finished applying cream to her face.

She passed the small pot over to Ellie, who sat on the end of her cousin's bed, still wearing her best dress.

Ellie smiled and sniffed at the perfumed face cream in the pretty little pot. There was nothing devious about Ruth. If she was sometimes hurtful or tactless, it was never intentional. She was

179

kind and good-natured, but she didn't believe in beating about the bush.

It was almost a relief she'd taken the chance of this quiet moment to ask about George. Although Ruth's visits to Salter's Grange were brief and infrequent, because she couldn't stand her Aunt Ellen, she'd been there often enough to have met George himself and to have cast an appraising eye over him. Unlike Daisy, at least Ruth had met him.

'I know you say you love him, Ellie, or at least you *think* you do, but you've never been out with anyone else. How do you know you mightn't love someone else far more if you ever let yourself give it a try?'

She broke off, instructed Ellie in the correct way to apply skin cream to her face, then continued.

'George is perfectly all right, nice looking, speaks well for a country boy, but has he any sense? It all sounded great going off to Canada, but how much has he saved? How long do you think it'll be before he comes home for you or sends your ticket? Besides there's *you* to consider too. Do *you* really want to go out there?'

The questions struck a familiar note. Daisy was younger, less confident than Ruth and much less willing to upset her, but she had asked the very same ones.

'But Ruth, even if I wasn't entirely happy about going, I've said I'll marry him and women have to go where their man's job is. You know that. That's why Polly went to Toronto and now Mary is going to Indiana. I'm sure if Florence

180

found a man she wanted to marry, she'd go wherever he went.'

'Aye, if she ever found a man,' said Ruth dubiously. 'Or maybe that's why she's never let herself find one. Anyway, you and George aren't engaged yet, are you?'

'Well, not exactly, but...'

'If he'd had any gumption about him, he'd have bought you a ring,' Ruth said sharply. 'It needn't have cost much. Even a dress ring would have done. It's more the look of the thing. And he could have borrowed the money from his uncle, given the big pay he was going to have,' she went on firmly. 'What did happen about that motorbike? Did you ever ask him?'

Ellie shook her head.

At twenty-two, it could certainly not be said that Ruth was uninformed about the ways of young men. Since she'd begun work in a small dress shop on the Lisburn Road itself, her one ambition was to get on, get a better job, earn more money, have enough to let her dress as she chose, go to the dances she preferred and mix with the kind of young man more likely to live in the leafy avenues of south Belfast than in the crowded streets off the Woodstock Road where she herself had first seen the light of day.

So far, however, Ruth had not found a partner that met her exacting requirements. She had plenty of invitations out, certainly, and she accepted many of them, but she would never go out more than twice with a young man who did not appear to have 'prospects'.

'What about this man you met at the Tennis

Club, Sam Hamilton? What's he like?' Ruth asked, as she took off her dress, hung it carefully on a hanger and shook out the skirt.

'He's very nice.'

'Oh, for goodness sake, Ellie, if the Devil himself put a hat over his horns and said "Good morning" to you, you'd say he was nice,' said Ruth irritably.

Ellie laughed. Partly it was the unfamiliar image of the Devil wearing a hard hat that flashed across her mind, partly the look of complete outrage on Ruth's face.

She stopped laughing and tried to see Ruth's point of view. Perhaps being much more experienced, Ruth could see things she couldn't see herself. But then, Ruth had made up her mind about what she wanted and she hadn't had to because George had always been a part of her life. He'd never been a boyfriend, or an admirer, or a 'catch', or any of the other words Ruth might use about the many young men she'd encountered.

'Ruth dear, I couldn't let George down when he hasn't done anything he shouldn't have done. He had to take the chance of going to Canada. I made a promise, or rather, we had promised each other ... well, as you know we'd planned to get married as soon as something turned up. We'd both been saving, but neither of us wanted to move in with the Robinsons. There wasn't room anyway...' she broke off, aware suddenly that what she was saying didn't seem to explain anything.

'I suppose it's different in the country,'

admitted Ruth grudgingly. 'There's not much work going apart from farming. Oh Ellie, would you really have wanted to be a farmer's wife?'

'But I wouldn't be "a farmer's wife", I'd be George's wife.'

'If a house had come up, do you really think you'd have got married?'

'Well, the problem wasn't *just* finding a house. We couldn't have lived on ten shillings a week. George's father would have had to give him a bit more to make up for his free bed and board and his clothes, but there was no use asking him about that until we had a place to go. So George said.'

'And I suppose Freeburn's wouldn't let you stay on after you were married, even for a few months.'

'No,' said Ellie shaking her head sadly. 'That's one advantage of the mills. They'll take a woman and not even notice if she's months gone, providing she doesn't take more than a week or two for the birth. At Freeburn's, like all the other good shops and offices, you get your wedding gift and you have to go.'

Ruth yawned hugely, a way she had of showing she'd had enough of a conversation. Ellie stood up, ready to step across the tiny divide between the two attic rooms.

'You know, Ellie, that blue really suits you,' Ruth added, looking her up and down as she stood in the doorway. 'You're a very good-looking girl if only you'd pay a bit of attention to yourself. Come to think of it, maybe George ought to pay a bit more attention to getting that ticket. Or someone will give him a run for his money.'

There was rain on Sunday night, but when Ellie went to the window next morning the sky was sparkling and mostly blue, except over the escarpment where a row of huge, grey-bottomed clouds sat lowering at her. They looked as if they'd come crowding down from North Antrim and were now elbowing each other sideways to get the best possible view of the city below.

The day was already planned and after a leisurely breakfast the two girls walked to the tram stop.

'Wouldn't it be nice just to go into town for a bit of shopping whenever the notion took you?' said Ruth, as she handed over the pennies for their fares. 'I could get used to a life of leisure, couldn't you?'

The tram pulled away with a whine as they settled themselves. Ellie had the window seat so she could look out at the view.

'Look,' she said, 'Uncle John's putting out more potatoes.'

They both waved and just as they thought he hadn't seen them, he straightened up, caught sight of them and raised a hand in salute.

'Does Auntie work in the shop now at all?' she asked, as they gathered speed, the whine of the tram now rising like the cry of a banshee.

'Oh yes. She does Thursday and Friday. They're the busiest days. She says she likes to keep her hand in, but she's glad it's not full-time any more. She can keep an eye on Bobby and do

184

her church work. She has a couple of old ladies she calls on.'

The tram was full and noisier than most, the hiss and whine of their progress and the rattle of the trolleys making conversation difficult. It didn't really matter as Ellie was soon absorbed in watching the bustle and activity beyond her window as they made their way down through Shaftesbury Square and along Great Victoria Street to the city centre.

It was even busier than she'd thought it would be, motors and horse-drawn carts all mixed up together, double lines of them moving in both directions. She wondered how the horses pulling the heavy drays could stand the noise of hooters, the hiss and rattle of trams and the blare of motor horns right beside them.

She rather dreaded getting off the tram. She remembered only too well from previous visits Ruth would be across the street before she'd even stepped off the footpath. She never quite grasped that Ellie needed time to get her bearings. It wasn't just the noise of traffic and the press of people. Everywhere she looked, there were posters and shop signs. They all seemed to require her attention and she couldn't take it all in quickly enough.

She'd tried to explain, but Ruth was not good at seeing things from any point of view other than her own, so she'd invented the joke about 'my wee cousin up from the country' to cover her puzzlement. It was not an unkind joke and Ellie always laughed at it herself, but however often she came to Belfast, she still felt as if her head was overflowing.

'Mind your step there, Miss,' said the conductor kindly, as the now familiar whine subsided and she looked down cautiously at the crowded pavement.

'Come on, Ellie, this way,' said Ruth, taking her arm firmly, and finding space for them to alight. 'Let's start with Cleavers, it's not far away.'

The pavements seemed even more crowded than she'd remembered. On every corner clusters of men in working clothes stood together. Some of them were passing a piece of paper from hand to hand. Others were gathered around one of their number who was reading aloud from a newspaper. As they drew level with the flower sellers outside the City Hall, she saw a news board. 'Strikers lie on...' But Ruth hurried her past so quickly, she couldn't see the rest.

'Here we are then,' Ruth said, a distinct note of relief in her voice, as she stopped outside the revolving door. 'You go first and I'll push. Just keep on walking...'

Ellie did her best to concentrate. She didn't like revolving doors. Once before, she'd tried to go the wrong way and hit her head on the glass. But this time there was no difficulty. In a moment, she was inside, walking on thick carpet. It was quiet, a smell of perfume on the air, and the voices spoke in hushed tones, almost like being in church. It was such a relief after the shouts and whistles of the men in work clothes and the roar of traffic.

'Good gracious, Miss Magowan, I thought you

were on holiday.'

A tall, elegant woman wearing a plain black dress decorated with jet buttons and tiny beads paused and looked them both up and down. Ellie was rather glad Ruth had insisted she wear her best dress, for there was something about the voice and demeanour of this woman that made Ellie think of Miss Walker.

'Yes, Mrs Patterson, I am indeed, but I wanted to show Miss Scott where I worked,' said Ruth, with what Ellie thought was a small curtsy and certainly a much clearer articulation of each word than she normally used.

'Miss Scott, how do you do. I take it you are not from the city?' she said, with a very brief smile.

'No, Mrs Patterson. I come from Armagh.'

'Indeed. We do a certain amount of business in Armagh. Perhaps you know Freeburn's.'

Ellie smiled broadly.

'I'm Senior Assistant at Freeburn's.'

'Well, now, you'll know Miss Walker, a distant cousin of mine,' she said, with a less formal smile. 'A very shrewd buyer, I must say, always aware of all the very latest changes in fashion. You're very fortunate to have someone so up to the minute. I'm sure Freeburn's is most successful.'

Ellie assured her that they were and it was and after confirming that Ruth would be returning to work on Thursday morning, they parted.

'Do make sure you show Miss Scott *all* our latest ranges, Miss Magowan,' said Mrs Patterson, as they turned away. 'It will make it easier

187

for her when she returns to Armagh and finds the items amongst those that Miss Walker is currently ordering.'

Ellie smiled to herself as they walked on. She wondered how Mrs Patterson would react if she were told the list from which her distant cousin had ordered was the list Mr Freeburn's senior assistant had compiled at his request.

As they penetrated deeper into the store, however, she soon forgot what she was thinking about Mrs Patterson's cousin, so full of interest were all the departments, particularly fabric and household linen. The bales of cloth and displays of curtains and nets were comfortably familiar and the quiet was so reassuring after the clamour outside.

'The pattern books and patterns are upstairs,' Ruth said, as they began to tire. 'It'll take a while to go through them all. If we do manage that we could go and recover over a cup of tea at the Milk Bar.'

She led them through another department, turned the corner, and there before them was the staircase leading to the upper floor. It was carved from white marble with wide, wide steps and very shallow treads, thickly carpeted in red. It rose from the lower floor and then divided, the steps continuing to both left and right. Ellie was quite overwhelmed. She had never seen anything like it in her life. Surely even in Buckingham Palace there was nothing as splendid as this.

'Come on, Ellie. I said it's upstairs. Are you tired?'

'No, no, not tired. I was just looking at the way the staircase curves,' she said quickly, glancing round as Ruth urged her on up the gentle stairs.

No, she wasn't tired, she was preoccupied. She was thinking about poor people with not enough to eat and all this unbelievable luxury everywhere around her.

Monday's shopping trip was a great success. Ruth had bought four dress lengths and three paper patterns, Ellie, two dress lengths and two paper patterns, one of them for Daisy. On Tuesday, they would study the ready-mades in the other big stores, acquire zips, buttons and trimming materials and visit the sportswear shops on Ellie's behalf. That would leave Wednesday for cutting out and pinning.

Ellie was not exactly looking forward to another visit to the city centre, but she was hoping she would find it easier. As she settled down in the window seat once more, ready for the whine and the shudder the tram set off, she certainly felt steadier. She didn't even fumble with the pennies for their fares, it being her turn to pay today.

The morning was fine, though not as sunny as the previous day. There was no sign of Uncle John as they passed the shop. They were a little earlier than they'd been the previous morning, so they had to stop at the entrance to the bakery to let the horse-drawn carts come out in front of them. Some turned off into the nearby streets and avenues, but two remained ahead of them, till suddenly they stopped, bringing the tram to a halt behind them.

It was difficult to see what the hold-up was. All around them the other passengers offered their explanations, though none of them were able to see anything more than Ellie or Ruth.

'There's an accident. It's all blocked till the polis come.'

'Someone's shed a load. Them bakery carts can't get roun'.'

Then two strange things happened. First of all, the two bakery carts turned round and came back towards them. Ellie noticed that both horses were shaking their bridles as horses always do whenever they're anxious or distressed. All at once, they became aware of a roar, a growing vibration like the grumble of approaching thunder. From behind them they heard the throb of motor engines and saw they were being over-taken on the wrong side of the road by Crossley tenders.

More and more vehicles in front turned off left into the side streets. There were no longer any vehicles at all approaching on the other side of the road. The tram driver didn't have the option of turning off the tramway, he stayed where he was, to be greeted by an outburst of motor horns from behind. Very slowly he inched forward and then the tram stopped again.

At last they could see what the trouble was. The road in front of them was entirely full of people, almost all men, though here and there they saw a grim-faced woman. All poorly clad, many of them barefoot. Amidst the huge, dark mass, the Crossley tenders were slowly forcing a

190

path.

'They're marchin' on the Workhouse,' said an elderly woman, peering out. 'They said they would if they got no offer. An' they've been offered nothin', God love them.'

'That's the Workhouse away over there,' said Ruth, her voice unusually quiet as she waved a hand beyond Ellie's window. 'Dunluce Avenue, that's where they're heading. Goodness knows how long we'll be stuck here,' she added, looking out at the tide of dark figures spreading down the Lisburn Road as far as the eye could see.

Ellie watched, tears springing unbidden to her eyes. Some women had small babies wrapped against them in shawls or strips of cloth. Men waved their fists, shouted slogans, encouraging each other. But it was the faces that affected her most. The pale, grey faces of people who are hungry and exhausted and driven to the limits of endurance.

Then there was a crash. Splinters of glass fell around them. A woman in the seat in front of them screamed, a trickle of blood on her face. Without thinking, Ellie brushed the splinters from her skirt and got one stuck in her finger. She pulled it out surreptitiously, not wanting Ruth to see. It was bleeding, so she slipped it into her pocket and pressed it against her handkerchief.

'They ought to be shot, the whole lot of them. Tryin' to kill us. Why don't the police get in there and see to them,' demanded a portly man carrying a rolled umbrella.

'What are we going to do, Ellie? There must be thousands of them. We'll be here all day.' Ruth's tone was sharp enough, but Ellie caught the note of anxiety beneath the irritation.

Three more pieces of brick were thrown. The driver's window was broken and two windows on the other side of the tram. Quite suddenly, it began to grow quieter. The last of the long, long procession turned into Dunluce Avenue on their way to make their protest outside the Workhouse.

Ruth breathed a sigh of relief, sat back as the tram started up, but it stopped again almost immediately.

'They're lying on the tramlines. We'll get no further till the police clear them off,' said the conductor, walking back from the front of the vehicle. He paused by their seat and looked at them both.

'I think you young ladies wou'd be wise to slip out and go down that road over there,' he said, pointing to a tree-lined avenue on their right. 'It'll take you out at the bottom of the Malone Road near opposite the University. There'll maybe be trams runnin' all right over that side. We might sit here all day, till they get word from the Guardians one way or other.'

He had hardly finished speaking before Ruth was on her feet. Ellie had just time to say 'Thank you' before she saw her cousin hop briskly down from the tram, stride across the empty road and turn and wait for her on the other side.

Twelve

Ellie was so exhausted on Tuesday evening, she began to wonder if she'd ever manage to get as far as her attic bedroom. Thanks to the young conductor on the tram, they'd succeeded in reaching the city centre and they'd done all the jobs they'd planned. For Ellie, there'd been little joy in doing them. As she and Ruth matched up ribbon and buttons and discussed yokes and collars, all she could think of were those grey faces, that dark tide of hungry and exhausted people.

There was nothing to comfort them when they returned home. The father of Bobby's little friend from Moonstone Street was a policeman. As he came off duty, he'd met the two boys coming from school, so he was able to tell them the Lisburn Road had been at a standstill for three hours and reinforcements had been summoned for the following day.

'I'm warnin' ye's both,' began Aunt Annie, when she'd sent Bobby to do his homework in the dining room. 'Say not a word about what ye's saw and what's happened today. Ruth knows what her father can be like, but you, Ellie dear, have never seen him when he's in one of his moods. Pay no attention. Let him have the last word whatever ye do, or there'll be no standin' him.'

They heard Uncle John before they saw him. With paper patterns spread out on the sitting-room floor, the largest space they could find for cutting out, they felt the whole house vibrate as he slammed the front door behind him and marched down the narrow hall.

'Annie. Where are ye, Annie?' he shouted.

They'd looked at each other, but said nothing. Aunt Annie had been right and the evening that followed was grim. To begin with, Uncle John had sat silent at the dining table staring at his table mat. When his meal arrived, he'd pushed his plate away and had to be encouraged like a child to eat his nice dinner.

'Sure ye need to keep up your strength, John dear. Don't we all have to try to do that.'

'Them buggers,' he said at last, having eaten a good meal in complete silence. 'Them buggers. Lying on the tram rails so that honest people couldn't go about their business. Not a soul in the shop half the day, and those that did, in and out in two minutes, for fear of what was happening. Police here and tenders there and no customers. Sure ye wouldn't see the days takings in the bottom of the cash box.'

Sitting quietly in a corner by the sitting-room fire after the meal had been cleared away and washed up, Ellie watched the other three and could hardly believe in that same room there'd been nothing but jokes and teasing on Sunday morning, Uncle John enjoying himself, delighted to have a new audience for his familiar stories.

He insisted they listen to the Northern Ireland News on the wireless. It told them nothing they didn't know already and that only annoyed him further.

'It's these Communists and socialists stirrin' things up, tellin' working people they've a right to this and a right to that. What about the rest of us? Aye, and the worst of it is, they're gettin' in on both sides, They're gettin' good Protestants to gang up with the Other Side, an' havin' them marchin' together as if they weren't marchin' with traitors.'

'What d'you think should be done, John, to get these people jobs? Isn't that the problem?'

'Sure there would be no problem with jobs if that other crowd took themselves off where they belong. Let them go down to the Free State and see what they can get there. Our government is too soft on them. This is a Protestant country for a Protestant people. Your man Basil Brooke was right about that. He said that ninety-nine per cent of them are disloyal and he wouldn't have one of them about the place. We should get rid of the lot of them.'

'Including wee Bridget?'

Ellie looked up sharply from the sleeve she was pinning on the first of Ruth's new dresses. Bridget was a saint's name, a Catholic name. One of the serving girls at Robinson's was called Bridget and she'd once told her the story of her namesake, a girl who had converted her dying father to Christianity while sitting by his bed weaving crosses out of the rushes on the floor to

195

pass the time.

'Ach, there's the odd one. You'd hardly know Bridget was one of them. She keeps quiet about it, an' she's a great worker. And very popular in the shop. I'll say that for her.'

'There's maybe the odd one of them *could* do a day's work,' suggested Annie.

'Aye, but not many.'

Ruth and Ellie said *no thank you* to the offer of cocoa. They were only too glad to be able to make their way upstairs. When they reached the top of the three flights they gave each other a hug, but no word was spoken between them about the troubles of the day or the oppressiveness of the evening as they turned in opposite directions and shut their doors behind them.

Ellie couldn't sleep. Exhausted as she was, she could find no comfortable position for her aching back. She knew why it was aching, but that didn't help much. At home she'd have filled the stone jar from the still hot kettle on the back of the stove, but here the thought of the long, cold journey down to the gas stove was too much for her. She turned over and tried again, but the echo of her uncle's voice wouldn't go away.

He'd gone on at great length about loyalty. As he saw it, you were on one side or the other. Whatever your side thought or did, it was right and what the other side did was wrong. The possibility of agreeing with something the opposing side thought was beyond his comprehension.

But how could he be right? Did those people crowding up Dunluce Avenue, desperate to persuade the Board of Guardians to increase their pittance, have a side? Did it make any difference to their common cause whether they were Catholic or Protestant?

She wondered what her father would say if she asked him what he thought. She tried to recall once more what Charlie Running had said. It had been clear to her then that he knew a lot more than her father did and he'd been rather sheepish when he'd said: 'If they're beat, there's always the Workhouse.' But you couldn't take all those people into a workhouse. It wouldn't hold them all.

Round and round it all went in her head and then she was in a forest. She thought of George.

'You have to be loyal to George,' said the big brown bear.

'What do you mean?' she asked, wondering if there was any point in trying to run away. Bears, he'd told her, could run very fast. And climb trees.

'Because he's a man. You have to be loyal to him and do what he wants, because he's on the Right Side and you are the Other Side. That's just the way it is.'

She woke up suddenly, the image of the bear still there, a cramp in her stomach. She'd have to go to the lavatory whether she liked it or not.

Uncle John was in better spirits next morning. Waking at his usual early hour, he had looked out of the bedroom window and seen Crossley tenders and Lancia armoured cars passing in large numbers on the road below.

Before leaving for work he'd told Aunt Annie that clearly the authorities were now doing what he paid good rates and taxes to have them do. It looked as if they were about to ensure his livelihood would not be interfered with for another day.

Although there was much activity outside with police vehicles moving in both directions, traffic was back to normal. Bobby went off to school ready to boast that his sister and cousin had seen the strikers lying on the tramlines, while Aunt Annie made another pot of tea, sat down gratefully by the sitting-room fire and offered to help with the dressmaking.

'My goodness, haven't these three days just flown,' she declared, late that afternoon, when she got up to start preparing the evening meal. 'Are you sure you don't mind being on your own, Ellie, when Ruth goes back to work tomorrow? I'd have loved to stay and keep you company, but with things the way they are, I think I need go to the shop as usual. Your Uncle John'll not get over yesterday for many a long day.'

Ellie smiled and told her not to worry. There was plenty of sewing still to do and if it was fine she'd go and have a walk in the park. What she didn't add was that she felt tired, after all that had happened, weary in spirit as in body. She rather badly needed a bit of peace and quiet, and time to herself.

There was no doubt the house was quiet on Thursday morning. Almost too quiet, the rooms empty and dim, the bright sunlight barely penetrating the sitting-room windows, shaded by the high privet hedge surrounding the minute square of neglected front garden.

She laid out the day's sewing. Feeling suddenly chill without the fire, lit especially for her and Ruth the previous day, she went upstairs to put on something warmer. She pushed open her window and looked out longingly to the slopes of the escarpment. Beyond the houses, the marshalling yards, the bog meadows and yet more rows of tiny houses on the other side of the valley, she gazed up at the fields. Some were green with new growth after the harvest, others still yellow with stubble, enfolded by hawthorn hedgerows, the tiny leaves, always slow to show the gold and red of autumn colour, still a rich dark green. The light was bright up there, with nothing between the fields and the sky except craggy outcrops too steep to cultivate, scarred here and there by quarries, the light glinting back off pale, new-cut rock surfaces.

She made up her mind, pulled on her jacket, collected the key of the door and walked quickly along the pavement until there was a gap in the flow of carts and motors large enough for her to cross to the other side of the road. A few minutes later, she was in the park, walking back up the narrow path towards the summer seat where she'd sat with Ruth and Tommy on Sunday.

It was cooler today, the sun less bright, but it was warmer here in the park than in the empty, unheated house. She was suddenly aware that the sight of flowers and the rustle of drifting leaves at her feet had made her smile. Moments later, as she came up the slope, she smiled more broadly as she recognised the pleasant-faced, white-haired, elderly woman who had greeted them on Sunday. She was sitting on the summer seat she'd thought of sitting on herself, feeding an array of small birds with crumbs from a paper bag. She paused on the narrow path as she spotted a robin, bolder than the rest, hop on to the arm of the seat, his eye cocked expectantly. A few minutes later, the crumbs had all vanished. The robin had been given some expected treat and had now flown away.

'Good morning,' Ellie said, as she came up to the seat, where bright eyes and a smiling face looked up at her. 'I didn't want to frighten your birds.'

'That was kind of you. I do hope you're going to come and sit down and talk to me. I'm fortunate enough not to be a lonely old woman, but I do miss talking to young people. Even some of my grandchildren are rapidly approaching middle age,' she said, laughing easily.

Ellie thought what a lovely face she had. Though deeply lined as one would expect with someone in their seventies, or even eighties, the lines were not harsh. There seemed to be a hint of laughter in the very face itself.

She sat down willingly.

'I saw the robin come to your hand. My father has a wren that sits on the anvil, or even on his hammer, but it won't come to his hand,' she said smiling. 'He says only a robin will do that.'

'So *you* don't live in Belfast, do you?'

'No, I'm *the wee cousin up from the country*,' she said, mimicking Tommy and laughing.

'We'll you certainly don't *look* like a country cousin,' the older woman replied, laughing heartily herself, as she ran an eye over Ellie's pretty dress.

As their laughter faded, Ellie saw her look away for a moment as if some sad or sudden thought had crossed her mind.

'And where in the country *is* home?' she asked, the smile returning as she spoke.

'Near Armagh, a little place called Salter's Grange.'

'Is your father the blacksmith there?'

Ellie nodded.

'Then your grandfather was Thomas Scott and your father is Robert.'

'Goodness,' said Ellie, quite taken aback, 'how on earth do you know that?'

'Because, my dear, my beloved John, who died six years ago this August, served his apprenticeship with Thomas and worked with him for many a long day,' she said quietly, wiping a tear unselfconsciously from each eye. 'And I once made a home in the old house opposite the forge, which I expect is a ruin by now.'

'Then *you* must be Mrs Hamilton,' said Ellie quickly. 'I've heard my father talk about you and your living opposite the forge. He said you used to sing when you were doing your work.'

'My goodness, what memories you bring...'

Ellie watched her face change as she caught a hand to her mouth, almost as if she were afraid she might be overwhelmed by them.

'You promise you won't let me bore you,' she said suddenly. 'Old people can be so tedious,'

201

she went on, 'telling the same old stories.'

'But it's not just old people that tell the same old stories,' Ellie protested. 'I've heard people not all that old tell the same old stories, but they're always stories you've never *asked* to hear.'

'Yes, you are quite right. It's not the stories that are wrong, it's the people themselves. The stories are what they want to believe. They don't always have much to do with how things really were.'

Ellie nodded, thinking of listening to Uncle John's tirade the evening before.

'Now *do* tell me your name, please. You must be Robert's youngest daughter, but I haven't seen him since John's funeral. He and your mother both came to Rathdrum that day.'

'That's near Banbridge, isn't it?'

'Yes, that's right,' she said, looking pleased.

'I'm Ellie.'

'Of course. Your mother was Ellen. I've only met her once and it was very briefly,' she said, a slight frown shadowing her face. 'And I'm Rose Hamilton. Please, *please*, call me Rose. I know it's not usually done, but I've no one to call me Rose any more,' she said sadly.

'Why is that?'

'Because Ellie, although I am so very fortunate and have sons and daughters and grandchildren ... and great-grandchildren,' she added, with a little laugh, 'I'm Ma ... or Mother, when they're being polite,' she added, laughing aloud, 'or Granny or Grandma or even Grandmother, depending on which family it is and what they've

202

been taught. But I no longer have my dear friends, Anne and Mary and Peggy and Selina and Elizabeth ... and ... others. So there's no one left to call me Rose now,' she ended wistfully.

'Rose is a lovely name. I think you grew roses once at Salter's Grange. I have a little garden in the ruins of the old house and there's a pink rose I found there run wild.'

'A rambler, with masses of tiny blooms and wicked little thorns?'

'Yes,' said Ellie, her eyes lighting up with pleasure. 'Could it possibly be what you planted?'

'I honestly don't know. Perhaps it's a great-great-grandchild. I'm not sure how long a rambler like that can go on propagating itself if it's left to get on with it all on its own. But I have a granddaughter called Rosie, who might know. She worked for McGredy's in Portadown. She still gardens though she's married now with three little ones. I'll ask her when James next takes me to Dromore.'

'Is James your son, the gentleman you were walking with on Sunday?'

'Yes, he is. He's my eldest. Rather an important gentleman now, so I'm told, though he's very modest about it himself. He's in one of the Government Departments. Economic Development, I think it's called. He's been very busy moving his office from the City Hall to the new building up at Stormont. But he's very good to me, drives me around to visit my family and takes me to the Mournes when I pine for the mountains. You can see the hills from this seat when the leaves fall, but I was born in Donegal and was brought up in Kerry, so these Antrim Hills aren't quite what I call mountains. Though I am very fortunate to have them and this park.'

'You can almost forget about the city when you're sitting here, can't you?' Ellie said, looking towards the hills, still hidden by the summer's growth, a quiet longing in her eyes.

'Don't you like the city, Ellie?'

'I don't know. I'm always glad to come and see Auntie and my cousins, but I don't think I'd like to live here. My bedroom is at the top of the house and I can see fields from my window. I think I was missing them this morning. And the little, humpy green hills of Armagh. I'm even missing the ride in and out to work in the town and getting wet as often as not,' she ended laughing.

'Where do you work?'

'Freeburn's. It's a drapery business. It used to be quite small, but my boss is very go ahead.'

'Yes, I think I can remember it. Just round the corner from the marketplace. It almost looks down Thomas Street. Mrs Freeburn used to sew mourning dress. She had a notice in the window ... that *was* a long time ago...'

'Were you remembering something very sad?' Ellie asked, as the silence grew longer.

'Yes, I'm afraid I was,' she replied, nodding rather sadly. 'One of my oft-told stories. About escaping with my children from a rail disaster, thanks to my son James. But it's much too sad a story for such a lovely morning.'

She paused and turned to look at Ellie directly.

'Would it be very rude of me to ask if you have someone you hope to marry?'

'No, not rude at all,' said Ellie promptly.

She wondered what to say, or where to start. She couldn't remember ever having talked to an older woman as lively or as interesting as Rose Hamilton. She found herself wishing they really could be friends, then she could ask to hear her stories. What was it like when she was young? How had she met her husband? And how did she know he was the person she wanted to marry?

She'd love to know about her children, daughters or sons, who they had married, what they'd done and where they all were. It seemed to her that if she were able to listen to Rose talking about her life, she would learn all the things that her mother had neither the patience, nor the wisdom, nor the interest to teach her.

Neither of them was aware of time passing as Ellie spoke of George and their plans, of her sisters and what she knew of Canada, until a tall figure stopped in front of them, tipped his hat courteously and said with a slight smile: 'Mother, I was told that you had gone missing without leave.'

'Goodness, James, it can't be lunchtime already?'

'I am reliably informed that it is.'

Rose and Ellie both laughed.

'James, this delightful companion of mine is Ellie Scott, Robert Scott's daughter. She's visiting Annie Magowan, Annie Scott-that-was down on the Lisburn Road. Can you believe it?'

205

'To my discredit, I seem to remember pulling that same lady's hair in the schoolroom beside Grange Church. And you say she lives locally?'

'Not only that, Mrs Wilson's been buying our vegetables at Mr Magowan's shop for years and we didn't know he was Johnny Magowan from Ballyards.'

'It is just possible that keeping the shop's previous name may have confused us.'

Ellie decided that James Hamilton was a nice man. He seemed to be laughing at himself very slightly all the time. His way of speaking was very friendly, even if it sounded a little bit formal to her and his accent was rather posh.

'My dear, I can't ask you to lunch, Mrs Wilson would scold me if she thought she wasn't fully prepared, but please, will you come and see me again? Can you spare the time? What about lunch tomorrow?'

'Not tomorrow, mother dear. Previous engagement.'

'Oh what a nuisance,' she said crossly. 'When do you go, Ellie?'

'Saturday morning. Quite early, I'm afraid.'

'Friday then. Can you possibly come Friday? Come to me here when you can and we'll have lunch and if you have to run away afterwards I'll understand.'

'I'd love to come,' said Ellie, as Rose began to get awkwardly to her feet.

She found it difficult to watch her struggle and wondered why James merely stood by, holding her stick till she was firmly on her feet.

'There, I'm perfectly all right, you see,' she

206

said, smiling up at James. 'Pleased as I am to see you, I would have come home by myself had I not been having such a happy morning.'

'Perhaps mother, Ellie, if I may also call you so,' he began, with a little bow towards her, 'might need to know the number of our house. Then your meeting may not be prevented if it has the bad taste to rain on Friday.'

Rose stopped, looked from one to the other, and laughed.

'Yes, we know. Old ladies are forgetful. But why not, when I have far more important things to think about! Thank you, Ellie, my dear, for a lovely morning. I shall look forward to Friday. Give my regards to your Aunt Annie, if she remembers me. Goodbye.'

'Now have you got everythin', love? Your ticket, your handbag and the carrier with the material, forby your wee case?'

Ellie smiled as Aunt Annie went through the routine she'd heard her use every morning with Uncle John and Ruth and Bobby too, on school-days. Perhaps because her own mother had never bothered to make such an effort, she found it very endearing.

'It's a pity you hafta go in to come back out again, but then I suppose it's only because you know the Armagh drivers that they'll drop you off here. Time ye were away now and don't be long till yer back, as the saying is. Tell your Ma and Da I was askin' for them.'

Annie came to the door with her, gave her a big hug and watched as she walked down the short

207

garden path and disappeared behind the overgrown privet hedge. Minutes later, beyond her
neighbour's more ordered garden, she saw the
small figure reappear, her case in one hand, her
purchases in the other, her bag over her shoulder.
Just as she reached the stop, Annie heard a tram
approaching. She closed the door, well pleased
her favourite niece had got off to a good start on
her journey home.

Ellie could hardly believe how quickly the
week had passed and how very varied it had
been. As they ran without any hold up past the
Bakery, past the junction with the avenue leading to the Workhouse and on towards the city
centre bus station, she began to wonder what she
would say when asked about her 'holiday'.
People always asked about holidays when you
came back.

It would have to be different things for different people, of that she was sure. Daisy and Susie
would want to know what she'd bought, which
of the new styles had most prominence in the
windows of Donegal Place and Royal Avenue
and what she and Ruth had done together. Mr
Freeburn would want a full report on leisure and
sports clothing as displayed in the city centre.
She might tell him she met Mrs Patterson in
Robinson and Cleavers, but she would most
certainly not mention her relationship with Miss
Walker or what she'd said about Freeburn's
having such a shrewd buyer.

She peered out of the window and saw the
news she'd expected to see on the news boards.
Further Rioting, said one. *RUC baton charge*,

said another. There was no doubt what Charlie Running would want to hear about. She had a lot of questions to ask him too, though not quite as many as she would have had if James Hamilton had not appeared for lunch the previous day.

He'd been to a meeting with the Mayor in the City Hall which had ended earlier than he'd expected and Rose had wanted to know what was going to happen. How did the Guardians hope to stop the rioting without making concessions? What point was there in delay when all the time distress was increasing and property being destroyed?

Ellie was quite surprised at Rose's questions, but it was clear she knew a good deal more about strikes and stoppages than she would have guessed. She referred to other labour troubles and asked why the government was still in recess. At one point she asked quite sharply why it had met in September merely to extend the recess to November when there was a full-scale crisis on their doorstep.

James was very proper and said nothing that was still confidential, but Rose made very shrewd guesses. When she said that they thought if they weren't in session they couldn't be blamed for what was happening James had to admit that 'she wasn't far wrong'. But after that, it was Rose herself who changed the subject and asked Ellie about her cousins.

The Armagh bus was not very full and the conductor put all her luggage safely up on the racks out of her way. At least this time she didn't have to worry about breaking the eggs.

Once out of the city, the journey went very well. She sat back and watched the line of the hills slip away behind them as they approached Lisburn. Gratefully, she ran her eyes over the trees lining the route. Even a week further on they were showing much more positive signs of autumn. In the main street of Moira, the four large trees that lined the road had spread inches of shrivelled leaves over the footpaths. Men with twig brooms were sweeping vigorously. Heaps of leaves, like small haystacks, were awaiting collection by a horse and cart, a big heavy horse with broad shoulders and gentle eyes. Just like the ones that came to the forge from the surrounding farms.

She thought of Robinson's next door and then of George. There'd been no letter in the week before she came away, so there should be a letter waiting. Yes, she was glad to be going home, whatever she might find there.

Thirteen

Autumn lingered that year, the weather still fine and pleasant as Ellie settled back into her routine at home and the young staff of Freeburn's began the customary preparations for Christmas and the January sale. Susie had her fifteenth birthday in November, invited all her colleagues to a party, which they enjoyed enormously, and began to make real progress with her ambition to get Joe to talk a bit more. Daisy continued to go out with Frank Armstrong, but now no longer blushed every time his name was mentioned. Nor did she try to convince anyone that his asking her out was just his 'being polite'.

There was no longer any tennis to look forward to, but it seemed that the redeployment of Miss Walker, the arrival of Susie, and Ellie's own promotion to Senior Assistant had brought about a marked change in the atmosphere in Freeburn's. Everyone seemed happier and little treats and outings were now planned every few weeks to help them keep their spirits up as the days shortened and got much colder.

December came with regular flurries of sleet, snow and chilling rain, as wet as July had been, but infinitely more uncomfortable. As Ellie bent her head against the bitter wind on her journeys to and from Armagh, she tried to keep her thoughts away from her cold, wet legs and the moisture running down her icy face, by thinking of all the pleasant things that had happened in the previous months.

There were small and slightly unexpected events, like the smile on Mr Freeburn's face when the items she'd recommended before her holiday had arrived and he'd seen them put on display. There was the success of her new dress. While there might be no opportunity to wear it yet, it was still a great pleasure to have something hanging on the back of the bedroom door that fitted perfectly and suited her so well. She'd never thought she could cut on the bias like the magazines had recommended, but she'd persevered and she'd managed it.

Then there was the big surprise her father had for her when she arrived home. To her amazement, he'd bought a new wireless. He hated buying anything new and avoided it whenever possible, but this time he was so pleased with himself he could barely disguise the fact.

He'd been thinking of buying one for a while now, he explained, though Ellie couldn't remember him ever having mentioned it. The Ecko they'd had since wirelesses first came out had taken to crackling in the middle of the news, or even in the middle of one of the few programmes he ever listened to. Just when he'd made up his mind to do something about it Charlie Running had recommended a particular make and had got one for him and one for himself, at a discount. Not out of the way expensive, he thought, and my goodness you could hear every word the man said as if he were standing beside you in the same room.

What had surprised her even more than the arrival of the wireless itself was that her mother had started listening during the day. Now, in the evenings, she complained about the programmes and that seemed to make her happier than complaining about how ill she was and how no one ever paid a bit of attention to her.

Beyond all this, however, was the news from George.

She'd been very upset when she arrived home and found no letter awaiting her. Or rather, there were three letters awaiting her and *none of them* were from George. She was so upset, she hadn't written him her usual letter and she felt badly that she hadn't when his letter eventually showed up a week later. That letter did change everything.

He apologized at some length for the delay. He'd been working up at the camp when his uncle sent for him to come down to Peterborough. They'd had a sudden staffing problem in one of the mills and couldn't get a qualified man for the job for some months. His uncle had arranged a week's special intensive training for him in the hope that he could make up for the absentee if he was given an experienced man alongside him. It had been terribly hard work at first, for there was so much to remember. The machinery they were using was highly dangerous if you didn't know exactly what you were doing, but he'd managed to get the hang of it quite quickly.

The long and the short of it was that his uncle was very pleased with him. He would still have to do another season in a different lumber camp to get more of the experience at that end of things, but as soon as the snow came next year, he'd be coming down to Peterborough to work in the mill. Wasn't that great news?

He also said that he and his cousin Jimmy were going to go down into the States for the winter to see what work they could find until the ice melted. That way, he could really begin saving. In no time at all they'd be together again. He could hardly wait.

* * *

213

If Uncle George in Peterborough, Ontario, was pleased with his nephew's prospects, there was someone else in that same rapidly-growing city even more delighted about the sequence of events at Peterborough Lumbering.

Polly McGillvray was now well settled in her small house in Hunter Street, a few minutes' walk from the side entrance to the Quaker Oats factory. Only a week after George's letter arrived at Salter's Grange, she received the first happy letter she'd had in months from her little sister. She was so relieved and so excited, she could hardly think of anything else for days afterwards.

She'd hoped getting away for a bit of a holiday would have given her sister a bit of a lift, even if it was just going to Aunt Annie. With all she had to do at home when their mother took to the couch, and with no George to take her out, she didn't have much in the way of pleasure these days. Aunt Annie was a kind soul and Ruth had always been fond of Ellie, though not as fond as her brother, Tommy. She smiled at the thought of her handsome young cousin arriving with his little box of chocolates. He'd always been sweet on Ellie.

But the first letter she'd had after Ellie's return home had really upset her. Ellie always wrote so clearly and openly, Polly couldn't fail to see how unhappy she was. She'd not mentioned George at all, which was a bad sign. What she had written about was the people she'd seen marching to the Workhouse and lying on the tramlines. In particular she'd told her about the death of a man

214

called Sammy Baxter. He was a flower-seller and a Protestant and he'd been shot by the police when he'd been demonstrating with Catholic comrades on the Falls Road.

Ellie had admitted to Polly that, when she found there was nothing to help her understand what was happening in Belfast in the Armagh papers, she'd walked up to Charlie Running's house on Sunday afternoon to see if he could explain to her why the poor man had been shot.

After a week of rioting, Charlie explained, the police had orders to clear the streets. They'd been issued with guns and it was common knowledge, the police only used guns in Catholic areas. In Protestant areas, they stuck to truncheons.

Polly knew that Charlie was a very knowledgeable man. She'd heard her father complain often enough he was never out of the Library and sometimes he talked like a book. He always said there was no use him arguing with Charlie for he had facts and figures at his fingertips you'd never even heard of yourself.

She'd read that October letter over and over again. Charlie had tried to answer Ellie's questions, rightly enough, but in the process he'd had to tell her about the problems unemployment was creating in other countries and maybe that had only made things worse. Apparently there were six million unemployed in Germany, something Polly herself hadn't the slightest idea about, and according to Charlie, there was a man called Hitler making speeches and holding great rallies and promising to put the country on its feet. Hitler seemed to be promising everyone what they wanted: jobs for the unemployed, opportunities for businesses to expand, even a husband for every young girl! As Charlie saw it, the man was on the up and up. There was no limit to his ambition and so far no one had lifted a finger to stop him.

Dear Ellie, she had such a soft heart, she'd end up worrying about all those poor people in Germany, just as much as she'd worried about the poor people in Belfast. As if she hadn't enough to cope with around her own back door.

On top of the letter, Polly had a dreadful week after it arrived. Everything that could go wrong did go wrong. Jimmy was moved to the night shift. Eddie threw a tantrum and said he didn't like school, so Davy played up too because he always did what Eddie did. Even little Ronnie, normally the most amenable of children, reached the next stage of teething and grizzled all the time.

So Polly could hardly believe it when, only a week later, the second letter had come like the sun coming out from behind a cloud. Ellie hadn't forgotten what she'd seen and heard in Belfast and she did mention again things that Charlie had since told her, but the whole tone of *everything* she'd written was so very different. When she asked about employment in Canada, particularly how things now looked for Jimmy, you could tell she was concerned, but there wasn't that awful sense of anxiety coming through what she was writing about, as if everything in her life was going wrong.

Polly read and reread the letter, just to reassure herself. Yes, it did sound as if George was settling down at last and beginning to think a bit more about the future and their plan to get married. Nothing would please Polly more than George not being able to wait to be reunited with Ellie. That was more like the way it should be.

More than once over the late summer when Eddie and Davy were finally asleep and she was waiting for Jimmy to come off the late shift, she'd sat by her own fire and tried to bring to mind all she knew about George Robinson. He'd only been fourteen when she'd married Jimmy and left for Toronto. Nothing wrong with him she could think of at that stage, and likeable enough. She'd never heard of anything he'd done wrong other than the mischief you'd expect from a young lad. No, there was nothing against him, but she did wonder if there was anything positive to be said on the other side. She asked herself if he *ever put himself out*.

She smiled to herself. She hadn't thought of those words for a long time. *Putting himself out*, was a phrase often used by her grandmother, Selina, a woman she'd loved dearly. *'Putting yourself out'* was what people did if they cared. About a person, about a task, about anything that mattered. It was a way of showing love and commitment.

Suddenly Polly remembered a particular day, when she was a good deal younger than Ellie was now, sitting in the forge house with Selina and asking her how she knew her first husband Jack had been the right man for her, and then

217

Thomas, her own grandfather.

'You see, Polly, if a man loves you he'll put *you* first,' she'd begun. 'Now, it's not that you might not always let him do that, but if that willingness is not there, then however much he says he loves you, however much *he thinks* he loves you, that love is not going to be durable. Life can be very hard for women in ways men can't always understand, but if they're willing to *put themselves out for you*, then you can do the same for them. They may be strong, and kind, and hard-working, but they have their weaknesses and soft spots just as much as women, though they're not supposed to show them. A wise woman knows a man's weakness and protects him from it. But he has to do the same for her and that means he's going to have to *"put himself out"*. Make an effort it would be far easier for him not to make.'

She wasn't sure she'd understood at the time. Looking back, she wasn't sure she'd even thought about what Selina had said when she met Jimmy at a dance at the Floral Hall in Befast when she'd had a holiday with Aunt Annie. He'd said he was going to Canada and asked her there and then to go with him.

No, she didn't regret it. Jimmy was a good man. He'd put his hand to anything she ever asked him to do and done his best for her, though he said he was no good with children, which was a pity. He hated to see her tired, or anxious. When he put his arms round her in bed at night, she sometimes thought those moments were the only comfort she'd ever have in a world so full of work to be done and children to look after.

Unless, of course, Ellie were to come out and marry George. The thought that she might have her sister, her dear, golden-headed little sister, living in the next street, or across the park, or anywhere she could reach on foot, or by bus, was such a joy that even when Eddie shouted downstairs for her to bring him a drink of water, closely followed by Davy, whom he'd wakened, she went upstairs to settle them yet again, smiling and longing for the time to pass.

Time always does pass. It might have slowed down during the dark days of January, but now it seemed to Ellie that no sooner had they had a day off work to celebrate Easter than May made a triumphant entrance with glorious sunshine, the countryside responding immediately with blossom and luxuriant growth.

Although the letters from George had not been very frequent since he'd gone back up to the camp, in every letter he now talked about returning to Peterborough, finding somewhere to live and saving up enough for their immediate needs. Surely by this time next year they would be together again, or, at the very least, she would be making her plans to welcome him home for their wedding, or saying goodbye to her friends, packing up her trousseau and sailing out to join him.

The Tennis Club reopened and she and Daisy had taken delivery of their new racquets. They were amazed at how much having one's own racquet improved one's game. They played at least three times a week and were looking forward to the Annual Tennis Club Dance at the end of the month. Although Daisy would be going with Frank, she had insisted Ellie must come with Susie, Harry and Stanley. She couldn't possibly let them all down by not going. As Daisy had said often, it was one thing going out with another fellow and quite a different matter going to support your own club along with other club members.

In one of her recent letters to Rose Hamilton, she'd admitted she was *looking forward to dancing again although I can't go with George, especially as I made a new dress last autumn and I haven't had a chance to wear it yet!'*

Rose had suggested they keep in touch after their lunch together the previous October and Ellie had been very happy to agree. She enjoyed writing and found it very easy to write to Rose because she remembered what she'd said about missing conversations with young people. So she wrote about the shop, about her friends, about their jokes and outings and the idiosyncrasies of the customers. In return, with only the slightest encouragement from Ellie, Rose wrote about her family and whatever thoughts or memories came to mind as she read her young friend's letters. She told a good story and she too enjoyed writing.

It was Rose who suggested on one occasion that, given all the practice they both had corresponding with the far-flung members of their families, they ought to embark on an epistolatory novel which could be published in weekly parts like Dickens's novels had been, until the entire ramifications of their two families had been laid out for the entertainment of their devoted readers.

Ellie had never heard the word *epistolatory* before but it wasn't too hard to guess what Rose meant. She'd laughed, thinking of the wide spread of her own brothers and sisters and intrigued by the even wider spread of Rose's much larger family. In her next letter, she'd asked her if she could tell her all the places she had family. She had a reply almost by return.

Here you are, my dear. I don't actually write to ALL of these places. I often instruct parents to pass on my news and greetings. Sadly, some of the grandchildren of my own older brothers, now long gone, are only in touch at Christmas, but here is a list of places *where Hamiltons are presently to be found: all the counties in Northern Ireland, County Donegal, Dublin, Scotland, Prince Edward Island, Cambridge and Gloucestershire, London, Paris, Berlin, New York and New York State, Pennsylvania, Vancouver Island and Sydney, Australia.*

Neither can I guarantee that these people are *exactly* where they last told me they were. Sarah was in Berlin with her husband, Simon, but she may have returned to their home in Cambridge, or be visiting her sister Hannah, either in Gloucestershire or in London. And then, of course, Sarah's eldest son, Hugh, may be nowhere on earth at all, but, like Miss Amelia Earhart, in the skies! Slater, James's son, last heard of building a bridge in Sydney, might now be in Ceylon or

221

the Caribbean. It certainly keeps *me* up to the mark trying to keep up with their activities.

Ellie often entertained herself on her journeys in and out of Armagh by trying to construct a family tree for Rose. Constructing such trees was, of course, a normal pastime in the forge. Ever since she'd been a little girl, she'd listened to visitors engaged in 'placing' someone.

'Now would those be the Taylors of Hockley, that had the farm down the back of the wall? The eldest girl was a teacher and married an Armagh man.'

'Not at all, man dear, they're a different family entirely. These Taylors lived over by Maghery and he was the land steward for Sir Capel Molyneux. The daughter went to New York and married some man with pots of money. They bought a big house in County Down for their holidays, but yer man couldn't stand the rain, so they went to Arizona or Mexico, I forget which...'

What Ellie found so extraordinary was the way people moved around, emigrating perhaps to Australia and then moving on to Canada. Some got rich and came home, wanting to spend their last years in the places they had once loved like Rose's younger brother, Sam McGinley. Others simply disappeared from view. They may have died, of course, or just never felt the need to keep in touch.

Rose had told her that John had had two brothers who went to America and never came back, though it looked as if one of them had left a son in Liverpool. He, poor child, had been sent

222

as an orphan to Canada with his name on the collar of his coat, but he'd come back to Ireland looking for his family. He'd found them too, married a local girl, and was now living in her own old home at Rathdrum.

Life was so full of these extraordinary stories of people travelling thousands of miles and meeting up with people from just down the road. It might not be thousands of miles, but her own meeting with Rose in Belfast was just such a story. Indeed, she'd heard from Charlie about how pleased her father was to retell it for the entertainment of visitors to the forge, though he'd never told it when she'd been present.

But an even better story than Ellie's meeting with Rose was already on its way to Salter's Grange. Before the apple blossom was well in bloom, Ellie had a letter from Polly, so thick she'd had to use a whole row of stamps to cover the postage.

It had happened like this. Jimmy had offered to look after the boys while Polly went to the shop, as long as she took the baby with her in the pram. He didn't think he could manage if the wee one cried with his teeth. Taking Ronnie with her was no trouble to Polly. Apart from the teething, he was the most good-tempered baby. He'd sit outside the shop and wave at the passers-by and with the carrier underneath she'd not have to carry home the potatoes.

It was only a short distance to the corner shop, but Polly set off as if she were going for a long, leisurely walk. It was as good as being out on her

223

own, walking in the sunshine with no Eddie and Davy pulling at her skirts and asking for sweets.

The Corner Store was a small, overcrowded shop full of the mixed smells of soap and candles, cured bacon and ham, spices and ginger cookies. Polly always enjoyed going there. She parked the pram where she could see it through the window, waved at her youngest child, who smiled and waved back.

'Good mornin', Mrs McGillvray. How are you the day?'

'Good mornin', Jim,' she said, returning his greeting, smiling at the familiar phrase 'the day' and the faint trace of an Ulster accent living in Canada had not entirely removed. Peterborough was full of people of Scots or Irish descent, but however often she met them she was still touched when she heard the sounds of home. 'No Rebecca today to help you? Is she all right?'

'Aye fine. She's away to our eldest granddaughter. Wee one due any time,' he said smiling. 'My son's giving me a hand, though he's supposed to be on holiday from Quaker. He's out the back fillin' up the paraffin cans.'

Polly had almost finished her shopping. She'd taken the potatoes out to the pram and found Ronnie happily entertaining a neighbour. She was busy fitting packets of tea and sugar into her shopping bag when suddenly a young man walked through the door from the back premises.

He nodded politely and said, 'Good morning.'

Polly opened her mouth to reply, but no words came out. She stood staring at him, her mouth still open till Jim caught sight of her and asked if

224

she was feeling all right.

'Jim, your son here,' she said, putting a hand to her throat. 'He looks so like my brother Bob, I thought I was seein' things.'

'They do say we all have a double somewhere, ma'am,' said the young man, smiling easily.

His accent had not a trace of Ulster in it, but when he smiled he looked even more like Bob.

'Jim, you wouldn't by any chance be a Scott?'

'Aye, surely. I'm Jim Scott. Did ye not know that?'

'No,' she said, shaking her head, 'I heard everyone callin' you Jim and you didn't seem to mind, so I called you Jim as well. There's no name on the shop and I never thought to ask. I'm Polly Scott. My father's Robert and you must be his brother James that went away.'

'Well indeed, you might be right,' he said very slowly. 'In fact you *are* right, there's no two ways about it,' he said, scratching his balding head, which she realised did look just like her father's. 'An' you and I seein' each other near every day this last year or more,' he added wryly.

'So what you are saying, ma'am, is that, not only do I look like your brother, I *am* your cousin. That would explain it, wouldn't it?' he added, laughing and shaking his head at his father who had begun to smile himself.

At that point Polly had had to suspend her furious scribblings because she knew she couldn't get any more pages into the airmail envelope, but it was clear to Ellie from what she'd already written, that Jim was not in any way displeased to have been found. Whatever the

225

reason for his departure from Ireland and his failure to keep in touch, he and his son had welcomed wholeheartedly the discovery of this totally unexpected family connection.

As Ellie had expected, Rose also thought it was a wonderful story and wrote straight back asking her to let her know how things worked out with the Peterborough Scotts. She was sure it would help Polly to have relatives literally round the corner and she wondered if Jim's wife, now revealed as Polly's aunt, might give her some help with the children.

Rose and Ellie had agreed Polly had been too easy with the boys and being easy with boys was never a good idea. It left her with seldom a moment to herself. Indeed, more than once she'd admitted writing her letters late at night when even Jimmy was in bed.

Rose's letter continued:

But my dear, before I get distracted by any further thoughts about Polly and the children, I have something to ask you. My birthday is on the twelfth of June, the same day as my daughter Sarah. I shall, of course, be eighty, a figure so advanced that I cannot quite believe it.

James has insisted that we have a celebration. I cannot very well say no. How could I say no to James? Without him being the means of saving us on the twelfth of June 1889, that fateful day of the Sunday School Excursion to Warrenpoint, there would be no Hamiltons to celebrate.

I should so like you to be here and to meet at

least some of the people I have talked about at such great length.

The twelfth is a Monday, but I see no reason not to have our tea party, or whatever James has in mind, on Sunday the eleventh. Could you possibly manage to come? I did mention it to your Aunt Annie when she came to see me last week and she says you could come up on Saturday night and perhaps catch the early bus home on Monday morning.

I'm sure your Mr Freeburn wouldn't mind you being just a little late if you asked him nicely ... which I am quite sure you are rather good at.

Please do try to come. I am forbidding birthday presents, I am much too old for those, but I would be happy to receive a piece of your pink rose just to see if we recognize each other!

With fondest love,
Rose.

Ellie smiled. Not just one opportunity, but two, to wear her new dress. As her father so often said 'It never rains but it pours.'

Fourteen

On Monday the eighth of May, sunshine poured down on the busy streets of Armagh as Sam Hamilton roared into the city. He slowed smoothly to a walking pace as he came level with Sleator's, dismounted, and wheeled his motorbike round the back of the garage to its parking place on the edge of the servicing and repair area. Today, was his twenty-seventh birthday.

He was in good spirits. He loved the sunshine and the warmth of the morning and his journey to work from the family home beside Richhill Station had been memorable. The bike always went better in dry air and today it had simply flown, the engine sweet, the road still fairly empty at this early hour.

Like people, machinery responded to the conditions in which it had to function, but it wasn't simply weather that affected them. There were motors he'd serviced that had nothing specifically wrong with them, but they'd still run badly and one look at their owners had told him why. Impatience, heavy-handedness, irritability, all had their effect on even the most robust systems. On the newer models, with their more delicate tuning and timing, it could be disastrous.

228

Yet you couldn't deny the air itself *was* a factor. No damp today, he thought, smiling to himself, as he peeled off his jacket and hung his helmet on a hook, ready to tackle whatever the day might bring.

'Rich ... Rich...'

He laughed quietly to himself. Peggy had just got engaged to a young schoolmaster. All his colleagues agreed she seemed like a different girl. She beamed at everyone, dressed even more smartly and said *please* when she wanted something done. Two things though hadn't changed. She was even more particular about her shoes, and neither love, nor the prospect of marriage to an educated fellow had done anything to soften the sharp edge in her voice.

'Rich, will you *please* take out that Chevrolet over there. It's not right. Here's the book and a note of what the chauffeur said to Mr Richard last night. He's not in this mornin',' she explained, handing him the papers and the ignition key. 'An' if you don't mind me sayin', you've got oil on your bottom.'

'Thank you, Peggy,' he said, trying hard not to laugh out loud. She now said *bottom* instead of *backside*.

'Would you have a newspaper?' he asked politely.

She disappeared below her desk and re-emerged minutes later red in the face and irritated.

'I don't know where all the old newspapers go. Do yous eat them out there in the yard?'

'Not guilty, ma'am,' he replied, interested to see how a little fluster brought back the old way

229

of speaking.

The Chevrolet started perfectly. He slipped out into the traffic without any difficulty. Not unusual, even with an underperforming motor, it didn't tell him anything. What he needed was to get up speed, so he could test acceleration and cornering. He eased his way down College Street, turned right along The Mall and decided to head for Hamiltonsbawn.

Of all the roads leading out from the county town, this one had the steepest slopes. Besides, he hadn't driven it for some weeks. He made a point of varying the road he chose for test drives, so he could keep his eye in. Roads radiated out of Armagh like a spider's web, so you had plenty of choice and the circle of outlying villages provided parking or an easy turn round.

He drove steadily, his ears tuned, his eyes free most of the time to enjoy the sparkle of Lowry's Lough and the view out over stretches of green countryside as he climbed higher. Driving to Hamiltonsbawn he always thought of the unknown ancestor who must have founded the village and the story his grandmother told about Aunt Sarah. Once, when they were staying with Lady Anne, over in England, at Ashley Park, she'd provided an extended history of the Hamiltons.

Apparently a Lady Something-or-other had asked Granny which branch of the Hamiltons she came from, assuming a landed family with a coat of arms. He'd always loved the way Granny admitted she hadn't a clue what to say. She'd heard of the Hamiltons of Clandeboye, but John

Hamilton of Annacramp was unlikely to be any relation of that affluent and titled family and it was obvious this woman expected a full family history.

She was only sixteen at the time, but Sarah had upped and given her one. She'd started with the Plantation of Ulster and explained how the Hamiltons had undertaken to plant good Protestant settlers and build fortified houses, known as bawns. She'd held the floor for goodness knows how long and when, at the end of it, your woman asked her if they *were* related to the Hamiltons of Clandeboye, Sarah had just said rather sharply that their branch of the Hamiltons, the Hamiltons of Ballydown, had been there *far* longer than them.

As soon as he got to Hamiltonsbawn, he turned round and drove back towards Armagh at top speed on the empty road, did an emergency stop, then slid into a space by the roadside that fishermen used when they were going down to the lough. He checked under the bonnet and shook his head. It certainly shouldn't be as hot as that. He could do nothing more till the engine cooled, so he walked away, leaned over a nearby field gate and looked about him.

This soft green countryside was beautiful. Damp in the bottoms between the little hills, but if it was, at least it was never other than green. He'd seen pictures of other countries with hot summers and parched, beige land. Not for him. He'd never really wanted to leave his home, but he'd come very near to it last year.

What had happened between him and Marion

231

had hit him so hard he just couldn't believe it. One day he was on top of the world, going down to Rountrees to buy the furniture for their new home, wanting to surprise her that he'd done so well, saving up enough money for all they needed, the next, she was making excuses, wanting to put the wedding off. Then she refused even to talk to him. Then she threatened him with her father if he came looking for her again.

Both his sisters had tried to talk sense to him. Each said the same thing quite independently, that he wasn't to think it was his fault. There had to be someone else. Well, now he knew there had been, he'd had to admit they were right, that it was Marion who'd let *him* down. But just knowing still hadn't helped him.

That's when he'd decided the only thing to do was go away and make a new start. He'd gone to the Guardian office and spoken to the woman there. Very helpful she was. She thought at first he wanted to go on holiday and gave him a brochure. New Zealand, the Land of the Long White Cloud, it said. That was what the Maoris called it. When he explained he wanted to emigrate, she was even more helpful. Told him skilled people were much in demand. There'd be no trouble at all with an assisted passage provided he was single and in good health.

Well, he was certainly single. Perhaps he wasn't as fit as he'd been when he and Marion played tennis at the club in Portadown, but that was easily put right. His wee cousin Daisy had been at him to join the RUC Club. He could take out his racquet again while he was making all the necessary arrangements.

'Son dear, do you think you're doin' the right thing?' his father had asked, one evening in the workshop in the barn, the pair of them sitting on two empty cans of lubricating oil.

'I know you've had a hard blow, but you're young and has every hope before you. You've your two sisters in particular who'd miss you terribly ... and, of course, your Ma,' he added quickly. 'I wouldn't stand in your way if it was what you wanted, but I'm not sure it would take away that pain in your heart. The only way with grief and loss is to turn and face it. If there's a hole in your life you must see what you can do to fill it.'

He'd looked hard at his father. He had a fair idea he was speaking from his own experience. He was grateful too that he never once mentioned God or faith whenever he tried to help him. Being a Quaker, his father had a deep commitment to his beliefs, but to his credit he never tried to push them at other people. His advice was always kind and practical and meant to help them, not to make himself feel he'd done the right thing.

'You know it might only be some wee thing at first,' he'd gone on. 'Maybe a small success. Something you're good at, like your job, or maybe somewhere you always wanted to go, or making a few new friends. You've been so long with the one person, you might have forgotten men and women you used to know. Would you not give it a wee while yet and see if anythin' comes that might lift your heart?'

233

His father *had* been right. He'd found there were good things. He'd met Richard Sleator through work, as great a follower of motor racing as he was himself. They'd become friends and together met a whole lot more people at the Tennis Club. He thought immediately of Ellie Scott. He'd told his father at one point that he thought he'd never even dance with a girl again, but he'd danced with her and if she'd not been spoken for, he might even have got as far as asking her to go to the pictures. But that, he hadn't told his father.

Rosie said he was too soft. It could be a nice fault in a man if he found the right woman, but it would cost him dear if he took up with someone who wasn't as kind-hearted as he was. Like his father, only she put it more bluntly, she didn't think New Zealand would solve anything. He'd still have the pain within him and maybe no one to take the place of their father or Emily and herself to help him live through it. He might end up even more lonely without all the familiar things one can hold on to in bad times.

He looked all around him at the burgeoning freshness of spring. This would always be something to hold on to. The little green fields, the hawthorn hedges sprayed with creamy-white blossom. This elegant motor was his till he handed it back, the better for what he'd be able to do for it when he got the engine stripped down.

He opened the driver's door. Disturbed by the light breeze from the open offside window, Peggy's newspaper slithered from the driving seat and fell at his feet. He picked it up, looked to see if there *was* an oil mark from his backside and found Marion's name in the Family Announcements.

Prentice – Ritchie. To David and Marion Prentice, nee Ritchie, a son, Richard David. Born 7 January 1933 at The Carlton Maternity Home, Portadown.

He had to read it through three times before it finally sunk in. January. For a moment the date made no sense. Then he heard his mother's voice. How often had she stood in the middle of the kitchen, the newspaper in her hand, and declared, *'Another premature baby. Sure you could hardly believe how many of them there are these days. The hospitals must be run off their feet.'* Dropping her sarcastic tone, she would then count up on her fingers and say. 'That must'ave been after the harvest home,' or, 'that was the holiday they had before they were married.' Sometimes she would say, 'Well *they* didn't waste much time.'

He had never paid any attention before, but now what he saw were her fingers. Long, bony fingers, the joints enlarged with work and arthritis. Counting up to nine.

For the first time in his life, he did the same. And what he found was that Marion Ritchie, his fiancée, had conceived a child with David Prentice before he had gone out to buy the furniture.

He put the newspaper back on the seat and slid his oily backside across it. It was a small gesture to make, but it eased the anger welling up in him. He drove back to Armagh so slowly he picked up another fault he would never have expected to find in a motor of this quality.

Ellie, too, had set off to cycle to work in the best of spirits. Not only was the countryside shining in the sunlight, the dandelions opening bright eyes all along the hedge banks, but on her way past Riley's Rocks she met the postman.

'Aye,' Stevie McQuaid said, getting off his bicycle before she'd even asked. 'There's one from your sister and one from that young man of yours,' he went on, beaming cheerfully, as he pulled his mailbag over his head, undid the buckles and went through the small bundles. 'I'll not give you the bill for iron from Shillington's. I think it would be more use to your Da.'

She slipped the two letters into her handbag, thanked him and sailed on, her good spirits buoyed up yet further by the thought that she could slip upstairs and read the one from George at the first quiet moment in the morning.

It came as a surprise to her when a mile or so later, walking up the steep slope from the Mill Row past the asylum, she discovered she was no longer feeling happy. By the time she'd re-mounted, pedalled past the small stone cottages of Gillis Row and bumped her way over the level crossing into Railway Street, she knew she'd grown anxious.

She'd thought by now she'd adjusted to the fact that George was no letter writer. At school, when they were asked to write 'compositions', he could never think of anything to say and she'd often had to help him out. It ought to be different between them now, but even when she asked quite specific questions, hoping they would help to get him going, he didn't answer them, or said so little he might as well not have bothered.

She still knew almost nothing about the camp, how it was organised, where they slept, or where they ate. As for the trees they cut down all day and every day, all he said in answer to her questions was that they were coniferous. She wasn't all that well up on trees herself, but she did know the difference between larch and spruce and if he'd told her about other varieties, she'd have been able to go to the library and look them up.

Every time a letter came, she'd open it full of the same excitement and pleasure and almost always ended up with the same disappointment, as if she'd been looking once more for something that just wasn't there. She had no idea what she could do about it.

Monday morning was always busy in the shop. It was not specifically customers, for that varied with the season and the weather, but the window and the aisle displays had to be changed first thing. Mr Freeburn was always in his office for the whole morning and frequently there were deliveries which meant at least two staff were needed out at the back to help with the unloading and checking the bill of lading.

Her main task was to ensure there was no disorder or dislocation while the displays were being done. Mr Magennis, Joe and Daisy looked after the counters while she and Harry, assisted by Stanley and Susie, dressed the models and draped swathes of new fabric. Trying to create something eye-catching week after week was not easy. She often wondered how they kept it up.

Even though all the materials had been prepared late on Saturday afternoon and Harry had made sketches of what they'd planned to do, it was late in the morning before they'd finished. She checked that Daisy and Susie had had a tea break earlier, then slipped quietly upstairs herself.

The staffroom, in Miss Walker's time little more than a repository for cardboard boxes and unwanted furniture, had been transformed and it had been entirely Susie's idea. First she'd persuaded the boys to rearrange all the storage above the shop to take what was in the room itself, then she'd got them to freshen the walls with a coat of distemper, paint the surround of the fireplace and varnish the bare floorboards.

That made a big difference, but Susie wasn't satisfied. Having draped the two sagging fireside chairs with brightly coloured remnants and seen how much better they looked, she'd got Joe to use his carpentry skills to mend the chairs. She then recovered them herself and made a re-markably professional job of it.

When he'd viewed the result, Mr Freeburn had been impressed. A few days later, he produced a third fireside chair for them, so that they would *all* be able to sit comfortably for those few minutes when they arrived upstairs weary after work, before the effort of going home.

Ellie took out her letter. Indifferent to the now pleasant surroundings, she dropped into the nearest chair, tore open the envelope and drew out the folded sheets. She read it quickly, sighed, and read it again. It was neither better nor worse than she'd expected. It didn't tell her anything about what he was doing or what he was thinking, or how he felt about this new life he was making in a new country.

He did say he missed her and longed to be with her. Unfortunately he'd used the same words, in the same way, in every letter he'd written since last October. It reminded her of the way mothers say the same things to children, night after night, when they put them to bed: 'Goodnight, sleep tight. See you in the morning.'

She smiled suddenly as she remembered Polly's less genteel version when she herself was being put to bed a long time ago: 'Goodnight, sleep tight. Don't let the bugs bite.'

She picked up Polly's letter and devoured it, dropped it to the floor and covered her face with her hands. She thought longingly of her. Long or short, her letters never disappointed. They were so alive, whether she was on top of the world or out of her mind with fatigue, or beside herself with frustration over the behaviour of the boys. With a letter in her hand, Ellie could see her, feel what she was feeling, but there were times when the distance between them brought such an ache of loss, it was almost unbearable. Nothing but a flesh and blood Polly would do.

She thought of what Daisy would say. She was

239

always so quick to support her, so ready to encourage her not to spend her precious days waiting for George to write, or send her ticket, or say he was coming home. Daisy was a comfort, yes, but it was advice about what to *do* that she needed and she knew it had to be someone older and wiser than Daisy.

When the answer came to her, she couldn't imagine why she hadn't thought of it sooner. She would tell Rose all about her problem over George and ask her if they could have a word, even if it was her birthday. She knew her friend well enough to know she wouldn't mind and she could be sure Rose would have wise words to offer her.

Whether it was the thought of Rose, or the sight of the bunch of flowers Susie had put in a vase on the mantelpiece, she felt her spirits rise. She got to her feet and picked up her handbag from its hook.

'That's what that display needs,' she said aloud. 'At the bottom right-hand corner. Red or yellow to offset the grey.'

Half an hour later, after consulting Harry and cheered by her new idea, she set off for the nursery men's trestles in the marketplace to see if she could find what she needed.

Monday was not a market day, but at this point in May people were busy with their gardens and the nursery men were well aware of the fact. When Ellie rounded the corner into the marketplace she found almost as many vans and trestle tables as on a regular market day, but today they

240

were almost all selling plants, flowers, shrubs and young trees.

What she needed was a plant in bloom for the corner of the window display of men's suits and suiting fabric. Something to contrast with the pale greys and blues and particularly the very pale grey with the fine chalk white stripe which was displayed in many of the magazines this season.

It was still too early for roses, even the early varieties, but some of the nursery men now had enormous greenhouses and were growing small bush varieties in large pots. Under one of the trestles she caught sight of some bright, red blooms. Hoping that it wasn't a salvia, or dahlia, or one of the other perennials that would never tolerate the shop window for a whole week, she hurried forward, gathered her skirt around her and got down on one knee to have a good look.

To her delight, it was a healthy bush rose with pretty little pale-green leaves and some buds just unfurling. It was rather expensive, but she was sure Mr Freeburn would refund at least part of the cost from the petty cash. She often bought flowers and foliage plants for the windows and this wasn't totally different. If he paid half she'd willingly pay the other half and take it home when it stopped flowering.

She was just leaning forward to pull the tub out from among its fellows when she collided with a leg, a brown, dungareed leg with a slight smell of oil clinging to it.

'Och, I'm sorry, I didn't see you,' said a familiar voice, as a hand came down to steady her.

'Ellie Scott. Will you say a prayer for me while you're down there.'

Ellie laughed and grasped his hand, got to her feet and saw Sam Hamilton looking down, amazement and pleasure in his startling blue eyes. She had never before noticed how blue they were.

'Is that the one you want?' he asked, nodding at her choice.

'Yes, it's a nice shape and it's going to flower soon. Probably tomorrow if it's indoors.'

'An' what about those two?'

'Nice plants, but a bit further behind. Should bloom next week.'

'Now isn't that just great,' he said, clearly delighted about something. 'I think this must be a lucky day for me, having an expert to advise me when I need to buy two presents. You see, it's my birthday and I want one for Rosie and one for Emily.'

Ellie put her hand over her mouth and laughed. For a minute or two she just couldn't stop. It wasn't *that* funny, but when she looked up at him, he'd begun to laugh too.

'Sam Hamilton,' she began soberly, 'has no one ever told you that on *your* birthday your sisters are supposed to give *you* presents, not the other way round?'

'Ah well, ye see, I've been giving the pair of them a bad time,' he explained more soberly, 'and today I made up my mind I ought to go and see them and say thank you. I can go and see Emily tonight in Stonebridge and then Rosie in Dromore on Sunday. And those two wee bushes

242

sittin' beside your one will go down well.'

'And what about a birthday present for you, Sam?'

'Would you like to give me a birthday present?' he asked, his eyes suddenly sparkling.

'Yes, I would,' she replied, wondering what he might have in mind.

'Well, the last time you and I were at a dance, I had the first and the last. D'ye remember?'

She nodded happily.

'Then, for my birthday, you can give me *two extra*. Four altogether,' he said firmly, holding up four rather grubby fingers. 'That'll leave you enough for all the rest of the Tennis Club queuing up to dance with you in between. Is it a deal?'

'Yes, it's a deal,' she said, as he picked up her plant and handed it to her.

'I'm sorry I can't carry that back to the shop for you,' he added, glancing at his watch, 'but I've got to go and see a man about a motor. I'll see you and Daisy at the club one of these nights,' he said. 'I've hardly been yet this season, but I'll have a bit more time now.'

He tucked his two plants awkwardly under one arm, paid for them and hurried off down English Street, a plant now under each arm. As he passed, he gave her a quick backward glance and such a smile as to leave her thoughtful all the way back to the shop.

Fifteen

Having started off so beautifully with warmth and sunshine, May suddenly turned wet at the end of the second week. For all the young people at Freeburn's, including Joe, who had finally been persuaded to join the Tennis Club, it was a great disappointment. On several evenings it was obvious by closing time that no play would be possible while there were other evenings when they all went hopefully to the court, only to be rained off later.

There was, however, no possibility whatever of the Annual Tennis Club Dance being rained off, for this key event of the season, a nine to two affair including a sit-down supper, was held in the City Hall, a large building which provided various civic offices as well as a ballroom, reported to have a beautifully sprung floor, and a stage fitted with deep-red velvet curtains which swung back just like the ones in the Ritz Cinema.

None of the three girls had ever been to a dance in the City Hall before. Susie was so excited about the prospect of her first grown-up dance she could think of little else. Since the advent of Frank, Daisy had been to many dances, but none as yet in the City Hall. She was almost as excited as Susie, who'd been allowed to go because she'd be accompanied by not only Ellie and Daisy but also her brother Richard, a member of the organizing committee.

Ellie herself had not danced since the night she and Sam Hamilton had won the Tennis Tournament the previous September and she had to admit to herself she felt nearly as excited as her two friends. For reasons not clearly known to herself, she did her best not to make it obvious to either of them.

It was Susie who insisted neither Ellie nor Daisy could go cycling home at two o'clock in the morning in their best dresses. She had spoken to her mother and persuaded her brother to go and stay with his older brother and sister-in-law in Abbey Street, thereby leaving an extra spare bedroom at the house in Beresford Row. They would all be able to get ready together, she said, and if it should rain that evening, her father promised he would drive them up the City Hall himself.

The evening of the twenty-sixth of May, however, was warm and pleasant, as perfect a summer evening as one could wish. Although Ellie and Daisy had been given a bedroom each, next door to Susie's own room, it was only a matter of time before Ellie's room, which looked out over the trees on The Mall, became their joint dressing room.

Susie's excuse was that the long mirror on the back of the wardrobe door was the best in the house while Daisy just appeared in her slip when she heard the voices next door. But Ellie wasn't in the least put out by this invasion, far from it, she found a great comfort in the presence of her two younger friends. After all their talk about the dance in the staffroom at Freeburn's it seemed very appropriate for them to be together now, doing each other's hair, sharing powder, or lipstick, or scent.

Susie's mother was so kind to them, smiling wistfully when she mentioned her own dancing days, admiring their dresses and ready to provide anything they might need. In a quiet moment she thanked both Ellie and Daisy for all they'd done for Susie, a much happier girl now than when she'd left school labelled a failure. She'd be only too pleased to have them both again, should there be another big dance they all wanted to go to.

'Chauffeur reporting for duty, ma'am,' said John Sleator to his wife, as he came into the sitting room where Ellie and Daisy sat politely and Susie hopped up and down, quite unable to keep still. 'You're in luck, there's a Daimler tonight. Came in this morning and Richard and my best mechanic worked on it all day, so we could drive you in style tonight.'

'My goodness,' said Susie, staring down from the first-floor window to where the gleaming vehicle was parked outside. 'Is that it?'

'That's it, Susie dear. A 1927 Double Six 30. Not as sensational as the V12, but both King George and Queen Mary ordered one of these when they first came out. Fit for royalty and for three lovely ladies. All thanks to Sam Hamilton who found out what was wrong with it. Now, time to go. Sorry I haven't got a peaked cap.'

There was a flurry of goodbyes and thanks. Mrs Sleator reminded Susie to make cocoa for her friends when they came in. 'Have a wonderful time, all of you. Oh, and Susie, don't forget your alarm clock, you know I can never waken you myself.'

'Right, Mummy, I promise. Thank you for letting me have Ellie and Daisy to stay, it's been lovely. They are so good to me,' she said, kissing her mother briefly and making for the door.

John Sleator drove the long way round to the City Hall and when they arrived within sight of it, he was delighted to see that there were NO PARKING notices outside. Then he laughed to himself. As the event was being run by the Royal Ulster Constabulary, it was hardly surprising they'd thought of controlling the traffic.

He glided to a halt in front of the entrance, jumped out, opened the rear door of the vehicle and handed out his three young ladies. The looks on the faces of the uniformed constables by the main door, clearly impressed by the Daimler and by its contents, was worth all the effort. As he drove home to his wife, he wore a broad grin. It was the sort of story you could be forgiven for telling more than once.

Although it was broad daylight outside, the ladies' cloakroom was a blaze of light, already crowded with women of all ages, wearing dresses that ranged from the very latest styles in short frocks to long skirted creations in silk and taffeta brought out yet once again for this yearly

247

occasion.

'D'you not think we're a bit early to go in?' asked Daisy anxiously. 'We wouldn't want to be the first.'

'That's probably why this cloakroom is so full,' suggested Ellie, 'they're all saying the same thing,' she went on, as they struggled through the press of bodies to hand over their coats.

'Oh, do let's go in,' said Susie. 'Even if we *are* the first.'

Ellie herself was finding the crush, the strong odour of perspiration and scent, the airlessness of the cloakroom, very oppressive and the longing in Susie's tone was so obvious. The dear girl had waited for months. What did it matter if they did turn out to be the first?

'Why not,' replied Ellie, looking into the shining eyes.

They squeezed out through the crowd and breathed again on the cool airy staircase, crossed the landing and stepped into the dimly-lit ballroom. The floor was empty, but as they entered, the band struck up the first number of the evening and the three young men standing with their backs to the entrance turned round and came towards them, revealing themselves as Sam Hamilton, Frank Armstrong and Richard Sleator.

Whether they had been waiting together, or whether it was just chance, Ellie never discovered, but as Sam Hamilton held out his arms to her, she had a sudden feeling that the evening was going to be a happy one.

They moved around the floor as if they'd been dancing with each other for years, saying little, taking in the fairy lights and the festooned decorations, the familiar faces of other couples on the still uncrowded floor. The bank of fresh flowers edging the stage gave off a fresh perfume. Above them sat the band, lined up in their smart dinner jackets, playing as if they would never tire.

'Well, that's number one,' said Sam smiling down at her at the end of the first sequence. 'First and last and two for my birthday,' he added, reminding her of their agreement, 'and maybe a bonus for fixing the Daimler,' he added lightly, as he walked her back to Daisy and Susie.

It was almost two hours later before Sam claimed his next dance. Ellie had been partnered for every one in between and had enjoyed all of them. First Harry, then Stanley and Joe, Richard Sleator and Frank Armstrong and, to her great surprise, the Club Secretary, Charles Merrick, the precise little man with the neat moustache who'd apologized to her for failing to find her a tennis partner for the afternoon of the tournament last year.

'Are ye not tired yet? You've danced every dance. How do you do it?' he asked, as they moved easily into a slow waltz. 'And you standin' all day?'

'And what about you? Don't you stand all day too?' she came back at him, laughing. 'And bending over as well.'

'Sometimes I get a wee lie down,' he said, his

249

eyes twinkling.

She raised an eyebrow at him.

'Mind you, the concrete's pretty hard and John doesn't provide cushions.'

'I've got plenty of cushions,' she retorted, laughing, 'all shapes and sizes, but very little chance to sit on them.'

'We could go up on the balcony and watch for a wee while. See how Susie is gettin' on, until they call us for supper.'

She nodded slowly. 'I hate to admit it, but I *am* tired but I still don't want to miss anything.'

'Well, we can see everythin' goin' on from up there, better actually than down here.'

They made their way up the two flights of shallow stairs to the next floor and stepped down the steep aisle between the rows of cushioned seats to the very front of the balcony. Here and there in the dimmer corners behind them entwined couples were quite oblivious of their passing.

They leaned over the broad edge and looked down. Picked out all their friends as they appeared. Said what a great band it was, how beautiful the lights and decorations were, and then sat back comfortably with a sigh in their cushioned seats, the long day catching up on both of them at last.

'Did your sisters like the wee rose bushes?' Ellie asked, when the silence between them seemed to have gone on for rather a long time.

'Aye,' he beamed at her. 'That was good luck meetin' you that day. You were a great help.'

'Oh Sam, I only encouraged you to choose

what you'd have chosen anyway,' she said dismissively.

He shook his head vigorously. 'It wasn't just that, Ellie. I'd had a bit of a shock that day. Ye helped me get over it.'

She looked at him, startled, concerned by a tone she'd not heard in his voice before. She waited to see if he would go on.

'Last year, I was engaged to be married, Ellie, and the girl broke it off,' he began, looking down at his large hands. 'I'd the furniture bought an' we were just waitin' for a house we could rent. I was that upset I thought of goin' to New Zealand. I had the plans made, though my two sisters told me it would do no good. The only way was to face it here.'

He paused for so long, Ellie wondered if he'd be able to continue.

'You said you'd given your sisters a bad time,' she prompted gently.

He nodded again. 'I blamed myself for what had happened. I thought it was me had done somethin' amiss and I couldn't face thinkin' about it every day, comin' and goin' to work, aye an' at work too. I never knew when it was goin' to come over me. I just wanted to get away from the thoughts of it. That day I met you in the market I'd found out it wasn't me at all. It was somethin' she'd done.'

He paused and laid his hand on hers as if to underline the point he was about to make.

Ellie didn't move her hand away. She just waited, anxious for him to finish the tale, for it had taken away the ease from his body and the

251

sparkle from his eyes.

'Ellie, the worst of it was I nearly made a terrible mistake.'

'What was that, Sam?'

'I nearly let that woman drive me away from here. From this place I love and my home and my family. If it hadn't been for Da and Rosie and Emily, I'd a' been away months ago.'

'Oh Sam, that *would* have been so sad. You've a good job and you've friends and sisters here. You might have been very lonely away on the other side of the world.'

'Aye, that's what Emily and Rosie said.'

'I'm a bit envious of you, Sam. My sisters are *all* away,' she said suddenly. 'When things go wrong for me, I so wish I had Polly round the corner.'

'I can imagine that all right after this last year. Where is your Polly?'

'Peterborough, Ontario.'

'An' does she like it there?'

'That's the trouble, Sam. You can't always tell. Her husband Jimmy is with Quaker Oats. It's only maintenance work, all he could get when his company in Toronto went down. She has three wee boys and they've not much money. I know she makes the best of things, but I often wonder if she wishes she was home.'

Ellie watched as he nodded vigorously. He seemed quite restored to his good spirits again after the tension and distress of telling her about what had happened to him. She was touched by his concern for Polly and the way he listened so carefully to all she'd said about her.

'My granny always says you hear so much about those who go and make a great success, but you hear less about those who fail, an' hardly anythin' at all about those who come home, or those who spend their life wishing they *could* come home.'

'That sounds like a very sensible granny,' replied Ellie, smiling at him. 'I haven't got a granny either,' she went on matter-of-factly. 'Does yours live near you?' she asked, thinking how fortunate he seemed to be with his family.

'No. I wish she did,' he said sadly. 'She lives in Belfast now with my Uncle James. She used to live over Banbridge way, a place called Bally-down, but then Granda died and she lost her great friends, Richard and Elizabeth Stewart, so Uncle James asked her to come and live with him...'

'In Cranborne Park, off the Lisburn Road?'

Sam stared at her, eyes wide in astonishment.

'How d'ye know that?'

So Ellie told him how she had spoken to a woman feeding birds in the park and how they had become friends.

'I can hardly believe it,' he said, shaking his head yet again. 'And did you not tell her *you* knew a Sam Hamilton?'

'No, it never occurred to me. There are so many Hamiltons around Armagh I never thought of you,' she said, laughing herself. 'She told me a lot about her family, but she said even her grandchildren were getting middle-aged these days. That could hardly include you. She *did* mention a Sam Hamilton, but that was her son.

She said he always wanted to drive road engines. I'm not quite sure what a road engine is, but it must be a long time ago. James, Sam, Hannah and Sarah. Four of them. She told me a lot about each of them, but she didn't get as far as grandchildren.'

He brought his other hand over to join the one already resting lightly on hers, took her hands firmly between his and squeezed them.

'Just wait till I tell her,' he said beaming at her, 'that I know her wee friend Ellie Scott. I'm going up for her birthday in a fortnight. She's going to be eighty. Did she tell you that? She'll never believe me that I know you.'

Ellie looked at his smiling face and laughed.

'I can always tell her myself, Sam. She's invited me to her birthday party, so I'll be going too.'

Before Sam had quite taken this in, the Master of Ceremonies announced that the First Supper would be served in the basement. They consulted their tickets, were pleased to find that First Supper included them, and five minutes later they were sitting down at a small table where Susie and Joe had kept seats for them.

The talk was lively, but did not interfere with the consumption of a generous supper of cold meats and salads, fresh rolls with butter, fruit trifle with cream, and coffee.

Ellie looked across the table at Susie to see if she was enjoying herself. To her surprise, she found that the girl who was always talking, joking and laughing was eating her trifle very slowly and listening with close attention to something Joe was saying.

'My goodness,' she thought to herself, 'how little we know of people if we always see them in the same situation.' She'd seen these two talking to each other over and over again in the last months, but there was something she saw now she'd quite missed. Susie wasn't just ensuring that Joe wasn't left out of things, she was quite absorbed in what he was telling her. For his part, Joe was talking to her with a quite new confidence. A moment later, he stopped and she laughed. An easy, happy laugh which clearly delighted him, a laugh that spoke of something more than friendship. Susie wouldn't be sixteen till November. But then, Ellie thought, she'd been younger than Susie when she and George first went out together.

'Could you manage another wee dance, d'you think, Ellie, now we've got a bit more energy?' Sam asked, as they rose from the supper table.

'That would be lovely,' she said, taking his hand as they wove their way through the next instalment of hungry people waiting expectantly outside the supper room.

The dance floor was emptier, the band reduced in number, the lights dimmed somewhat further. They said little to each other but when the dance sequence ended, they made no move to separate and when the Master of Ceremonies announced the Last Supper they laughed with everyone else.

Moments later, they moved into a vigorous quickstep as the band got their second wind, much refreshed by their supper and the encouragement of the dancers.

'You're a lovely dancer, Ellie,' he said, as they paused once again, stood side by side, clapping the band.

'You're not so bad yourself,' she said lightly.

The moment she spoke a wave of sadness swept over her just as it had in the supper room when she'd looked at Susie and Joe and heard them laugh together. It was so unexpected, she nearly missed her step as the band struck up again.

In the relative quiet after the applause when the dance ended, they noticed the Master of Ceremonies bend down to the dance floor and take a note from a member of the committee. He came forward to the microphone, his face inscrutable. He waited and waited, till he had all their attention.

Ellie wondered what on earth could have created such a solemn face and began to feel uneasy. Sam fidgeted at her side, then suggested it might be the winner of the raffle.

'Ladies and gentlemen. It has been suggested to me by your committee that you might like to make requests for particular numbers. I cannot promise that we will be able to play them all, but we shall try. I have already received the first request. I have it here.'

He paused yet again, then his face broke into a broad smile.

'We will be delighted to play *If you were the only girl in the world*, for Sergeant Frank Armstrong and his partner Miss Daisy Hutchinson who have just become engaged.'

There was a riot of cheering and stamping and clapping. Without any previous signal, all the dancers moved to the sides of the ballroom, leaving Daisy and Frank quite alone. Daisy looked rather pink, but Frank was perfectly at ease. He put his arms round her and they circled the ballroom twice to the continued shouts and cheers of Frank's colleagues and the clapping of all their friends in the Tennis Club.

Ellie clapped as hard as everyone else but she had no idea at all what she was going to do if Sam should look down at her and notice the tears streaming down her face and splashing on the soft blue fabric of her best dress.

'I'll walk over to Sleator's with you, Ellie,' Sam said quietly as the last strains of *God Save the King* faded away. 'What about wee Susie? I can't see her anywhere, can you?'

Ellie looked around. Moments ago the members of the Constabulary had been so obvious by the set of their squared shoulders and the solemn look on their faces as they sang the National Anthem. Now they relaxed, moved, became again just young men at a dance. She scanned the faces that streamed past and spotted Daisy and Frank but there was no sign of Susie.

'I'll probably find her in the cloakroom.'

'Most likely. I'll wait for the pair of you outside. I don't think Daisy will need us to see her home,' he said nodding back over his shoulder.

But Susie had no more need of a companion than Daisy. As Ellie retrieved her coat, she saw

257

her meet Joe on the staircase.

'No Susie?' asked Sam, a hint of anxiety in his tone.

'I don't think we need worry. I saw her go off with Joe.'

'Ah well, she's safe enough with him. I always thought he was a desperate quiet lad, but there's a big improvement there. He seemed to be enjoyin' himself tonight. And so did Susie.'

He put an arm round her, drew her through the crowd milling through the double doors and out on to the pavement, waiting for friends, or getting into the few motors that had drawn up outside.

There was no moon and the only lamplight was the single gas lamp outside the Post Office, but the sky was perfectly clear and there was a mass of stars. Their pale light gleamed on slate roofs and was reflected back from the glass in the dark shop windows.

'D'ye mind the day you brought the parcel for wee Johnny?' he said as they moved quietly past the front of Sleator's.

'I do. I didn't know what to make of you that day,' she said easily. 'You gave me such a strange look, but then you weren't expecting to see anyone...'

They paused, crossed the empty street and slowed their steps. Ahead of them, Susie and Joe were walking very slowly, their arms entwined.

'Dear be good to them,' Sam said unexpectedly. 'If that's a match, it'll hardly suit the Sleators. Sure what prospects has Joe as a shop assistant?'

'He's a clever boy,' said Ellie, 'if he weren't from a big family, he might have gone to college and become a teacher or something like that, but he certainly won't be able to marry on what he'll ever earn at Freeburn's. Just like George and his ten shillings a week, clothes and his keep. That's why he went to Canada.'

Ellie stopped abruptly, amazed she had spoken so freely. But then, why shouldn't she? Sam was just as open with her. If we're going to be friends, then that's the way it should be.

'And does he like it out there?'

'I don't think he's terribly keen on the lumber camp, but it's a stepping stone. His uncle is a partner in a big lumber business in Peterborough, but he wants George to get experience in the camps before he comes down to the mills.'

'And the money would be good there, wouldn't it?'

'Oh yes, when he first told me he was going, I couldn't believe how much he'd earn.'

Sam smiled and nodded. 'Aye, I know all about that. Emily went and got a job in Macy's.'

'But I thought Emily was married and lived at Stonebridge.'

'Oh yes, she does. She met her husband out there. But he's from here, just outside Monaghan, and the two of them saved up to come home. He has a wee business now making car bodies, specialist work. Emily keeps the books. She's always been great with money.'

'Like Daisy,' she said, laughing. 'She can do a sum in her head while Susie and I are still looking for a piece of paper.'

259

They paused at the steps leading down to the broad walk crossing The Mall, the short way home to Sleator's house on the other side.

There was no one anywhere in sight. The green space at the heart of the city with its surrounding trees, lay absolutely still in deep shadow. Ahead of them, the marble slabs laid edge to edge all the way across to the matching steps on the other side shone like a bridge through the darkness.

'Wonderful night, isn't it?' he said, stopping and scanning the sky.

'It's a long time since I've seen so many stars,' she said wistfully, 'but then I'm not often out at two o'clock in the morning.'

'Ach, it's a pity that. Do you think George would be annoyed if you went out with your friends now and again?'

'I don't know, Sam. You know how people talk,' she began thoughtfully. 'The Club is great. I must say I'm grateful to Daisy, I'd never have thought of joining if she hadn't kept on at me.'

'Aye, she's good at that. Sure that's why I joined as well.'

'Aren't we lucky, Sam, we have such good friends?'

'We're lucky all right. We've an awful lot to be thankful for, the way things are these days. There's a lot worse off than we are.'

They walked together across the shining path, up the steps and turned along the pavement under the trees. They could see a light in the bedroom that was Ellie's. As they watched a light came on next door.

'That's Susie,' she said quietly.

260

'It might be a while before Daisy appears,' he said lightly.

She nodded, suddenly feeling sad that the evening was over, that he would turn away into the darkness, walk back up to Sleator's and ride home. In the deep silence, she would probably hear the roar of his motorbike as he headed out the Portadown Road.

'Ellie, I want to ask you somethin'. I don't want you to take it amiss.'

She looked up at his face, now visible in the spill of light from the windows above.

'If you and George hadn't grown up side by side and you hadn't been spoken for long ago, an' if you'd met me, like Frank met Daisy, or Joe met Susie, d'you think I *might* have been in with a chance.'

For a moment she felt overwhelmed with anxiety. What *could* she say? Then it came to her. There was no question about what to say. He'd been truthful with her. She could only be as truthful with him. She nodded.

'Oh yes, Sam. You'd have been in with a chance.'

'Good,' he said firmly. 'I'm glad about that,' he added as they crossed to Sleator's front door. 'I hope you're not tired out in the mornin'.'

'If I am, it'll have been worth it,' she said, putting her key in the door.

He stepped back, watched till he saw the door swing open.

'Goodnight, Sam. Thank you for a lovely evening.'

'Goodnight, Ellie. It was great.'

261

Sixteen

Ellie woke early on the morning of Rose's birthday party, blinked in the June sunlight, looked at the clock and gave thanks there was no need to get out of bed for another half-hour. There was a great deal to be done at home before Sam Hamilton and his father arrived to collect her for the drive to Belfast. As they were due at twelve noon, however, it meant she couldn't go to church and that would give her a bit more time.

Her father liked her to go to the parish church on the hill most Sundays, though he never went himself. She'd never managed to discover what had caused the falling out between him and the Rector. Even Charlie could only say it was about money. Though he couldn't be sure, he had a feeling that, once, when the Rector had come looking for subscriptions for the church fabric, Robert had told him he thought the church was too interested in money for its own needs and too little concerned for those in real poverty.

It had surprised her that her father should have spoken out so strongly, for he always tried to be on good terms with everyone, unlike Charlie, who didn't care who took offence at what he said provided he knew what he was saying was true. But then, she reflected, people were always capable of surprising you.

She thought of Susie and how slow she'd appeared when she first came to Freeburn's. And Joe, who'd been good enough at his job but so desperately quiet they could hardly get a word out of him. As she'd gained in confidence, she'd revealed just how practical and imaginative she could be. Since she'd finished redecorating the staffroom she'd been looking out for other ways of making life easier and more comfortable for all of them. As for Joe, he'd amazed everyone including Mr Freeburn himself.

'Miss Scott, I wonder what you think of these,' he'd said, as he waved her to a chair one morning only last week.

He'd passed over some documents he'd been studying.

She leafed through a collection of graphs and diagrams beautifully drawn and neatly labelled in Joe's small but very legible hand with coloured inks to distinguish particular points he wished to emphasize. She'd been so fascinated by them, it was several minutes before she realized exactly what Joe had done.

'So this graph is the turnover for the shop and this is the breakdown by department,' she began, running her eyes up and down the coloured lines. 'And these circular charts show which lines are most profitable and at which time of the year.'

He nodded and looked pleased. 'Are there any surprises there, Miss Scott?'

'Well, yes. I know we sell a lot of curtain fabric, but I didn't think there was quite so

263

much, or so profitable. And I didn't know, or had never noticed, we sell most of it in October and November. I suppose if I'd guessed, I'd have thought it would be the springtime.'

'It seems Mr Hanna has been most observant,' he said, nodding vigorously.

For a moment, Ellie couldn't think who Mr Hanna was. She smiled to herself when she realized it was Joe. But it was significant Mr Freeburn had never mentioned him before. This was the first time he'd done something on his own initiative.

The thought of Joe's achievement and Mr Freeburn's enthusiastic response delighted her. It was one more thing to add to the pleasures of this summer, the dance, the evenings at the Tennis Club, and Daisy's engagement.

It was hard to believe that only a year ago, Daisy was distraught because their landlord had served notice and the anxiety it produced had made her mother even iller than she'd been. But all that was over and gone. There'd been no more difficulty with the landlord since Mr Free-burn had intervened and her mother was now completely recovered thanks to Doctor Richard Stewart.

She'd doubled her flock of hens last summer and added some turkeys to rear for Christmas. Since then, they'd had no trouble paying the rent. Daisy said they still hadn't paid the arrears, but they were saving up a little each week in case the outstanding debt should suddenly be presented.

Daisy looked so happy these days, the ring on

her finger still so new she kept glancing down at it as she cut cloth or made up a parcel. It was not a diamond ring, but it was old and pretty and had once belonged to Frank's grandmother. He'd had it in his pocket the night of the dance, not sure if it would even fit, but it had. Ellie would never forget drinking cocoa at three o'clock in the morning with Daisy and Susie, both of whom were far too excited to want to go to bed.

It was a year now since she'd waited so anxiously for George's first letter. He'd said before he went it would need a year, or two, to save up for her ticket, or come home to marry her. Yet not once since he'd gone had he mentioned a time or a date. All he ever said was how much he missed her and longed to be with her again which might be true enough but wasn't much to help her with the waiting.

She turned on to her left side, stared at the beam of light striking the rag rug in front of her washstand and found herself thinking of Sam Hamilton. A dozen times now she'd caught herself going through that last little piece of conversation they'd had after the dance, standing under the trees on The Mall opposite Sleator's house.

If there had been no George, might he have been 'in with a chance', he'd asked. And there was only one answer she could give. Indeed, yes, he would. He certainly would. She'd never met anyone she'd liked better nor felt easier with. Except always George, of course.

Sam was someone she could talk to. He listened and he shared his thoughts with her. He'd told her about his bad upset as well as about his good fortune in having father and sisters to help him see that running away wasn't the answer.

If he'd gone off to New Zealand, they'd never have met, never danced together, never walked home in the starlight and she wouldn't be going up to Belfast today by car to meet his sisters and to talk to Rose. It would have been such a pity to have missed all that.

She had no idea what she was going to say to Rose about George and his letters and their plans for the future, or rather, the lack of them. But perhaps it would come to her on the drive. There was something about Sam's presence that always made her feel steadier.

Suddenly, she felt uneasy and anxious. It still wasn't seven o'clock, but she slid out of bed and poured water into the china basin from the tall, flower-scattered jug. There was no doubt about it, every time she thought about George and the fact he'd still offered no plan for the immediate future, it made her feel uneasy. That was what she needed Rose to help her sort out in her own mind.

Sunday was the day Ellie did all the household chores her mother could not or would not do during the week. She had long since stopped asking herself whether her mother was really ill, whether it was simply 'nerves', as the doctor from Armagh declared on his regular visits, and if so what that might mean. Sometimes, when she thought no one was looking, Ellen could be quite vigorous. She'd clean out the hen-house or wash the floor, peel vegetables and make a stew, or even polish the furniture, but there was no method to her work. She did what she felt like doing and ignored the rest, knowing that her daughter would do it for her.

Normally on a Sunday morning before church, Ellie did the weekly wash and hung it out behind the gable of the old house where no one would see it, then caught up on the pans and saucepans left soaking in cold water under the kitchen table. She changed beds and ironed shirts and was grateful for the hour of physical rest provided by the Episcopalian service before she came home to cook a midday dinner.

Today, along with the rest, she made time to scrub the kitchen floor, then she emptied her bucket, rinsed her cloth and retired to her room to change out of her oldest skirt into her blue dress.

'Sure you're well late for church, Ellie. Could ye not read the clock?'

'Not going to church, Ma. I told you. I'm going up to Belfast to visit a friend I made when I stayed with Aunt Annie.'

'An' how long are you stayin' away? Who'll bring me the spring water if you're away?'

'I'll be back tonight, Ma, and Da brought two buckets in a while ago. Did you not see him?'

'Ah sure I can see nothin'. I've lost my glasses.'

By the time Ellie had found the spectacles, collected her jacket and handbag, the sitting-room clock had struck twelve. It was always ten minutes fast, but she still looked out of the kitchen window. A car was parked down on the road and Sam Hamilton was walking up the lane. Before she could go to the door, she saw her father put down the buckets of water he was carrying to the forge. He stretched out his hand to the young man.

'Sam Hamilton, I'm pleased to meet you. I'd have known you anywhere,' he said, his voice echoing on the silent air. 'Yer even more like your grandfather than yer Da. Is he in the motor?'

'No, Mr Scott, he isn't. He said to apologize to you. He wasn't planning to go to Meeting today, but there's a Friend from Belfast has come to talk to them about destitute children. He said he had to go. So I'm collectin' your Ellie first and then Da and Emily on my way through Richhill.'

'Ach, tell him I'm sorry I missed him. Is he well?'

'He's the best.'

'An' Rose, your granny?' he asked, a softness in his voice.

'She's rightly, too. To be honest, she's amazin' for her age. I hope I'll be as sharp if I get to eighty.'

Ellie heard her father laugh as she said good-bye to her mother and walked down the path to join them.

'Tell Rose I was askin' for her,' Robert instructed Sam as they both turned towards Ellie. 'Is that a birthday present?' he went on, nodding and laughing again as he caught sight of the carefully wrapped long stems of pink briar rose she was holding.

'Oh no, Mr Scott,' said Sam, 'we've been well warned. No presents, she says. That must be somethin' between her an' Ellie.'

'Aye an' there'll be somethin' between you an' me if ye go on callin' me Mr Scott,' said Robert with a short laugh. 'Sure didn't your grandfather serve his time with my grandfather and your Da an' I chase one another up an' down that field there.'

'I thought maybe I should use a Sunday name on a Sunday,' said Sam, his blue eyes twinkling. 'Especially when I've come to chauffeur this young lady of yours,' he added easily.

'See ye enjoy yourselves. An' tell yer Da to take a run over. Even if he hasn't some fancy motor home from work with him he can surely still ride his bike this far.'

'I'll tell him what ye said, Robert, and I'm glad to have made your acquaintance after all I've heard about you, one way and another.'

The two men shook hands. Sam took Ellie's jacket to carry for her and together they made their way down the lane to the car parked on the opposite side of the road in the entrance to Robinson's field.

Sam did a neat turn in the road and Robert watched and waved to them as they headed back towards Richhill.

He scratched his head and wondered if he'd made a mistake. Surely Sam was the young man who had bought the furniture for the girl that had let him down. Hadn't he told his father he wouldn't even look at another woman for many a long day.

269

Or could it be that Ellie had looked at him? Well, if she had, she could do a lot worse.

'Isn't it a lovely mornin',' he said glancing at her, as they drove slowly down to Scott's Corner and turned right through Annacramp. 'Granny's going to get a good day for her party. We'll be able to go out into the garden.'

'It's a lovely garden, Sam,' she nodded. 'She and I sat out there after lunch the day I went to see her last October. She says the only thing James hasn't done for her is move the Mourne Mountains to the bottom of it where she can see them.'

Sam laughed. 'Aye, Da says he's good to her. He's more than made up for the past, as it were.'

'What d'you mean, Sam? What happened in the past?' she asked, anxious that she might have misread a man to whom she'd taken a liking.

Sam drew in a deep breath and drove more slowly.

'James was very ambitious,' he began. 'An' as ye can see he's a big man now in the Government ... but he started off with Harland and Woolf as an apprentice. I don't know the ins and the outs of it, but he got very full of himself and very bitter. He couldn't say a good word about Catholics and I'm sure ye know Granny's father was Catholic and all that side of the family still are. There was a big row and James went off. He married into a wealthy family in Belfast but then he disappeared and nothin' was heard of him. Da thought he might be dead, but Granny said no. An' she was right. He came back, maybe eight or

270

nine years ago ... it was the year Rosie got married, for it was she who first met him at a Trade Fair in the City Hall. That was when she was with McGredys. After his wife died and his son went to live with his grandparents in Belfast, James went off to Australia. Slater is his son's name. He's an engineer. Goes all over the world. I've never met him, but Uncle James comes to see us and brings Granny regular. He and Da get on the best.'

'My goodness,' Ellie said, 'that's a story, isn't it? At least it has a happy ending. Poor Rose, she must have been heartbroken when he went away. She never mentioned that to me, though she's told me so many stories about her family. I loved the one about Hannah and Teddy, who was really Lord Cleeve, and how Sarah married Hugh Sinton when she was only eighteen. It's like something you'd read in a book.'

'Aye, and Granny herself, a wee chile thrown out on the road in Donegal that now has one daughter a countess and one a lady and a son up at Stormont ... and my Da, God Bless him, away at Meeting this mornin' to try and see how the Friends in Richhill can raise the money for another orphanage in Belfast.'

'Is that what he's doing?'

'Aye, otherwise he was lookin' forward to seein' your Da. They don't see each other often, but they seem to be very great, as the sayin' is.'

He broke off as they drove round Cannon Hill and he slowed on the steep downslope beyond.

'If you look over there to your right, ye'll see where we live. It's just over the level crossing,' he said, starting to laugh. 'I don't know why they call it a level crossing, it gets bumpier every year,' he added as they bounced across.

To the right, Ellie saw a wide-open farm gate. Beyond it, a long, low house, freshly whitewashed, a tall barn and a line of outbuildings standing opposite. As she looked, the small dark figure of a woman walked down the yard, a bucket in one hand.

'Isn't your mother coming to Belfast?'

'No, no, she isn't,' said Sam shortly.

Ellie took a cautious look at him and decided to say nothing, but she felt suddenly sad. All his liveliness and good spirits seemed to have evaporated.

A moment later, she caught him looking at her.

'My Ma doesn't get on with Rose, never has. Can't say a good word about her, though her an' my grandfather were very good to us when times were hard and there were nine of us to rear,' he said, matter-of-factly. 'Maybe it's jealousy. She's always resented Rose having a bit of money, though from what I hear Granda worked hard for anything he got. But then, maybe, it's that she and my Da don't get on. She hasn't a good word to say for him either. He just keeps on working, gives her money and says nothing. I don't know what went wrong between them. He'll never say a word against her.'

'Oh Sam, I'm so sorry. And there was I envious of you and your nice family,' Ellie began. 'We don't know the half of it, do we?'

Sam laughed heartily and Ellie paused, taken aback.

'I'm not laughin' at you Ellie,' he said quickly, 'it's just that all their lives Granny and Granda had that saying goin' back and forwards between them. She always said he never told her the whole story about anything. She'd have to question him to get it out bit by bit. But that was no hurt between them. They both knew he could never get things out. So they laughed about it.

'They were a great pair,' he went on sadly. 'What one failed, the other managed, and the other way about,' he added softly, a hint of sadness and longing in his voice.

'That's a good way to be,' Ellie replied. 'Two's better than one. It can be awfully lonely if you haven't someone to fall back on.'

'Aye, I agree with you there. An' when times are hard or you're hurt about somethin' that's when you know the real value of someone bein' there,' he said firmly as they slowed down outside the Quaker Meeting House in Richhill.

A tall, broad-shouldered man in a dark suit and well-polished shoes stood on the pavement looking round him and enjoying the morning sun. He walked over to them as soon as they stopped.

'Hello Da, this is Ellie Scott.'

'I'm very pleased to meet you, Ellie,' the older man said, shaking Ellie's hand. 'No, sit where you are, we can change over when we pick up Emily,' he added, getting into the back.

Ellie could see now why Sam's father had been such a help to his son. He had the loveliest smile. Slow and almost wistful, but full of a warmth and kindness she had seldom seen before.

Ellie quickly found out what good company Emily was and they talked away in the back seat, leaving Sam and his father to discuss in minute detail the performance of the engine, the fuel consumption and what they considered to be the design weaknesses. A new Morris, not long out of the showroom, it belonged to one of the Lamb brothers, a kind man who regularly lent Sam's father his vehicle for family visits.

'What about your wee ones?' Ellie asked. 'Did they not want to come?'

'Oh they wanted to come all right,' said Emily, shaking her head vigorously, 'but Rosie and I decided there'd be no great-grandchildren and James agreed with us. Rose is great as you know, but there's a limit. Sure they have me worn out and me about fifty years younger than she is,' she went on laughing. 'I'm sure Kevin will be exhausted when I get back, but bless his heart, he never thought twice about tellin' me to come on me own.'

'That's good of him. I wish my sister's husband could do the same. It's not that he wouldn't, he's not lazy or anything like that,' she explained, 'he's just no use with children. I suppose some men are like that.'

'You're right there. Some men has no notion what to do with we'ans. But of course, there's some takes advantage of having no notion. There's maybe some things ye just have to learn if you're goin' to bring up a family. Sure I'm no hand at all at cookin', but I have to make the effort. Mind you, Kevin helps me out. He'd make a good chef if he had the time.'

Ellie laughed, delighted by Emily's ease of manner, her openness and good nature. They talked about Macy's and why the pair of them had come home. About saving up and trying to make a living. About Emily's knack with figures, just like her cousin, Daisy Hutchinson. Then they spoke of Daisy and Frank's plan to marry in a year's time before Frank's transfer to another town was due to come up.

It seemed no time at all before they were parking under the trees outside the broad, double-fronted house in Cranmore Park. They walked in through open doors down the wide hall through into the high-ceilinged sitting room.

Ellie couldn't see Rose at first, which was hardly surprising. She'd never been very tall and she'd grown smaller with age though she had no stoop on her shoulders like some old people she knew.

Suddenly there was a burst of laughter and a group of people over by the French windows moved apart and Rose was revealed in their midst. She caught sight of them and came over at once, holding out her hands to embrace each of them in turn. Ellie thought she looked quite lovely. She was wearing a lavender blouse with a brooch at the neck and a dark-purple skirt. Her hair was pure white and caught up in a pleat at the back with a little beaded decoration round it that matched her earrings. She was not using her stick.

'Poor Ellie,' she said, as she kissed her, 'you've managed James, two of my Sams and

Emily, but you'll have a whole roomful of people you don't know. Except that you do in a way, don't you? You've got their stories, so all you need to do is attach the right story to the right person. I'll give you a start. That couple coming down the hall...'

'Rosie and Richard,' Ellie said promptly.

'Oh, well done,' Rose cried, 'how did you manage that?'

'Sam told me once that Rosie looked like you and she does.'

'Well, I'm not sure it's a compliment to Rosie, you'd better ask her,' she said as she put her arms round Rosie, then Richard and introduced them both.

James came and joined them, bringing with him Helen Sinton and her husband David, a tall, elderly man called Billy Auld, and a darker man with a Canadian accent, called Alex, with his wife, whose name was also Emily.

The sitting room was beginning to get very full and very warm so James urged everyone to go outside. Ellie thought it had been done so cleverly. As you moved out through the French windows you stepped into a marquee. It had been put up *over* the garden and you could walk around among the flower beds and shrubs while still being under cover. Now there was plenty of space and it was cooler. Although the sun was beating down on the white canvas of the canopy, a small breeze flowed in where two of the sides of the marquee had been rolled up. It moved the heads of the flowers and made ripples in the tiny garden pool.

Suddenly, Ellie thought of the roses she was still carrying. This certainly wasn't the time to give them to Rose, so she bent down, removed their wrapping and placed them in the pool. As she stood up, she found a slender, elegantly dressed woman with blonde hair streaked with grey looking down at her.

'I'm sure you're Ellie,' the woman said easily. 'Ma said you had a garden where we used to live as children and the briar rose might still be going. I'm Hannah,' she went on, bending to touch the pink roses. 'I remember playing weddings with a piece of curtain for the bride and a bouquet of pink roses. Could it possibly be those?'

'I don't know, but it would be nice, wouldn't it?' Ellie replied. 'To think of something from childhood still going on. I'd love to think that something I planted would survive long after me.'

Hannah nodded, her eyes sparkling.

'Yes, I often think the world I live in now is so far away from everything I ever knew as a child and a young woman. But then, when I married Teddy, all I wanted was Teddy. I never thought of having to leave Ireland or live in a big house with servants or going up to London ... and certainly not of having to play the Lady,' she added, laughing.

'Would it have made any difference?' asked Ellie.

'No, I don't think it would,' Hannah replied promptly. 'I think if I hadn't been *sure* of Teddy I would have worried about all those other

277

things, wondering if I could cope with the sort of people who lived in his world, though his mother, Lady Anne, was lovely. She'd have worn wellington boots at the Palace if she thought the lawn was going to be wet,' she said laughing again, a lovely soft laugh that made you want to laugh with her, even if what she'd said hadn't been funny in the first place.

'Are you about to get married, Ellie?'

'I was, but we had no money, so George went to Canada to save up. That was a year ago.'

'How long did he think it would take?'

'A year or two, he said.'

'And would you like Canada?'

'I'm not sure. I do have a sister there and I'd so love to see her. I miss her terribly.'

'Yes, I miss my sister too, and I'm an awful lot older than you. And I have lovely daughters as well, so I've no excuse.'

'Isn't Sarah coming?'

'No, I wish she was, but she's in Berlin with Simon. Have you heard of a Herr Hitler, recently come to power?'

'Oh yes. My friend Charlie Running says he's a dangerous man. That he needs to be watched.'

'Your friend is wiser than most of the British Cabinet,' she said with a sharpness that surprised Ellie. 'Indeed he does need to be watched. That's why Simon is in Berlin. Officially, he's part of a so-called Trade Mission, so it's important his wife is with him. It makes it look innocuous. Anyway, Sarah is not keen to leave him. It's a quite dangerous situation. I shall be so grateful to have them back in Britain even if she's stuck in London and I'm in Gloucestershire. Poor you, with Polly so far away.'

'But Rose has been very kind to me. She knows I don't have anyone older to turn to. I'm going to ask her what to do about George.'

'Is there someone else?'

'Oh no,' she said, quickly, 'it's just very hard to know what to do for the best. He's not very good at writing letters and he doesn't always answer my questions.'

'Doesn't that tell you something important about him?'

'Well, yes, but George has always been like that. He doesn't think a lot about things. But he's very good-natured and a hard worker.'

'How long have you known him?'

'All my life...'

Ellie might have said more but the vigorous banging of a gong and the movement of people back through the French windows prevented further conversation.

'Ellie,' said Hannah, taking her arm and walking with her, 'sometimes if we are too close to people we cannot see them at all. Take your time and talk to Ma when you can. She knows you better than I do, she'll be able to help.'

They parted as James directed traffic through to the dining room where he had somehow managed to seat some thirty people in a normal family-sized room.

Seventeen

Ellie had thought the sit-down supper at the Tennis Club Dance was very pleasant, but when she saw the laden tables in the dining room at Cranmore Park she was quite overcome. To begin with, it looked so lovely. The large platters with a variety of cold meats were decorated with sprigs of parsley and quarters of little tomatoes, lemon slices and miniature carrots. Set at intervals along the narrow tables in china bowls or dishes, themselves decorated with tiny flowers, were salads and side dishes of rice or potato or crisp green leaves.

Despite the narrowness of the tables, a line of posies ran the whole length of each one with buds and blooms from Rose's own garden set off by white daisies and feathery green fern which must have come from a nursery or a florist. The whole effect was so colourful, she felt quite sad when everyone sat down and began helping themselves and their neighbours, passing dishes backwards and forwards.

'I think you'd prefer this one, Ellie,' said James, smiling as he leant over and filled the slim wine glass by her plate with a sparkling white wine. 'If you don't like it, give it to Richard here. He'll drink anything, won't you

Richard?'

'Everything in this house is worth drinking, James,' he replied with a grin, as he nodded towards the bottle in James's other hand.

James poured a glass of red for him and waited while Ellie took a cautious sip.

'Well?' he said, encouragingly.

Ellie nodded and thought for a moment. 'It's like spring water at first, but then it tastes like the smell of flowers.'

James nodded and looked pleased. 'I'll remember that, he said, holding up the white wine bottle so that Richard could see it. 'Remember this is the one for Ellie when the next lot comes round,' he said, as he moved on along the tables.

She had Richard Stewart on her right and a man whose little place-marker card said Brendan McGinley on the other. He was a strongly-built man with dark hair and brown eyes that moved continuously, taking in everything around him. Beside him, across the end of one of the three long tables lined up parallel to each other was Ned Wylie. Directly opposite her sat Sam and Rosie.

Ned and Ellie looked at each other in amazement as they sat down.

'I didn't know you knew Rose,' said Ellie.

'I could say the same to you,' replied Ned.

'Now hold on here,' said Brendan, who had a soft southern accent. 'I don't know either of you good people nor that handsome young man over there,' he added, nodding at Sam. 'I met Rosie and Richard in the hall, but who are you two for a start?'

'That's a good question, Brendan,' said Rosie, laughing, 'but might I suggest we fill up our plates first, before our friends and cousins further up the table start sending down for re-inforcements.'

'What a practical lady you are,' said Brendan. 'You are certainly a Hamilton. They're a very practical lot.'

'Now what makes you say that, Brendan?' asked Richard, eyeing him with interest.

'I was just thinking back to one night in Dublin when I dropped in on your Aunt Sarah,' Brendan began. 'There was a wee bit of bother goin' on at the time. Easter time, 1916, it was and I had the misfortune to be on the losing side, but Aunt Sarah took it all in her stride and fed me jam sandwiches. I hadn't eaten for a while and I'll never forget the taste of those sandwiches. Then, if memory serves me, while I was being escorted to the docks to be entertained by His Majesty in Wales, a whole battalion of Hamiltons drove down from the North, penetrated the barricades, and sprang Aunt Sarah with Helen and Hugh and returned them to the safety of Ballydown. I'm sure they're here today but I'm not sure I'd recognize either of them.'

'So you must be one of the Donegal McGinleys,' said Rosie, beaming at him. 'Aunt Sarah used to play football with you in Creeslough.'

Brendan nodded.

'And you went back to Ardtur with your Uncle Sam, who was Rose's brother and he found the doorstep of the house from which they had all been evicted in 1861,' said Ellie slowly, as she

282

recalled the details of the story Rose had told her.

'Right, young lady, right,' said Brendan, bowing to Ellie. 'Now will someone introduce me to this lovely young lady. Is she a Hamilton or is she just thinking about it?'

'Brendan,' said Richard, putting down his knife and fork, 'let me introduce Ellie Scott, granddaughter of Thomas Scott, with whom John Hamilton served his time...'

'And with who's help, my brother Sam, sitting here beside me, managed to win the Tennis Tournament at the RUC Tennis Club last year, the first sporting achievement by any known Hamilton,' added Rosie, who was enjoying herself enormously.

'Now, I've got you nearly all,' said Brendan. 'Two Hamiltons, one Stewart, one Scott, now how about the Wylie?' he said, picking up Ned's place marker and peering at it.

'Well, you could say I got thrown in with the Hamiltons,' said Ned.

'Or thrown out,' said Ellie soberly.

'Or even threw another Hamilton in,' said Sam laughing.

It was Ellie who explained the riddle to Brendan when they all stopped laughing.

'Ned lives not far away from where I live at Salter's Grange and when he was a wee boy he went on a Sunday School Excursion. His mother, Mary, and Rose were close friends. James and Sam and Hannah and Sarah were all there. They got out before the train ran away. Ned's mother didn't, but she had just enough time to throw him out. He was only small.'

'And he landed in a briar bush,' added Ned cheerfully.

'Then,' added Rosie, 'when our cousin Alex arrived back from Canada looking for his family, Ned found him at Annacramp and brought him to Ballydown.'

'So that's what you mean about him throwing in another Hamilton?'

'Yes,' said Sam, who had been watching Ellie and taking it all in. 'That's Alex over there with his wife Emily. His young son was born the week Granda died, so there's another John Hamilton at Ballydown.'

'Aye, and there's a couple more Rose McGinleys around, come to think of it,' said Brendan. 'My Uncle Sam had six sons and there's more than a few Roses among their daughters in New York State and thereabouts.'

As the meal went on and Brendan asked his questions about people he could see but didn't know, Ellie would have liked to have known more about the man himself. He was comfortably dressed, very relaxed in his manner but she'd noticed he never missed anything that was said.

'Rose told me her brother left you his little farm in Donegal, but you don't look like a farmer to me,' she said quietly.

'Quite right, you are, Ellie. Even when I did my best to cultivate the said acres I wasn't much of a hand at it. I made quite a good rebel in that I managed to survive, which was more than some of my friends did,' he said matter-of-factly.

'I fear I'm very respectable now,' he continued. 'I run a small bookshop in Dublin. After the excesses of my youth it appears I have inherited my uncle's passion for text. I'm not a millionaire, but I own millions of words,' he said, his eyes twinkling with pleasure.

She'd have liked to ask him how he'd come to run a bookshop, but unfortunately the opportunity disappeared when two young girls in summer dresses and white aprons and two young men in shirts, ties and flannels with similar white aprons came into the room and did a remarkable job of disappearing the central table while leaving its former occupants comfortably seated at one end of what had now become a hollow square.

With this new arrangement, Ellie could now see a short table running across the room. Rose was seated in the middle between her son, Sam, and her daughter, Hannah. Next to Hannah was an empty chair into which James descended at intervals to speak to Hannah or to catch up on his own lunch. Beyond Sam's father sat a very attractive, dark-haired girl with a most lovely, lively smile and a rather serious-looking young man.

'Richard, do you know who the two people at the end of the little table are?' Ellie whispered, in the growing silence which had descended at the end of the meal and continued through the rearranging of the room.

'That's Aunt Sarah's daughter, Helen Sinton, by her first marriage. And that's Hugh, her brother. He's an old friend of mine so I'm hoping to get a word with him later. You know there's going to be an airport in Belfast very soon, don't you?'

'Goodness no, I didn't. Where will it be?'

'Not very far from the city. Up towards Antrim, place called Nutts Corner, so Hugh tells me. He designs aircraft but he has his pilot's licence. He's thinking of doing some flying to help them get started. Not many pilots around yet.'

Into the sudden hush, the four young people appeared carrying a birthday cake with a single candle. It was not a huge affair, but they'd put it on a small table and now carried it, one at each corner, to place close against the short table exactly opposite Rose. James leaned forward and lit the candle.

'Happy birthday, Mrs Hamilton,' they said in chorus.

'Thank you, my dears. You've been splendid. Please don't go till I've sent you out some cake to take home.'

Rose paused and looked around the room, everyone now completely visible to everyone else.

'Blow out the candle, Ma,' said Sam quietly.

'Oh yes, of course...'

The candle went out first time and as it did everyone stood up and sang Happy Birthday. They clapped and clapped and Ellie wondered why it was that tears should spring to her eyes when she looked at the small, composed figure. Then there were cries of Speech, Speech, Speech.

Ellie assumed that James might say a few well-chosen words. She rather gathered that he often had to address large audiences and sometimes audiences of very prominent people. But James kept his seat, his eye on his mother.

Rose got to her feet.

'Well now,' she said, 'as you've all come because I asked you to come and many of you no doubt at some inconvenience,' she went on, casting her eyes round the gathering, 'you are entitled to whatever you might ask for. Even a speech,' she said, shaking her head, as everyone laughed.

'I am indeed unaccustomed to public speaking,' she began, to further laughter, 'but I have never failed to say what I thought to any member of my family ... and I hope they'll forgive me for that...' she added, dropping her voice slightly.

Ellie was amazed. She had always enjoyed Rose's capacity to laugh at herself, but she'd never imagined she'd be able to stand up in front of so many people and make them laugh and wait upon every word.

'But I've never had the chance to speak my mind with so many of my family all at once. It is an occasion too good to miss.'

There was another burst of laughter as Rose looked around her assembled guests.

'Over forty years ago, too many over for my arithmetic to be more exact, my two sons, James and Sam, told me to jump out of a moving train. Often, it is only after one has acted that one knows it was the right thing to do. So it was on this occasion. I jumped and took Hannah and

Sarah with me. The Sinton family from Armagh followed behind, together with two girls and their boyfriends, young shop assistants in Armagh.

'Had we not jumped, not one of us would be in this room today,' she went on matter-of-factly. 'It is not simply that I would not be here, my children and grandchildren would not be here, and there wouldn't be great-grandchildren waiting at home. Think also of the husbands and wives, the old friends and neighbours and the new friends I've made, who would not be here either. And those four lovely young people from the University who've been looking after us.

'This is not simply "my birthday" therefore. It is a moment to give thanks. However much we may have lost, and we have *all* lost someone or something dear to us, nevertheless, today we *must* celebrate. We are here, we are alive. The most precious thing in life is to have someone you can love and trust. I have been fortunate. I have had not just one very special person in my life, I have this whole room full of people I love and trust. Is it any wonder I don't need birthday presents?'

There was a moment of stunned silence, then a huge round of applause as Rose reached out her hand for the knife, pulled the cake towards her and began to cut it up in a most businesslike manner.

'Ellie, there you are,' said James, as he walked down the garden path. 'Was my lovely niece able to cast any light on the origins of your

288

rose?'

All around the garden, in the filtered sunlight of the marquee, Rose's guests sat or stood in twos or threes. Only her neighbours from the adjoining houses and her former housekeeper of many years had slipped away to leave her with her own immediate family.

'Probably no,' said Ellie, who was on her knees looking at a border plant she'd never seen before, 'but we decided we wouldn't let the facts get in the way,' she added, smiling at James as she stood up. 'Everyone remembers the pink rose, even Sam's father, and Sam says his father is no good at flowers. Wouldn't know a daisy from a dandelion. So Rosie and I have decided *this is* the Hamilton Pink. She's told me how to take cuttings in the autumn and how to bud, so by this time next year I hope to have lots to give away. Hamiltons first, of course.'

'That's a lovely idea,' said James nodding. 'Ma will be delighted. In fact, you've completely upstaged me,' he went on, laughing wryly. 'I was seriously thinking of asking McGredys or Dicksons to name a rose for her. It's quite expensive, but that doesn't matter. Knowing my Ma, she'll be far happier with what you produce. You must tell her about it yourself, right away. She did go up for a little rest, but she sent me to fetch you. She wants to have a word with you before she comes down.'

'Oh,' said Ellie, taken aback, 'are you sure she doesn't just want to be quiet a bit longer?'

'Quite sure. I had strict instructions. Ellie and only Ellie was what the lady said. She's in her bedroom, but she's not even lying down,' he said as he turned and strode away.

'Oh Ellie, what a pretty dress. Is that the material you and Ruth bought when you were up on holiday?'

'Yes, it is, the one I was worried about because of cutting on the bias,' she admitted, smiling ruefully when she remembered sharing her anxiety with Rose.

'Come and sit here. I must go down *quite* soon, because there are people who have a long way to go and they'll want to say goodbye,' she explained, moving over on the window-seat to leave room for her.

'Now, tell me. Any news from George since you wrote to me? Or, more precisely, has he said anything since then about coming home or setting a date?'

Ellie shook her head. 'No, all he says is that he misses me and longs for us to be together. But he says that every time,' she confessed sadly.

'Well, he needs to do better than that, Ellie. He may not be naturally thoughtful, but in this situation, he simply has to learn and learn quickly. Now I think it's time you took more thought for what *you* want. No, let me finish,' she said, as Ellie opened her mouth to protest.

'We all have things we can do nothing about, like working in a lumber camp with no accommodation for women, but that doesn't mean that we don't talk about them, share them, see what could be done. Remember Ellie, in every situation there's always *something* a person can do. That's why so often, in the face of even a great disaster, people make a cup of tea. And one action often leads to another and that is when things start to improve. Do you see what I mean?'

'Yes, I do,' Ellie said firmly, thinking of the night when Daisy and her family were faced with eviction and they went together for an ice cream.

'I think you should tell George how difficult it is for you here at home, not knowing what he's thinking about your future. I also think you ought to make it clear that you want him to come home to be married.'

'But why so, Rose? I really don't mind where we're married, just as long as we can be together again.'

'But Ellie dear, you and the George that went away are unlikely to be at all the same people by the time you're able to meet up. It's just over a year since he went, isn't it? Well, he's clearly not coming this season, so it won't be before the ice melts in March next year. He doesn't say enough for you to know if he's changed, and besides, don't you think you yourself have changed if you think about it?'

Ellie blushed slightly. 'Well, no, I don't think I had thought about it.'

'I didn't imagine you had. I've noticed you tend not to think about Ellie, so that's my job. Old ladies shouldn't give advice, but some of them can't resist, so I'm going to ask you to do one thing for me. Don't *go out* to marry George. Stay here at home. Let him come to you and then make sure he really is the man you want, not just a man that looks the same as a man you loved when you were younger. Do you understand?'

Ellie nodded and caught her lip.

'Now we must go, but you'll be up again soon for your holiday won't you? I think Annie said August. We can talk about it then, but in the meantime, remember to tell George what *you* want. If he loves you, then he'll want that too, whether it's possible or not. At least he can write about it, can't he?' said Rose crisply, as she got to her feet, kissed her and gave her a hug.

'Ellie dear, would you go and fetch me a Hamilton, son, or grandson, any one of them will do. I'm too tired for the stairs without my stick and I refuse to carry a stick on my birthday,' she said, her eyes sparkling with laughter.

Neither Emily nor Ellie said very much on the way home. Between wine and food and the excitement of talking to so many new people, they were both tired out, but very happy.

They dropped Emily first at a small cottage in Stonebridge. Before the Morris had even come to a halt two little boys had run from the dwelling to climb up on the yard gate and shout their greetings. Kevin followed behind, a child in his arms, picking his way between pieces of axle and chassis overflowing from the barn opposite the house which he'd turned into his workshop.

He came and shook Ellie's hand, leaving it slightly sticky from the babies' bread and jam, while Emily told her to come over and see them whenever she got a chance.

As they headed down the steep lane towards

Richhill Station she heard Sam's father ask to be dropped on their way past the farm. When they stopped, he got out and opened the door for her to come and take his seat in the front.

'I've a wee job I need to finish while Sam sees you home, Ellie,' he explained, as he shook her hand. 'Tell that good father of yours, I'll take a run over one night this week, all being well.'

'I will indeed,' Ellie said, as he looked in at the two of them. 'He'll be pleased to see you, I know.'

They drove off and bounced back across the level crossing. She could hardly believe it was only this morning Sam had made the joke about how unlevel it was. She looked at him sideways, his eyes firmly on the steep and twisty road ahead. The same square frame as his father, powerful shoulders, broad forehead, skin tanned, but not so weather-beaten. What was so different were the eyes. His father's were large, solemn and a misty grey. His, a startling blue. Even concentrating on the road ahead they seemed to be taking in more than most.

'Did you enjoy yourself, Ellie?'

'Oh yes, Sam, it was a wonderful party. I only had one bad moment.'

'What was that?' he said, startled, as he glanced sideways at her.

'When the two uniformed policemen came down the hall as I was coming to look for you or your father to help Rose downstairs. I thought something awful must have happened the way they just walked through the open door.'

Sam laughed.

'Ah dear, my fault. I should have warned you. That was Billy and Charley, the two eldest. They were both on duty. There was a meeting somewhere in Belfast this Sunday prior to next week's commemoration of Wolfe Tone. There's Protestants going to march down at Bodenstown, so they were called in reserve in case there was trouble. But whatever trouble they were expectin' mustn't have happened. So now you've met near all of my family.'

'Yes, and all you've met of mine is my Da.'

'Ach, never mind. I feel like I know Polly. She writes a good letter by the sound of it.'

'Yes, she does. When I read her letters, I can almost hear her saying the things. Like the time I told you about her finding Uncle Jim in Peterborough.'

'Aye, that was a good one. Does she ever think about comin' home?'

'I don't know, Sam,' she said thoughtfully, as he slid neatly into the entrance to Robinson's field. 'She might think about it on her bad days, but to be honest they couldn't afford it. Not with three wee ones.'

'It's a pity isn't it that so much comes down to money in the end?' he said, his blue eyes looking directly at her before he got out and came round to open the door for her.

'Lovely evenin' isn't it?' he said quietly, as they paused by the motor and looked out over the meadow beyond, the shadows of the cows long in the lowering sun.

She guessed what he was thinking. A lovely evening to walk the lanes with a friend. But however innocent their intentions, someone would see, jump to conclusions, and carry word of it back to the Robinsons.

'It's been such a lovely day altogether, Sam. Thank you for collecting me and bringing me home. I expect I'll see you at the Club,' she said, smiling at him.

'Oh indeed you will,' he replied, perking up visibly. 'We'll have to practise for the tournament, won't we?'

She crossed the road and stood at the foot of the lane to wave to him as he headed back to the farm. Then she walked up the lane, picked her way through the ploughs and harrows and half-constructed gates, and found herself thinking of Emily and Kevin who had saved up together to come home and to face the difficulties of one being Protestant and the other being Catholic.

'Ach, hallo son, did ye get wee Ellie home all right? There's tea in the pot. I think all that food and wine made me thirsty.'

'Thanks, Da. A mug of tea would be great. Aye, she's home safe and her Da'll be expectin' you next week,' he said, as he filled up a mug beside the paraffin stove on the workbench and added milk from the open bottle.

'Great day, wasn't it? Granny was in good form. I wish we could see your Auntie Hannah a bit more often and I missed Sarah,' said the older man sadly. 'But then, as Granny said, we're lucky to be here at all.'

Sam nodded as he drank his tea thirstily and made up his mind.

'Da, I want to marry Ellie Scott.'

'Ach, Sam, that's great news. You couldn't pick a nicer wee girl. When did this all come about?'

'No Da, it hasn't come about, I wish it had. Ellie's spoken for. Or rather, she was going to be married, but they'd no money so your man's away to Canada to save up.'

'Ohhh, so that's the way of it. I'm sorry, Sam. That's hard on you and you just getting' on your feet. Robert told me they were expectin' a wedding in the family, but I was a bit mixed up between his two younger daughters. I thought maybe it was Florence, who's older than Ellie.'

'What am I goin' to do, Da? I thought I loved that other woman but it was nothin' like this.'

'Well, aren't you that much further on? Now you know what you're lookin' for. An' all's not lost yet. Is the date set? Is she goin' out to him or is he comin' home for her?'

'I've no idea, Da. I couldn't bring m'self to ask.'

'Now you're not usin' your wits, son. Who do you think would know, barring Ellie herself?'

'A girlfriend maybe. Daisy? Or maybe Granny.'

'Yes, I think both of them would have a fair idea. It would do no harm to find out. As the saying is: *There's many a slip twixt cup and lip.* I know that went against you last time. It might be different this time,' he said reassuringly. 'I'll tell you this, however, that young woman will never do what a certain other young woman we know did. She's too straight for that. She'll not

296

break her word unless there's good reason. But there may well be good reason if she finds she doesn't love him as much as she thought.'

'So I might be in with a chance, Da.'

'Oh yes. If you bide your time you might well be in with a chance. That wee girl would be worth waitin' for,' he ended before lapsing into his more familiar silence.

Eighteen

The summer of 1933 had begun so happily for Ellie and it continued to bring small pleasures among the daily tasks. Although July turned out to be considerably wetter than June and most Orange men returned home from The Twelfth demonstrations 'with the shine off their shoes' as the country expression had it, August was continuously sunny, with just enough rain to plump up the ripening crops and satisfy the farmers need without spoiling the pleasure of young people who walked, cycled, or played tennis.

The very warm and fine September which followed such a good summer was a surprise to everyone. By the end of the second week, it had been so sunny, day after day, that the rainwater barrel at the side of the house was bone dry. A delph mug, lost for a year or more, reappeared at the bottom, cushioned on a thin layer of dried and cracked mud, none the worse for having

297

been dropped in accidentally and forgotten.

The unusual extension of summer was welcome to everyone. Usually by mid-September, one had only to step into the forge to hear a note of sadness, even anxiety, as the drop in the nights was observed and commented upon. By then, even on the finest of evenings, the sunlight was paling into dusk by nine o'clock whereas at midsummer the light had lingered till eleven.

It was the change in the mornings that affected Ellie most. Though she seldom complained about what could not be changed, she was always aware of the mornings growing darker. She dreaded the short winter days, having to get up and dress by candle light in a stone-cold room, a pattern like frosted ferns decorating her window and the odd sliver of ice floating on top of the water she'd have to use for washing.

Now, however, for the first time in her life, the thought of ice brought her some slight comfort. Yes, there were six months to go till the Spring, but thanks to Polly's encouragement, Ellie's mind was already moving forward to the first possible opportunity for George to come home.

Over the summer she'd taken Rose's advice and written more firmly about her need to know his plans for them. She told him that she wanted to know what he *would like to do*, even if it wasn't entirely possible. True, he'd made some attempt to reply, but he ended up saying he really couldn't tell her anything until he was back in Peterborough and could find out what plans his uncle had for him. Of course, he wanted to be with her, but until he was settled in his new job in Peterborough, he just didn't see how he could plan ahead. He was sure she'd understand.

What he said was perfectly sensible, but it was not exactly encouraging. As she admitted to Polly in one of her letters:

I don't see much point in saying anything more until he comes back down to Peterborough. When he does, I'll ask him to come and see you and Jimmy, if that's all right with you. It could be you'll get more out of him face to face than I've yet managed through letters.

Polly had thought that having George to visit them was a good idea. She'd done her best to encourage Ellie by saying the winter in Peterborough ought to give him long enough to see his way ahead. If he came down in October, he had five months before the seaway opened. Surely time enough to make things much clearer.

Ellie wasn't familiar with the St Lawrence Seaway. Beyond knowing where it was, she had no idea why its opening was in any way relevant to George. But Polly had been finding out on her behalf and it seemed that Uncle Jim was something of an expert on the subject.

They do try to get the St Lawrence Seaway opened at the beginning of March. As soon as there's the slightest rise in temperature or movement in the water, the ice-breakers are out, working up and down, opening the channels and encouraging the ice to break up even more.

It never occurred to me, Ellie dear, why they were in such a hurry but, of course, as the saying is, time is money. Well, it certainly is on the seaway. Uncle Jim says there's a fortune tied up in cargoes just waiting for the minute they can go. It's a loss to the owners if the ice keeps them back even by one day. So, set your mind at rest, by mid-March George ought to be able to get a sailing from Montreal.

The news that Uncle Jim and his wife Rebecca had become friends with Polly and Jimmy and now visited the little house in Hunter Street had pleased Ellie very much, but there'd been even better news from Polly in the course of the summer. Jimmy had been given a big step up at Quaker Oats. He was now in charge of a whole section of machines. Not only was the job more interesting and enjoyable, but his pay had been almost doubled.

Polly said she couldn't be sure, but she did think that Uncle Jim had had a hand in it somewhere. His son Tommy was a foreman at Quaker. He was the one who had given her such a turn the morning she went into the shop and thought she'd seen her brother. He'd been on holiday from Quaker then, just helping his father out. Now that he knew Jimmy himself, she did wonder if his father had asked Tommy to put in a word for him.

It wasn't just the extra money that was such a relief, Polly wrote, it was Jimmy being more like

300

himself. Doing a routine job, a menial job, had had a very bad effect on him. He was brighter now, in much better spirits and even making more effort with the boys.

Now Davy would be going to school as well as Eddie, she hoped she might be able to do a bit of dressmaking again. She missed her sewing and she was fairly sure she could find customers once she'd got her hand in again. As well as being good-natured and very kind to her and the family, Aunt Rebecca was one of those women who knew everyone. She didn't gossip, but she took in everything she heard, had a good memory and would be sure to know who would be in need of someone to sew for them. She was beginning to appreciate having an older woman she could talk to, Polly had added. It didn't make up for missing her little sister, but it was a comfort.

It gave Ellie such pleasure to think of Polly and Jimmy and her other friends here at home as she cycled to work on the first damp morning in mid-October. Leaves blowing in the fresh breeze and hawthorn berries gleaming red in the hedgerows reminded her, however, that her one sadness was that she was unlikely to see Sam Hamilton again till the Tennis Club opened at the end of April.

As the thought crossed her mind, she checked herself sharply. By then she might be Mrs George Robinson and be on her way to Canada.

She was shocked to discover the thought did not bring the glow of pleasure she had expected. What could be wrong with her today? Why did the thought of marrying George and sailing off together on the white hulled ship set against a blue sky she'd so often imagined no longer bring the same comforting feeling?

She tried to put the question out of mind, but once asked it wouldn't go away. Suddenly, she noticed she was cycling slower and slower as it buzzed round and round in her head. Even as she forced herself to speed up, she felt she could almost hear Rose, asking the same question herself, on the day of her birthday party.

Now the day came back to her, there was something else as well. Was it Rose, or was it Hannah who'd said that if you were quite sure of the man you never gave a second thought to the place or the situation? Yes, it must have been Hannah. She'd said she never even thought of having 'to play the Lady', because she was so sure about Teddy. Rose herself had left her home in Kerry, her mother and her friends and the mountains she so loved, to come to an unknown place called Annacramp, about which she knew nothing whatever, except that it was at the far end of Ireland and it was John's home.

Suddenly, it all went very quiet inside her head, as if the nagging buzz of questions and answers had simply stopped of their own accord. All she was aware of was the fresh, rain-washed sky, the patches of blue between the moving clouds and the slight hiss of her tyres on the wet road. Perhaps they *had* gone away, but even if they had, she was far from sure she'd answered any of them.

* * *

'Come in, Miss Scott. Do come in.'

Charlie Freeburn moved a comfortable chair for her to sit in front of his desk.

'Please sit down. Would you like a cup of tea?'

'Thank you. That would be very nice. Milk please, but no sugar.'

She smiled to herself as she saw him pour tea into cups normally reserved for distinguished visitors. She wondered if there was even a slight shake in the hand that held the silver teapot. Certainly he did not seem quite his usual self.

'I'm afraid I've had some rather bad news,' he began, glancing at her briefly as he passed over her cup, then staring into his own.

'Oh, I *am* sorry,' she replied quietly, wondering what on earth could have disrupted his usual imperturbable manner.

'Miss Walker has inherited a rather large fortune from an uncle in America,' he began matter-of-factly. 'She has given me neither a month's notice, which would have been courteous, nor a week's which is the normal requirement.' He paused for emphasis. 'Nor even a day's. She has simply telephoned to say she will not be coming to work today, *or ever again*, to quote her own words.'

'Oh dear,' said Ellie, dropping her eyes, and barely controlling the sudden urge to giggle at Miss Walker's most unladylike behaviour.

She took a deep breath, looked across the well-polished surface of the desk and found herself feeling enormous sympathy for his distress. However difficult he could be, he was always straight. He was invariably polite, even when someone had done something unfortunate, and he was perfectly capable of admitting that he was wrong, even to the carriers or the youngest member of his staff.

'The situation would be serious enough at this close point to Christmas, but how are we going to manage in the New Year? Miss Hutchinson has been most courteous in telling me of her marriage plans. She hopes to be with us till the end of April, but that depends on her fiancé's posting, which could come even sooner, and I am aware, Miss Scott, that you yourself may wish to leave for Canada in the spring.'

Put like that, his problem was glaringly obvious. The buyer, the Senior Assistant and an experienced member of staff all leaving within months was enough to upset anyone and a serious threat to the well-being of the business. She hadn't really thought about the fact that Daisy and herself might be leaving almost together and now Miss Walker had taken herself off, virtually without warning.

'Do you have any thoughts as to what we might do, Miss Scott?'

Ellie sipped her tea. It was beginning to get cold and she really was very thirsty. To her great surprise she saw a slight smile touch his lips as she collected herself and nodded.

'As for the buying, Mr Freeburn, I could take that over. Since I became Senior Assistant you've given me a great deal of freedom to make decisions. If you're happy about that, then it's only a matter of carrying the decisions through by going up to Belfast from time to time myself.'

304

'You would be prepared to take that on?'

'Yes, I would. Buying, yes, but accountancy, no. I have no gift with figures, but you have two members of staff who have, Miss Hutchinson and Mr Hanna.'

He nodded slowly.

'You are quite right. There is no reason why the buyer should also be the accountant,' he said matter-of-factly. 'It was simply a matter of convenience and it suited Miss Walker.'

He sighed.

'You have certainly solved the immediate problem,' he said, nodding vigorously. 'But where am I ever going to find a buyer when you leave me, Miss Scott?'

He looked so crestfallen, she almost wished she wasn't going.

'I do have one suggestion,' she said tentatively.

'You do? You know a buyer?'

'I know where we could get one.'

He opened his hands in a gesture of amazement.

'Mr Hanna,' she said, pleased with herself for remembering not to say 'Joe'.

He looked quite startled, peering at her closely to make sure he was hearing her properly.

'But the Ladies' Department?' he spluttered. 'Underwear? Corsetry?'

'I think that Mr Hanna would see such items merely as stock. Merchandise. You remember his graphs and charts. Besides, I think he could draw on Miss Sleator's knowledge. She may have been rather slow to accustom herself to how we work, but she hasn't any difficulty now.

305

If she had another six to nine months training with the idea of supporting Mr Hanna in view, I think she might surprise you.'

'Well, *you* do surprise me, but then you know the young lady's work much better than I, though I confess I can find no fault with what I see of it,' he said warmly. 'I must admit her mother has spoken to me most enthusiastically about her progress here.'

'Susie is entirely practical,' she began smiling. 'She needs to see a problem. Preferably lay her hands on it, like those old chairs in the staffroom she transformed,' she said, with a little laugh. 'Then she can work out a solution. She can't do things in her head in the way that Mr Hanna can.'

'My dear Miss Scott, I haven't offered you a second cup of tea. I'm so sorry. I confess I was somewhat dispirited this morning and totally preoccupied with my own problems.'

'When I have a problem, I cycle very slowly,' she began laughing. 'I forget that, at that speed, I'll be late for work.'

'I hope you don't have problems, Miss Scott. If I could be of any assistance...'

'That is kind of you. My problems are really more uncertainties. Things over which I have no control. Like not knowing when my husband-to-be will be able to come home from Canada to marry me.'

'May I ask what the possibilities are?'

'The earliest he can possibly come is mid-March when I'm told the ice breaks on the St Lawrence Seaway, the latest would be October, though of course, I hope it will be long before that.'

'Perhaps I might be able to make you an offer for our mutual benefit,' he began, completely restored to his normal self. 'Obviously your salary will be increased when you become our buyer, as from the beginning of this current month. But if you were able to stay till the end of June, to assist with Staff training in addition to buying, there would be a further increase. Perhaps helpful in setting up a new home?' he suggested, with a slight smile, as he named a remarkably generous figure.

Ellie began to shape a courteous refusal, then changed her mind.

'Perhaps you'd like to think it over,' he said, seeing her hesitate.

'No,' she said, somewhat to her own surprise. 'I think it's a generous offer and I'd like the new experience. Let's say the end of June. The summer is a much better time for travelling back and forth to Canada.'

18, Hunter Street,
Peterborough, Ont.
30 November 1933.

Dear Ellie,

Well, we finally managed it. George seems to have been so busy since his uncle sent for him a month ago now that it was only last night that he managed to fit us in and come for his tea. I had telephoned Robinson Lumbering as I thought he had gone back to the section he was in last year, but the foreman there told me he wasn't in the mill itself and to try Head Office.

Anyway, he came, looking very fit and well. He's very suntanned and seemed in very good spirits. He very kindly brought us all presents. Jimmy got a bottle of whiskey which was more than generous. I had a very nice plant and the boys had toffees. I think he enjoyed his tea. I did a big fry-up like we would have had at home when we had visitors and he tucked in and left a clean plate.

He told us a lot about the company and the opening up of new sections. It appears that lumbering was terribly important to the first settlers back in the 1800s but the whole business has changed radically since then. He explained how in the old days trees were cut in winter and sledded to the rivers over the snow to float down in the Spring. It was most interesting to hear about the different methods of controlling the logs. Sometimes rafts of logs were constructed, but this was not suitable for every location. In many rivers the logs had to be controlled by men who rode the logs, breaking up the logjams by rolling the logs loose with their spiked footwear. It sounded very dangerous to me.

I did ask exactly what he did at Head Office, but he said for the moment he was 'getting the feel of things' but it seemed to me he would be on the sales side. Huge amounts of timber go to Europe and he did talk about exchange rates and European currency. To tell you the truth Ellie, I didn't follow that bit as I was getting tired. I'd had a long day wanting to have the house nice for them coming. He was to have brought someone called Jimmy (was that the cousin from Portadown?), but he didn't show up.

I asked him what he thought of your new job and he said it was great, just great. He was sure you'd be very good at it. Finally, I asked him when he thought he'd be able to go over for you and he said: 'Now you're asking.' Then he said it was a very critical time for him, that what happened now would make a big difference later on. He was sure you'd want him to do the best he could.

He didn't stay late as he said they have to be in the office at 7.30 in the morning because of the invoices for the outgoing timber from the mills. He said he had to wash and iron his own shirts and he wasn't very good at it. But I must say the one he was wearing looked brand new. In fact, when he arrived I was worried the boys might climb up on his knee and mark his suit. It was very smart. He says all the young men have to wear smart clothes in his office.

Now Ellie dear, I hope I've told you everything. I'm very tired today for some reason or other though we weren't late in bed last night. I'm off to post this right away as I know you've been waiting to hear.

With lots and lots of love from us all and especially from your loving sister,

Polly.

She added a generous row of kisses, read the letter through again and sighed.

'Jimmy, I know yer readin' the paper, but would you just cast yer eye over this.'

He put his paper down, saw the look in her eye and reached out for the pale-blue sheets she'd been about to fold to fit the pre-stamped airmail envelope. Jimmy was always a slow reader and Polly sat fidgeting as she watched him working his way down the pages.

'Aye, well,' he said handing it back to her, the question unspoken in his eyes.

'D'ye think I've told it right?'

'I think ye've done a great job. Ellie's no fool. I think she'll read between the lines.'

'What d'ye mean? I was just trying to tell her all about him comin'.'

'Aye, an' I've said ye've done a grand job. It's a pity the man's so fond of the sound of his own voice and full of himself as well. If Ellie's any wit, she'll see it for herself. I don't think George Robinson has any plans for anyone other than George Robinson.'

'Oh Jimmy, you don't mean it do you? She's been goin' with him since goodness knows when. She loves him.'

'Aye, but does he love anyone but himself? Ask yourself that, Polly?'

Polly had known for a long time that something wasn't right and now Jimmy had put his finger on it. Just like him. He said nothing and said nothing and then when he did say something you knew he was right.

'What am I goin' to do, Jimmy? What am I goin' to do?' Polly asked, as she dropped her head down in her hands and burst into tears.

Jimmy let the newspaper fall on the floor and put his arms round her.

Nineteen

Although the February day had been bright and sunny the fields beyond the train windows were still iced with snow. Only where a south-facing slope showed green, a patch in the sparkling white carpet, or a bare hawthorn hedge had provided shelter and created a ragged edge, was there any break in the crisp blanket spread by a brief but determined flurry the previous evening.

The sun was going down in a blaze of gold, the sky almost cloudless, the River Bann full to the top of its banks, a perfect mirror of the pale sky above, as they steamed along through the quiet, empty countryside. No sign yet of even the earliest ploughing, the land still asleep. No animals either. Cows still indoors in warm barns, the hay stacked high to keep them fed.

Ellie took in every detail of the wintry landscape, delighting in this new perspective. This was the first time she'd done the weekly trip to and from Belfast in snow and she smiled to think what Polly would make of this light dusting.

Jimmy had bought a Box Brownie for Christmas so they could take pictures to send to family and friends and the ones she'd had of the snow in Peterborough showed it knee-deep compared with this little skim. Some were taken outside their small terraced house and even the window sills carried a depth of a foot or more. The pavements beyond were piled high, the cleared snow a compacted wall with a fresh coating on top.

The boys were shown up to their waists in the park where they'd built a huge snowman with other children from their street. Polly and Jimmy had posed in front of the enormous figure, and little Ronnie, held aloft on Jimmy's shoulder, peered down curiously, while the others all smiled for Uncle Jim who'd come with them to take the group picture.

It looked like a different world under the extraordinary thickness of snow and Ellie had wondered how people got to work and did their shopping and dried their clothes, but when she asked, Polly wrote back that people went on just as if it were perfectly normal. She thought the inhabitants of Peterborough would be just as amazed at the way everyone in Ireland expected to be rained upon, regularly and heavily, and didn't let it bother them unduly.

The train was warm and the regular rhythm was soothing. Ellie felt her eyes close and smiled to herself when they jerked open again as the train moved across a set of points. She didn't want to go to sleep. It was much too lovely watching the shadows lengthen and the last rays of the sun flash like fire behind the bare hedges on the horizon.

312

It wasn't surprising she was tired. It had been an early start and a busy day, but it had all gone very well. She had little idea of how much money she'd spent on behalf of Freeburn's, but she knew the prices of the individual items were right and the quantities she'd ordered were what would be needed. Joe would work out the figures from the invoices she had in her bag and she would laugh at the sheer size of it when he announced the final figure.

She thought Joe actually liked her to be so amazed at how much she'd spent. She'd told him once it made her feel like royalty. She'd heard they never handled money, just left it for someone else to see to the payment for whatever they required.

She leaned back comfortably in her seat and thought how amazing it was that tomorrow would be the first of March. Admittedly March could be as cold and unpleasant as January or February, but somehow one always felt better once March came. You knew the worst was over and however bad locally things might be, one could be sure they would improve.

Thinking of it now being March brought back into her mind the vexed question of George coming home. Long ago, she had taken Rose's advice and told him she would prefer to be married in Grange Church rather than go out to be married in Canada. At the time, he'd said that was fine, just fine. Whatever she wanted was all right with him, but he'd been gone almost two years now. 'A year or two,' was what they'd said when they parted, but two years on, they were no nearer to setting a date than before.

She couldn't bear the thought that George might no longer be the person she'd loved, or that she herself had changed in the time he'd been away, but she knew that could not be resolved, one way or the other, until they were face-to-face. She would just have to wait. It would be bad enough having to make such an awful discovery here in Ireland. The thought of it happening once she arrived in Canada she couldn't bear.

More than once over the winter, she and Rose had spoken about George and she felt what Rose had advised made good sense. Nothing that had happened since they'd first spoken about him had done anything to reassure her, and that's what was so troubling. No matter how she put it to him he still insisted he wasn't free to plan ahead for them. Now he was saying he couldn't leave the new job for any length of time, or not for a few months yet.

Sometime in January she'd suggested he come home for *a holiday* in May or June. By now, she felt, he *must* be entitled to some holiday. They could get married then and she'd follow him back when she'd completed her commitment to Mr Freeburn.

But, so far, he'd not said anything at all about the possibility of taking a holiday, though recently she'd had several letters that talked at some length about re-organization. New methods of marketing were also involved, about which he seemed very excited, though he didn't explain how these changes would affect him.

So absorbed did he seem to be in all the new possibilities now opening up for him in Robinson Lumbering that he'd managed to upset Polly, usually the most easy-going of people. She'd invited him to come and visit them at Christmas, but it seemed he was already booked up for all of the Festive Season. He'd told her he'd come and see them in the New Year. However, as Polly said crisply in her last letter: 'He's still comin' an' it's near the end of February.'

Now the sun had dropped below the horizon, the shadows were thickened very quickly, the landscape had grown bleak and unwelcoming, except where a farm set amid the fields, sheltering behind its windbreak, threw out sparks of light from windows and doors in both house and barn.

By the time the train picked up speed outside Portadown Station, the fields had moved from grey to black. As she looked out, all she could now see was her own face and the empty carriage reflected back at her.

'Rich-hill ... Rich-hill...

She glanced up from her book, thought back to the delight of a June day and wondered if the lights of the Hamilton farm would show in the darkness.

'Hello, Ellie.'

The young man opened the carriage door, climbed in and sat down, his clothes bringing a great waft of cold air with them.

'Hello, Sam.'

It was difficult to know which of them was

more surprised and they laughed as they explained themselves.

'I've a couple of days owing to me, so I've the motorbike stripped down,' Sam began, 'but there's a special solder I need an' we're out of it. They might have it at Turner's, or failing that, I'll borrow some from work. But I have to have it to finish the job otherwise it's the train or the bus tomorrow. Were you up in Belfast shopping?'

Ellie smiled at the way he ran his eyes over her smart hat and dress, her coat, neatly folded on the seat beside her, and the heavy, leather briefcase she'd inherited from Miss Walker in the rack above her head.

'Oh, yes, I've been shopping all right. You'd drop down dead if you knew how much I've spent,' she said, shaking her head, 'but it's not for me. It's for Freeburn's.'

'Ach aye, of course. You're their buyer now. Sure I forgot. Daisy told me all about it. She's terrible pleased about it. I think if it weren't for Frank, nothing would shift her from Freeburn's now. She says it's just great since that Miss Walker stopped bossing everyone around. She thinks even yer man himself was afraid of her.'

'Oh Sam, how funny! When he "promoted" her and she was no longer in charge of Daisy and me, I guessed that maybe he thought we'd do better without her, but I never thought of him being afraid of her. Maybe Daisy's right, she doesn't miss much. But I'm going to miss *her* when she goes,' she added sadly.

'Maybe you'll be goin' yourself very soon,' he

said promptly.

'Not before the end of June,' she replied, matter-of-factly. 'I'd expected it to be sooner, but I couldn't bear to see Charlie Freeburn left in the lurch by Miss Walker and then Daisy and me going at the same time. He's been good to me. I'm rather young to be a buyer, you know.'

'I always heard he was shrewd,' Sam replied quickly. 'That just proves it. You'd be good at whatever you put your hand to, Ellie,' he added, equally matter-of-factly.

'I'll take that as a compliment,' she said, looking across at him, aware of the brightness of his eyes even in the low lighting of the carriage.

'Aye, ye were meant to. You look powerful smart in that outfit.'

'It's a bit like a uniform, Sam. These women in Belfast would look through you if you just wore ordinary shop clothes. It's all about style. My cousin Ruth works in Robinson Cleavers. She says they don't give as good discounts if they think you're "up from the country". She and I have a laugh about me being "the wee cousin up from the country", but when it comes to business, it's no laughing matter. That's why I'm so smart,' she ended, turning her head and holding her hands out, so he could view the little close-fitting hat more easily.

'It suits you,' he said, honestly, 'But you're still yourself, thank goodness,' he added, as they slid into Armagh station and the squeal of brakes drowned out whatever he said next.

'Can I give you a lift, Sam?' she said laughing again, as they came out of the station.

A waiting taxi drew up and the driver gave her a wave and a smile.

'Dear goodness, I'm surprised you even speak to the likes of me. Hats *and* taxis,' he said, shaking his head in disbelief.

'Back up to the shop, Bob, please,' she said through the window. 'And can we drop Sam here at Sleator's. Unless it's Turner's you want,' she said, suddenly remembering and turning back towards him.

'Sleator's will do nicely, thank you ma'am,' he said solemnly, touching his forelock, as he opened the back door for her.

Ellie looked at his face, collapsed on to the back seat and had a fit of giggles.

'Sam, would you look at the shoes? How would I walk to Freeburn's from here in those,' she said, sticking out her small feet for his benefit. 'It's all part of the job.'

'So how'll you get home?' he asked, suddenly concerned.

'I'll get out of these clothes, put on my own things in the staffroom and add a pair of wellington boots if I think it's going to snow again.'

'Sounds like Cinderella?'

'Not as long as my bicycle doesn't turn into a pumpkin,' she said cheerfully, as Bob stopped opposite Sleator's.

'So long, Ellie. Hope I'll see you again soon,' he said quietly, as he stepped out on to the pavement. 'Thanks for the lift,' he added, before he shut the door and raised a hand in farewell.

She watched him as he walked across the road and disappeared between two parked vehicles.

As Bob drove off and headed up English Street, she caught herself wishing it wasn't two whole months till the opening of the tennis season.

It was already six o'clock before Ellie had gone through the invoices with Joe and had a chance to talk to Daisy and Susie about what they'd managed to do during the day. For a long time now, the three girls had agreed that they could keep things looking really nice if it wasn't for the customers. The shared comment kept them going when the customers were so frequent, or so difficult, that at the end of the day there was a pile of jobs outstanding. Then they had to decide what could be left for the critical half-hour in the morning before the shop opened and what simply had to be done before they were free to go.

Today, it looked as if the afternoon had been cold enough to keep customers away, so there was no backlog of garments to be folded and bales of cloth to be re-rolled. The sales ledgers and stock books were up to date. With three of them working, the sweeping, and dusting, and polishing of glass in the showcases, wouldn't take more than another twenty minutes.

'See you in the morning,' they chorused, as they parted in the entry, Ellie and Daisy wheeling their bicycles, Susie dropping into step beside Joe who had been waiting to walk her home.

Because she was later than usual, English Street was almost empty, the wet surface shining under the gas lamps. As she pedalled slowly along Railway Street, she realized there was no moon. By the time she crossed the railway line itself and headed out of town, it would be pitch black, only the light of her bicycle lamp to pick out the grassy verges with their surviving sprinkle of snow.

She was tired and cold and felt suddenly alone after the company and shared activity with her friends and colleagues, but there was no traffic on the road, the air was still, there was no more snow and she made good progress. After twenty minutes she found herself making a final effort up the hill to her own lane, the fresh white smoke from the forge billowing out against the dark sky, the faint glow from its main window a real encouragement.

'Hello, Da, Hello, Charlie. What's new?' she said, trying to keep her voice light.

Charlie made some sharp comment about politicians but she didn't catch it properly, the final words lost in a bout of hammering.

'Yer Ma's lyin' down,' her father said, as he thrust a horseshoe into the fire. 'But there's some dinner at the back of the stove. Yer woman Jinny is a right han' at a stew. She made it before she went.'

'That's good news, Da. I didn't know she could cook.'

'No more did I, but when yer Ma went to lie down, she said wou'd she put a bit of somethin' together and I said yes.'

'Glad you did, Da. I'll see you later. Cheerio, Charlie.'

Ellie wheeled her bicycle up to the house, parked it under the shelter of the elderberry

320

bush, pushed open the outer door, crossed the small, unlit hallway and went in to the kitchen. The room was empty, but the Tilley lamp was lit and sat hissing quietly on the table and the stove had recently been made up. She opened the metal window at the front and warmed her hands at the flickering glow. On the back of the stove, she found a dinner plate sitting on top of a saucepan of water with a lid over it. When she lifted the lid, she smelt the warm aroma of meat and potatoes.

She dropped down on the wooden settle and held out her feet in front of the stove. It was always a relief when her mother took to her bed and she didn't have to listen to a monologue of comment and complaint or sort out her confused questionings. She and her father had found Jinny to help with the housework when her new job no longer left her time to do all she'd been doing. It would be such a relief if she could help them out with some cooking as well and it would ease her mind to know there was someone to do it when she herself left home.

Although she was hungry, she found she had little appetite, but she finished her meal, washed up her plate and cutlery and put the teacloth to dry. As she straightened up from spreading the damp cloth on the metal bars over the stove, she saw two airmail letters, resting against the clock.

She felt her heart jump to her mouth, more with anxiety than excitement, as she reached up and brought them across to the table where the light was better. They were both for her. One was from George, a little thicker than usual, the other from Polly. Instead of a fat letter with extra postage it was only an official pre-stamped Air Letter.

She sat examining both envelopes, studying the postmarks, the stamps, the handwritten return addresses on the back, as if they would tell her what to do next. Then she collected herself, took a knife from the drawer in the table and sawed carefully along the inside of George's envelope to avoid damaging the thin folded sheets.

There were three sheets, not the usual two, but his writing seemed to have got larger. She read the short letter quickly, jumped to her feet, then read it again, anger and disbelief overwhelming her, as she walked up and down the kitchen.

Dear Ellie,

You know I am not very good at writing letters, but I do think of you so very often and I think I must explain why I have not been able to plan a holiday or a visit.

You see Canada is such a very different place from anything you have ever been used to. Peterborough is such a lively city, full of activity and large enterprises, not just Robinson Lumbering but Quaker Oats and the biggest electrical works in Canada and many others I may not have told you about. It is a very busy, noisy place.

The more I think of it the more I think you just would not be happy here. You are used to living in the quiet countryside and Armagh is only a wee country town compared to Peterborough. You are a home bird and now that I've lived in Peterborough for a while and have got to know it I think it would be wrong for me to take you away from all that you know and all your friends and family to bring you here.

It may be several more years before I have the opportunity to come home but I shall certainly want to see you. We had some good times which I shall never forget. I'm sure when you think it over you will see that I am right and that I have your best interests at heart.

Sincerely, your friend,
George.

She dropped the flimsy sheets on the table and burst into tears. It had happened. Some part of her had always known it would happen, but she'd never imagined it could come as a miserable letter full of absolute rubbish. For a moment, she was so angry she almost thrust the letter, envelope and all, into the cheering flames of the stove.

'No, Ellie, don't do that,' she said, jumping to her feet again and tramping up and down the empty room. 'Come on, dry your eyes in case Da and Charlie come up to the house and catch you.'

She did as she bid herself, then she fetched a glass of spring water from the enamel bucket in the press and forced herself to drink it slowly.

'A home bird,' she repeated furiously. 'He makes me sound like an idiot. A poor wee thing that has to be looked after. If he'd read his history of Peterborough, like I have, he'd have found that some of the settler women that came out from wee country places like here were every bit as tough as the men. Providing, of course, they had a decent man to work with. AND he's forgotten that he once said HE was a home bird.'

She paused, hearing a sound, thinking it could be a foot at the door, but a moment later the sound came again, clearer and sharper. It was the barn owl that lived somewhere nearby.

The lonesome cry of the owl in the darkness made her think of the book Polly had sent her, an old, musty-smelling book she'd bought at a sale in aid of the church. It had been written by a woman who'd arrived in Peterborough when it was still Scott's Plains. She'd gone north with her husband and young children on a trail marked only by blazes on the trees, to what would later become Smith, except there was nothing there at all, only a concession and a Lot number. This was a woman who'd braved the Atlantic and an unknown world full of danger, Indians and fevers, hunger and cold in the winter months.

George had no idea what a woman was capable of, had he, but then George hadn't much idea about people in general. In fact, she thought bitterly, he didn't have much time for thinking about other people, he was far too busy thinking about himself.

She stopped, startled. It was not like her to be so uncharitable, but perhaps that was *her*

324

mistake. Daisy always said she'd let George off too easily, he could do more. There was no doubt that listening to Daisy talk about the plans she and Frank were making had made her feel sad and lonely. She kept remembering the night he'd told her he was going to Canada. They'd gone on his motorbike to a dance and he'd never even noticed how cold she was, nor how long he'd kept her standing while he took care to see it wasn't stolen. Yet today, Sam Hamilton had worried about her shoes, and how she'd get home, dressed in her going-to-Belfast outfit, and he was just a friend.

She sat on the settle looking into the fire, determined not to cry. She felt if once she started she could cry all night and that would not do. Sometime soon her father would be coming up weary from the forge needing water to wash and a cup of tea. She drew forward a kettle on the stove, removed the dry tea cloth and remembered there was also a letter from Polly.

My dearest, dearest Ellie,

I am so upset I hardly know what I'm writing but Jimmy says I must tell you right away. I didn't believe it at first and thought there was some mistake, but Uncle Jim came last night and told us and then Rebecca came today with the wee newsletter thing they give out at Church. She has a friend goes to that Church and it was in it. <u>Robinson and Marriott</u>, an engagement. It's George and the daughter of his uncle's partner. Rebecca's friend Mary goes to that church and that was how Rebecca first heard that Gwen Marriott had a new boyfriend that was the nephew of the other partner. Then Uncle Jim got someone he knew to try to find out. That didn't work, but then Mary brought Rebecca the Newsletter. There it was in black print in the Church Notices.

Oh Ellie, I wasn't happy that time he came to see us in November, but I thought Jimmy was wrong, but when he didn't come and see us at Christmas and made no effort in the New Year, I began to think something wasn't right. This Gwen is quite a bit older than he is, but if she has set her cap at him he's old enough he should know better. And maybe the uncle has encouraged him. Nothing like having business all in the family.

I am so, so sorry Ellie that all our lovely plans have gone wrong, but please God there is a good man somewhere waiting for you. Please write soon and tell me you are all right. Jimmy says you're better off without him, but that's poor comfort if you are upset.

Your loving sister,
Polly

Ellie pushed the letter quickly into her pocket as she heard voices on the path and steps in the hall.

'Kettle's boiling,' she said, with a calmness that amazed her, as her father and Charlie Running came in, bringing with them with a draught of icy air.

'A cup of tea would go down well,' said Charlie, standing to one side of the stove to let Robert draw off a basin of warm water from the tank.

'You timed it well, Charlie,' Ellie said. 'I'd just pulled the kettle forward thinking you might be up,' she went on, surprised at her own steadiness, as she reached up to the mantelpiece yet again, for the tea-caddy with its silver Coronation spoon.

George's letter still lay on the table, but she swept it up deftly into her other pocket as she went to trim the lamp. Neither of the two men even noticed, as she moved around the room collecting cups and saucers and making the tea.

Twenty

Friday the first of March, 1934, was a mild, breezy day in Armagh, glints of sun falling on green fields where every trace of snow had gone. The road was bone dry as Ellie set off for work, the *wee country town* of George's letter as busy as ever when she paused at the Post Office to send off a note to Polly.

Written by candlelight in her bedroom, a blanket over her shoulders, she knew it was neither as legible nor as coherent as she would wish, but she needed to tell Polly not to worry. However upset she felt at the moment of writing she was grateful that Polly's note had come when it did. It had made things a lot better and would be very useful when she came to write to George herself. But that, she said to Polly, would have to wait till it suited her.

She had taken off her coat and was changing her shoes in the restroom when she heard the strident ring of the telephone at the back of the shop downstairs. Minutes later Susie hurried in, her face flushed, her eyes bright.

'Poor Daisy,' she began, 'that was Frank. He says he thinks she's got flu'. He was out seeing her last night and she started sweating and couldn't breathe. She got in such a state because she couldn't breathe he asked if he could stay and he sat up with her all night.'

'Oh dear, Susie. Is she any better this morning?' asked Ellie anxiously.

'No. He says he's getting the doctor to be on the safe side,' Susie said, bending down to change her shoes. 'It must have come on terribly quickly, though she had a funny little cough yesterday. I thought it was just dust from some of the boxes...'

Susie broke off. Glancing up she'd discovered to her amazement that Ellie was as white as a sheet and had tears in her eyes.

'Oh Ellie, Ellie, what's wrong? You don't think she's going to die?' demanded Susie, a stricken look on her face.

'No, of course not,' Ellie reassured her, coming and giving her a hug. 'Daisy is perfectly healthy and Frank and her Ma will look after her well. I'm just being silly. I didn't sleep very well...'

'Something's wrong. I know it is. Is it George?

Has he killed himself up a tree?'

Ellie tried not to laugh, but she failed. As George had treated her like an idiot, perhaps it was a good thing if Susie returned the compliment on her behalf. But one look at Susie's face and she knew she'd have to tell her the truth. There were rather a lot of people she'd have to tell, so she might as well start with those who knew her best.

'Susie dear, George has got engaged to someone else. He doesn't know that I know, so he tried to say that Canada might not suit me.'

'Oh the so-and-so! Aren't you absolutely furious?'

'One bit of me is, but another bit is very upset with myself. When you talked about Frank sitting up all night with Daisy, I thought immediately of what George would have done, or rather, not have done and I felt I should have known better, or at least *sooner*. I'm blaming myself for being so trusting.'

'For making a mistake you mean?'

Ellie nodded.

'And what did you say to me about making mistakes when I first came?' Susie demanded.

'I've no idea.'

'You said that unless you make mistakes you can't learn. That it's all very well having rules and guidelines and all the rest of it, but the thing that really teaches you is when it goes wrong and you need help to put it right,' she said, with a firmness and a fluency that left Ellie quite speechless. 'Then you remember next time and as well as that you start to see a whole lot of

329

other things as well, because mistakes often happen by doing the SAME thing when you need to do *different* things.'

'Did I say that?' she asked softly.

'Yes, you did. And it's been a great help to me and to Joe. He used to be so afraid of making mistakes that he hid inside the books he read. Now he does all sorts of things. He's really quite clever, isn't he?' she ended, shyly.

'Indeed he is, Susie. I can't believe how clever he is with those awful invoices,' she said weakly, quite overcome by the idea that Susie had encouraged Joe to start using talents no one else had seen.

'You need a nice cup of tea, Ellie. I'll go and tell Joe and the boys that Daisy won't be in and we'll be down soon. They can start our jobs until we come. It was your idea, Ellie, that we all do as many of each other's jobs as we can and that no one would be cross if we made mistakes. So you can't be cross with *you*. I won't allow it.'

Susie lit the gas fire, switched the kettle on and hurried off downstairs, leaving Ellie to recover her composure as best she could.

As Daisy said when she came back to work, she had no notion of dying, but never having been ill before, she'd been in a bad way. Fully herself again, she threw her energy into running the shop while her colleagues dressed the windows with spring fashion and fabrics and planning her wedding. Frank had had his promotion and his formal transfer to Fivemiletown would come through at the beginning of May. They'd been told there was a police house available with the job so there was nothing now to stop them going ahead.

'There's only one thing I want from you as a wedding present,' she said to Ellie, on a mild April day when they were both free to take their sandwiches to The Mall.

'What's that then?' asked Ellie, cautiously.

'I want you to forget all about George Robinson,' she said firmly. 'I know you say you're over it, but yer not right. I don't know when I last heard you laugh.'

'Oh dear, I'm sorry. Have I been a misery?'

'No, I didn't really mean that,' said Daisy more gently. 'You *do* laugh and you can always take a joke, but...'

Ellie looked at her friend and saw her struggling to find words.

'You *are* right, Daisy, I'm not feeling very happy these days,' Ellie said quietly. 'I don't really know why. The more I think about George the more I know I'd never have been happy with him. He's just not reliable. And the thought of being in Canada with him, even with Polly there, makes me shiver. Imagine being married to someone and having his children, yet knowing all the time you were on your own. Not physically on your own like women who lose their husbands, but knowing there was no help for you from the person you loved and who you thought loved you.'

Daisy looked at her closely as she crumbled up her last piece of crust for the sparrows who were watching their every move.

'Ellie, you shouldn't be thinkin' about what *might* have happened. It didn't happen. It wouldn't have happened. If he'd have come home you'd have taken one look at him and known it wasn't right. You'd have broken it off yourself.'

'Would I?'

'Yes, you *would*. Are you afraid you mightn't have?'

Ellie nodded and brushed the crumbs from her skirt to the great delight of the waiting sparrows.

'Then that's what's wrong with you,' Daisy declared. 'I *know* you wouldn't make that mistake, but *you* don't seem to know that. What are we goin' to do about it?'

'I honestly don't know, Daisy, but I know what my friend Rose would say. *Well, it didn't work out but you're that much further on*. And I am, thanks to you,' she said, nodding quietly. 'It's awfully hard to put something right until you know it's wrong in the first place.'

'Aye, d'ye mind the day we thought the bailiffs were comin' to put us out? Sure it was *you* sorted that out. It'll be all right, Ellie. You wait an' see. You'll not make the same mistake twice. You're not stupid.'

'Thank you, Daisy, I'm glad you think that,' she said, beaming. 'I don't think I'll ever get over George Robinson trying to tell me I was a poor wee thing that couldn't leave her *quiet wee place* in the country.'

She said it with such unaccustomed vehemence that Daisy burst out laughing and went on laughing till Ellie herself started laughing too and so startled the sparrows that they made a hasty retreat to the railings nearby.

Daisy's wedding was a small family affair. As neither of them had any significant church connection, they were married in the Armagh Registry Office late on a Wednesday morning, so that at least some of their friends could come for what Daisy called 'a wedding breakfast at lunch time' set out at her own home.

Ellie and Richard Sleator had been asked to provide the necessary witnesses to the marriage and Richard's car provided transport. They arrived back at Daisy's home to find Susie, Joe, Harry and Stanley had all managed to squash in to a somewhat larger vehicle lent by John Sleator and driven by Sam Hamilton.

It was not simply the bride who looked radiant in a new dress worn with Ellie's close-fitting, going-up-to-Belfast hat, the groom beamed on everyone as he poured whiskey for the men and port for the ladies. The cold lunch required two sittings in the farm kitchen, but afterwards everyone squeezed in to hear Richard and Frank's speeches which were short but very witty. Full of food and good spirits of both kinds, they then trooped out into the well-swept farm-yard where the cake sat on a borrowed milk-churn, all three tiers iced to perfection and decorated with silver paper good wishes and edible lucky horseshoes.

Stanley and Joe took photos with their Box Brownies and a friend of Frank's from the Allison Studio took four formal pictures with a large plate camera. The bride and groom cut the cake several times before he was satisfied and then he requested that every chair, stool, or wooden box, in house or barn, be brought out so he could take a picture of the whole wedding party.

One or two of the older people said, 'Ach no, I've too many wrinkles,' when what they meant was that there were not enough chairs, but eventually, everyone was accommodated, the smaller people standing on chairs at the back, the tallest in the middle and the immediate family sitting on either side of the bride and groom. Daisy's brothers and a few small cousins obligingly sat cross-legged on the ground.

The cake was now taken into the kitchen, carved and distributed, none the worse for so many insertions from the borrowed silver knife. Under the crisp, white icing the fruit cake Daisy's mother had baked was rich and moist.

'Hello, Ellie,' said Sam, handing her a piece on a tea-plate.

'Hello, Sam,' Ellie replied. 'Where's yours?'

'I'll have mine later. I came to see how you're gettin' home. You can't very well go back with the bride and groom when Richard takes them to the train.'

'And I haven't got a taxi handy like the last time we met,' she said laughing.

'Well, actually I'm the taxi man here today, but I think I'm fully booked for the first few trips,' he said smiling. 'Richard's organizing it. Some need to get to Portadown. Some back to Armagh. Could ye wait till I've done those?' he asked, looking somewhat anxious.

'Of course I could,' she said easily. 'I wasn't going to leave Mrs Hutchinson with all the clearing up. Don't hurry, there's a fair bit to do.'

A little later, the bride appeared in her going-away outfit, a pretty summer dress with the very smart shoes she and Ellie had bought together in Thomas Street. In her hand, she carried the spray of flowers her mother had ordered specially from Blakeley's nursery.

Richard looked up at the sky, decided the odd large cloud was harmless enough and put the top down on the motor before ushering the bride and groom into the back.

'Remember to throw your flowers, Daisy,' he said, as he walked round to the driver's side.

'Not on your life, Richard,' she came back at him. 'I'm not taking any chances with these. Come here, Ellie,' she called, as she stood up and leaned out, flowers in hand. 'You were never much good at catchin' things, but why bother when I'm puttin' them right into your hand,' she said, giving her a kiss.

There were shouts and cheers as Ellie took the flowers and Daisy's younger brother hopped up on the running board of the motor to pour confetti liberally over the bride's hair and down the groom's neck.

Richard drove through the cheering guests at snail's pace, still unaware that the same young man had managed in complete secrecy to do a thorough job of tying tin cans to his well-polished rear bumper.

The first thing Ellie did after Sam Hamilton

drove her home late in the afternoon was to take Daisy's bouquet carefully apart. Having sat in a bowl of water while the remains of the wedding party were being cleared up, the beautifully matched blooms were not even wilting. As she carefully removed the pieces of wire and the made-up bows and streamers of white and gold ribbon, she transferred the individual stems to a vase and a small collection of jam pots.

She studied all the containers closely and was delighted. On several of the creamy-white carnations and the two blending shades of heather, there were small side shoots just big enough to handle. With care, they were pieces she could root. She spent the evening finding exactly what she needed to encourage her slips to grow before putting them on the windowsill with the already vigorous cuttings of Hamilton's Pink.

As she got into bed that night, she decided it had been the happiest day she'd spent for a long, long time.

There were many happy days to follow over the summer. To begin with, she was able to take her week's holiday in June. She and Ruth went window shopping, took a day bus tour to the Glens of Antrim and visited Belfast Zoo.

Ellie spent a good deal of time with Rose and was there for her birthday, a quiet affair, a special lunch cooked by the housekeeper. James teased them by insisting he had cut a meeting with Lord Brookeborough himself in order to be free to join them at lunchtime. He'd been quite right about Hamilton's Pink. The home-grown cutting which had amused the bus conductor on the way up to Belfast, delighted Rose as much as he'd said it would. It looked so flourishing, a minute set of buds already in place. As she examined the little bush carefully, Rose said she agreed with her granddaughter. Even if it wasn't a successor to the one she'd tended all those years ago, then it was a cousin. It was, she said, still one of the family and a joy to have.

They mentioned George only briefly, the news of his departure and Ellie's subsequent low spirits having been written about and dispatched long ago. Instead, they talked about Daisy's wedding, Ellie's experiences buying for Freeburn's and Rose's most recent news from her family.

Sadly, they had to agree that Charlie Running was right. This man Hitler was on his way to the top. It seemed there was nothing he wouldn't do to gain power and, worse still, no one was lifting a finger to stop him. But it did look as if Sarah and Simon would be coming home. They'd done their tour of duty in Germany with the so-called Trade Mission. Sarah said it would look suspicious if they weren't replaced in the normal way and Rose confessed how grateful she was they'd be out of that country before anything worse could happen.

Back at work, Ellie began to encourage Susie to study fashion, not just read the magazines looking for things she'd like herself. She spent a lot of time too with Helen Adams, their new assistant, a pleasant, rather quiet girl who'd joined them straight from the High School at the end of the school year.

Helen had wanted to go to Queen's University but her father had died suddenly in April and she had to get a job. Ellie felt so sad for her. It was just like Daisy all over again, except that, unlike dear Daisy, and particularly unlike Susie, Helen was bright. You only had to tell her something once and that was that. By the end of September, she had mastered all the routine tasks and procedures and was literally looking for new fields to conquer.

Susie continued to walk home every evening with Joe, talk to Joe in her lunch hour when the rota permitted, and play tennis with Joe several nights a week. She had finally prevailed upon her brother Richard to intervene on her behalf with the Club Secretary. Susie, he argued, was in her seventeenth year. More to the point she was a better player than many of their older women.

Always a reasonable man, Charles Merrick proposed a trial game. Picking names at random, he set Susie and Richard to play against Harry Wright and Mrs Edwards. The score in favour of Susie and Richard was six games to two and to Ellie's great delight, Susie Sleator became the youngest member of the Club.

By tradition, the Annual Tennis Club Dance took place at the beginning of the season, but this year that had not been possible. The City Hall was in need of routine repairs and redecoration and the summer was the best time for the work, both indoors and out. So this year the last event of the season was not the tournament, but the Annual Dance, now to take place on Friday the seventh of September.

Ellie felt strangely apprehensive about the event and couldn't think why she should feel so. It wasn't that she hadn't a rather nice new dress, blue again because it seemed to suit her so well, but different in texture and a completely different cut from her last one. Nor was it that she enjoyed dancing any less than sixteen months ago. But some unease seemed to fill her with agitation every time she thought about it.

Sam was looking forward to it very much, however. Over the summer, they'd met often at the club and they'd gone to the pictures several times when the staff at Freeburn's had organized one of their treats. Emily had asked Ellie to come and see them, but knowing it was a long way for her to cycle, she'd suggested Sam go and fetch her on a Sunday afternoon. It had been a most happy visit and they'd gone again several times over the summer.

Ellie couldn't help noticing that the first time Sam arrived on his bike at the forge house, he'd brought a windproof jacket for her in case she hadn't one of her own. It was indeed far more effective than her warmest cardigan would have been. As for riding pillion, she was surprised at how much she liked it. But then, with Sam, she always felt safe.

As before, Mrs Sleator had invited Ellie to stay overnight for the dance, and Helen as well. She was a very generous woman and Ellie saw as soon as she arrived that Mrs Sleator had already decided Helen would be made to feel as welcome as Ellie herself. For his part, John Sleator was only too happy to repeat his chauffeur duty, this time with a new Chevrolet.

It was after supper that Ellie decided she needed a little rest. She and Sam went upstairs, tramped down to the very front row of the balcony and peered over.

'Look, there's Helen,' said Sam, nodding downwards.

'And there's Susie and Joe,' she replied.

A silence fell between them then, each absorbed in their own thoughts. Daisy and Frank were certainly part of them for the news had just come that Daisy was expecting a baby in February. After a little while Ellie felt ready to break the silence.

'Sam, there's something I want to ask you,' she began quietly.

'Ask away,' he replied easily.

'If there hadn't been a woman that hurt you and a man that let me down, do you think we'd be in with a chance?'

'Ellie,' he said, startled. 'Do you *know* what you're asking?'

'Yes, I think so,' she replied steadily.

'You're asking me if I think you and me would make a good pair,' he said, his blue eyes entirely concentrated on her face.

'Yes, I am,' she replied.

'Well, yes we would, but that would mean you'd have to marry me.'

She looked him steadily in the eye and said nothing.

'D'you mean, you're sayin' you'll marry me?'

'Yes, I am. If that's a proposal, then the answer

340

is yes.'

For a moment he sat stunned, unable to grasp his good fortune. His father had told him to wait. His Granny had told him not to hurry her. And he'd waited as best he could, knowing he would always love this woman whether she would have him or not. And now she'd said she'd have him. With Ellie, there'd be no going back.

He slipped his arm round her and kissed her.

'Ellie, I want to tell the whole world. Do you mind?'

For a moment, she didn't quite grasp what he meant, but then he took her by the hand and led her downstairs back into the ballroom. It began to dawn on her as he looked around, found the person he wanted, led her across to him and bent to speak into his ear.

Ellie was amused to see the slow smile and the bright gleam in his eye. Such a proper little man, the Club Secretary, so formal and yet so good-natured, he was now composing his features as the dance ended and the music stopped.

'Stay right where you both are,' he said firmly, patting Ellie on the arm before he ran lightly up the steps on to the platform, spoke to the large Master-of-Ceremonies and had the microphone lowered by at least a foot.

'Ladies and gentlemen,' he began, in his usual slightly clipped and precise tone, 'you are aware that, for our Annual Dance this year we have been forced to break with tradition. Instead of being May, we are now in September. I am, however, glad to tell you that we appear to have established an important *new* tradition,' he continued, pausing for effect.

'Last year, the band, who have given us such pleasure, kindly agreed to play requests from the floor. I am happy to be able to make the first request myself. I should like them to play *again* this year; *If you were the only girl in the world*, this time to celebrate the engagement of Ellie Scott and Sam Hamilton.'

Ellie thought she would never till the end of her life forget the shouts and cheers and clapping that completely drowned out the band for the first bars of the song. The floor cleared, as it had for Daisy and Frank, and she and Sam stepped out together, moving as they always did, as if they'd been dancing together all their lives.

Twenty-One

Of all the people who heard the news of Ellie and Sam's engagement in the days that followed the Annual Dance, there was only one who was not truly delighted. Charlie Freeburn expressed the most genuine of good wishes and did his best to feel pleased at what was clearly a happy match, but he found it hard to do other than regret that Ellie Scott would no longer brighten his life with her quiet presence, her smiles and gentle gaiety.

He did feel somewhat comforted when she said it would probably be some time before they could afford to get married and he felt better still when she went on to say they had the usual problem of having nowhere to live.

'I think I might be able to be of some assistance to you there, Miss Scott,' he said, brightening visibly. 'Do you know Edward Street?'

'Yes, I do,' she replied, wondering what could possibly be coming next.

'I have quite recently purchased a couple of properties there,' he said in a rather casual fashion, as if not to make too much of the fact that he was now buying property, 'three in fact, adjoining each other. They do all have what are known as "sitting tenants",' he explained, 'but one family is definitely finding the house too small and looking for something larger. One is occupied by a very elderly lady and one by a young couple planning to emigrate next year. I think we could be sure of finding something for you, if you thought the property suitable.'

Ellie did. A well-built brick terrace house, small, but with a yard at the back, the windows on that side looking out over playing fields. At the front, a wide, little-used street running between Cathedral Road and Abbey Street and only a short walk from both the shops and Sleator's garage.

'Of course, all these properties have been somewhat neglected,' he went on, 'they do need to be repaired and redecorated, which is my responsibility, of course. Perhaps that is actually a good thing,' he said, smiling, as the thought occurred to him, 'then you can choose your own colours for paint and wallpaper.'

Ellie could hardly wait to tell Sam. It would make up entirely for the very bad time he'd given himself after two days of going round excitedly sharing his good news with any friend or acquaintance that crossed his path.

'Ellie, I've some terrible bad news for ye,' he said, as they got out of sight of the forge and headed for the lane leading up to Church Hill.

She looked at him, startled, but failed to imagine anything that could have occurred since Friday night to make him look so distraught.

'You married someone else yesterday?' she said quickly.

'Oh Ellie, it's not a joke. I should have told you before you said yes. Ellie, I've no money.'

Ellie laughed.

'Sam, I wasn't actually marrying you for your money, but just as a matter of interest, what *have* you been doing with it all?'

'Well, you know about the bike, and that's still worth not far off what I paid for it, but all the rest I'd saved up for that furniture I told you about, I gave to Emily and Kevin to help them get the business started,' he said, with a great sigh.

'Good for you,' she said promptly. 'I nearly gave my savings to Daisy when we thought the bailiffs were coming, only I knew it wasn't enough anyway. How much *do* you have?'

She laughed again when he told her.

'Oh, Sam dear, that still seems an awful lot to me. When did you start saving again?'

'The night you said I'd be in with a chance.'

'You've done awfully well,' she said honestly. 'I've got about the same, but it's taken me *four*

344

years. It's only in the last year since my salary was raised that it's grown a bit faster. If I did another year, we wouldn't be so badly off at all.'

'And you wouldn't mind having to work another year?'

Ellie turned and looked at him full in the face.

'Sam Hamilton, the only thing I'll mind for the rest of my life is not being with you. But if we could both manage to save for a year it would give us a better start, wouldn't it?'

Ellie and Sam's wedding a year later was an even smaller affair than Daisy and Frank's had been, but it was an equally happy occasion and the joy of the young couple as they welcomed their guests to their own new home in Edward Street was clear to everyone.

They had worked so hard on the house, helped well beyond the call of duty by their landlord. Weeks before the wedding, they had already recreated Ellie's garden in the narrow backyard. For the marriage service itself, she was able to make her posy with Hamilton's Pink, creamy-white carnations and two shades of heather and the bows and streamers she had saved from Daisy's own bouquet.

There was one big difference, however, between their respective weddings. While Daisy and Frank had spent only two nights in a hotel in Bangor, before setting off for Fivemiletown, Ellie and Sam drove off from Edward Street in a gleaming blue, three-seater Lagonda for a week's touring in the west of Ireland.

They had certainly not planned such an adventure, but a month before the wedding a present arrived from Rose. They found enclosed in the carefully packed box of china, the tea set she herself had used for thirty years and an envelope addressed to Sam containing a note and a cheque.

My dear Sam,

As I know you both quite separately, as grandson and as dear friend, I decided you ought to receive TWO wedding presents. Then I had a better idea. I may be somewhat forgetful at times but I'm very grateful that my mind does still function perfectly well.

My dear Ellie has never seen what I call a proper mountain and more particularly she has never seen MY mountains. Kerry, I know, is too far away for a week's holiday, but you could take her to Donegal and then down to Sligo where my Lady Anne's husband owned so much land and then perhaps you might go on to Clare and watch the sun go down on Galway Bay, as the song has it.

The enclosed cheque would serve to hire a motor. I would love to think of Sam driving something he could never afford to buy like my dear John did when we finally went to Kerry. I remember it was a Lagonda, though I confess I still know very little about motors however much I did try to grasp all I was told over many years.

Please, to humour me, go and enjoy the freedom of not counting your pennies. It's only for a week and perhaps the only time in your life you will not have to count pennies. Please do bring back something special, an object, a particular memory, something you will always have.

I shall think of you on your special day and on your travels and hope to see you soon after you come back

With the most loving good wishes to you both,

Rose.

At last Ellie understood just why Rose loved her mountains so much. Donegal was magnificent in October, the heather still bright on the hillsides, the valleys a rich green, the moving clouds changing the mountain slopes from sombre masses into glowing rock faces as the sun came and went. The sea was ever with them, the Atlantic itself, only a name in a battered atlas, now sometimes a brilliant blue or turquoise, now a wild, heaving mass dashing against cliffs, throwing spray so high that they saw rainbows before the brilliant drops fell back again into the water below, now so calm the sea birds rode on it like little celluloid toys.

Sam drove and drove and enjoyed every mile, pressing on as much as Ellie would let him. He took joy in her delight with each new vista, the varied colour and texture of a part of Ireland of which she had only read.

At the end of their fourth day, full of wind and sun, they got as far as the famous Cliffs of Moher which everyone told them they must see. They parked in a rough space with a single

347

strand of barbed wire to prevent them from falling over the precipitous edge. They stared across at the layers of rock piled up like thick pages in a book and gazed up at the wide sky arcing from the land behind them to the furthest horizon. In the middle distance the Aran Islands lay quiet in the westering sun. From whitewashed cottages and pale stone walls the light reflected back so strongly they were visible across miles of dark blue ocean.

In a field nearby, less dramatic than the shadowy cliffs, they spread a rug, poured tea from a flask, ate the last piece of their wedding cake and gazed out towards the setting sun.

'Well, we can tell Granny we did it. We watched the sun go down on Galway Bay,' Sam said quietly. 'Are you happy, Ellie?'

'I've never been so happy in all my life,' she said simply.

For a long time they sat quietly, then Sam reminded them they would soon have to go for they still had to find a place to spend the night. Tomorrow they'd have to turn for home.

'Sam, do you remember Rose asked us to bring something special back, an object, or a memory...'

'Aye, I do. We'll have a lot of memories, won't we?'

She nodded happily, slipping her arm round his neck.

'Sam, I'd like to bring *this* back, you and me here, looking out into the far distance.' She paused. 'Do you know what else I'd like?'

'What?'

348

'If we have a wee girl, I'd like to call her *Clare*, then we'll have this day, all day and every day as long as we live.'

Sam nodded slowly.

'I think that's a great idea, just great,' he said taking her in his arms.

By one of those coincidences which often happen but which many people refuse to believe, their first child was born almost a year later on the day of her parents' first wedding anniversary, the eighth of October, 1936.

It was a long labour and having had to leave her in the Nursing Home on The Mall, late in the evening, Sam was beside himself with lack of sleep when at 7.30 next morning, he heard the bars of a bicycle scrape against the wall next to the front door as he stood drinking a cup of tea by way of breakfast.

'It's a wee girl, Sam,' said the elderly woman standing on the doorstep. 'She's a brave girl, your Ellie. It was hard, but she's all right,' she added quickly, seeing the look on his face. 'About half an hour ago. She's asleep, but you can come down from work an' see her then. I'm away home to m'bed.'

'Thank you, Nurse, thank you. It was good of you to come up here out of your way.'

'Not at all. Now away man and eat a good breakfast, for you look just dreadful,' she said, wheeling her bicycle into the street and riding off.

Sam was so unable to collect his wits that he went and asked John Sleator for the day off. He came home, cut a posy of flowers for Ellie and left them at the nursing home, then collected change for the telephone in the Post Office. He rang Freeburn's and spoke to Susie. Rang Irish Road Motors and told his father. Rang Cranmore Park and asked for Rose.

'She's not just feeling too good, Mr Hamilton. Mr James has sent for the Doctor. Could you perhaps ring again or can we ring you?' the housekeeper said. 'It's lovely news and she'll be delighted, but she's asleep at the moment.'

A shadow passed across Sam's mind, but he set it aside, got out his bicycle and made the forge in record time.

'Ach dear,' said Robert, 'an' both well?'

'Aye fine,' Sam reassured him. 'Nurse herself came an' told me on her way home from night duty.'

'Have ye any ideas about what'll ye'll call the wee lassie?' asked Robert suddenly, rubbing at something he seemed to have got in his eye.

'Indeed yes, we have the name ready. Clare. And Alison as well, just in case she doesn't like Clare when she grows up. That gives her a choice.'

'Clare Hamilton,' said Robert nodding. 'That sounds nice. Just wait till I tell Charlie Running I'm a Granda with a wee girl.'

It was obvious to everyone that Rose was fading. She slept a lot, though she was still perfectly coherent when she was awake, but she was having great difficulty getting out of bed.

Sam and Ellie took it in turns to telephone

350

James, Sam from work, Ellie from the call box at the Court House where she could watch the sleeping child through the glass panes.

After two weeks, by which time Ellie looked less pale and Clare was already waving small fists in the air, they decided they must go and see Rose. Richard Sleator, the kindest of friends, brought his motor round on Sunday morning having placed extra rugs in the back to make sure there would be no draughts to trouble either mother or child on the drive to Belfast.

Rose was in her bedroom, but she was sitting in her armchair by the window. She was not dressed, but this was not obvious for she had replaced her slippers with shoes and wore a pretty silk scarf over the collar of her dressing gown. Her hair was brushed back from her face and caught up gently in a clasp at the back.

'Come in, come in,' she called, as James pushed open the door and stood back to let them past.

'Ellie and Sam and Clare,' she said carefully, as if to make sure she did not forget there were now three of them and that she had acquired yet one more great-grandchild.

'She's lovely,' she said, as she took the child in her arms. 'But aren't they all? Was there ever such a thing as an ugly baby?' she asked, never lifting her eyes from the small moving scrap in her arms. 'You did so well, Ellie, to manage first time. I miscarried twice or even three times, I forget which, and my poor John was out of his mind with anxiety before I managed to produce James. But it *did* get easier,' she said, seeing the

351

stricken look on Sam's face.

Although Rose looked so easy and happy, James had warned them how she would suddenly become tired. It would be a pity to spoil such a happy meeting by staying too long, so after an hour they stood up to go just as the November sun was setting and a slight mist had begun to rise from the grass in the park opposite.

'I've just been thinking, and you must correct me if my arithmetic is wrong, but if little Clare lives as long as I have lived, she will end her life in another century. Imagine that! I was born in the nineteenth century, you dear children in the twentieth, but little Clare Hamilton, may well see the twenty-first.'

There were kisses and hugs and goodbyes. As they parted with James in the hallway Ellie knew they would not see Rose again.

She had quietly said her goodbye in her own inimitable way. She had left them with the wish that they would be happy together for many a long day.